Hea

And Then You Dance

Volume 2 in the
Crested Butte Cowboy Series

And Then You Dance
© 2013 Heather A. Buchman

All rights reserved. No part of this book may be used or reproduced in any manner whatsoever without written permission, except in the case of brief quotations embodied in critical articles and reviews.

This book is a work of fiction. The names, characters, and incidents are products of the writer's imagination or have been used fictitiously and are not to be construed as real. Any resemblance to persons, living or dead, actual events, locale or organizations is entirely coincidental.

ISBN 10: 1494243814
ISBN 13: 978-1494243814

Cover and content design by Sparrow Marketing & Design

Available from Amazon.com and other retail outlets.

She danced
She sang
She took
She gave
She loved
She created
She dissented
She enlivened
She saw
She grew
She sweated
She changed
She learned
She laughed
She shed her skin
She bled on the pages of her days
She walked through walls
She lived with intention…

—Mary Anne Radmacher, *Living Eulogy*

More from author Heather A. Buchman

CRESTED BUTTE COWBOY SERIES
And Then You Fall
And Then You Kiss
And Then You Fly

COMING SOON
And Then You Dare

EAST AURORA LINGER SERIES
Linger - Book One
Linger - Book Two: Leave

For the kind of cowboy

who makes

a girl's heart beat

just a little faster.

Table of Contents

Acknowledgments ix
Chapter One 1
Chapter Two 14
Chapter Three 29
Chapter Four 47
Chapter Five 60
Chapter Six 78
Chapter Seven 92
Chapter Eight 103
Chapter Nine 114
Chapter Ten 125
Chapter Eleven 137
Chapter Twelve 152
Chapter Thirteen 160
Chapter Fourteen 172
Chapter Fifteen 188
Chapter Sixteen 201
Chapter Seventeen 213
Chapter Eighteen 227
Chapter Nineteen 240
Chapter Twenty 252
Chapter Twenty-One 266
Chapter Twenty-Two 282
Chapter Twenty-Three 299
About the Author 313

Acknowledgments

Thanks to my readers—Angelina, Catie, Cathy, Eileen, Erlinda, Jacki, Kym, Stacey and Vicki. As always, I don't know what I'd do without you.

My inspiration comes from so many places. Music is at the top of the list. I make playlists when I start writing a book, and those songs become the music I hear when I'm writing, or reading, whether it's actually playing or not. If this book ever becomes a movie, I have the soundtrack ready to go. There are too many musicians, or bands, to list them, but I give my thanks for their inspiration anyway.

Chapter One

October

Billy stood out on the deck, the baby monitor in his back pocket. She'd probably sleep for at least an hour, maybe even two. He hoped so anyway, for her sake as much as his. She was a much happier baby after her afternoon nap. If she didn't wake up on her own at the end of two hours, he'd wake her.

Dottie, his mother, told him he should never wake a sleeping baby, but he didn't listen. By then, he'd miss her so much that watching her sleep wouldn't be enough. He'd want to feel the warmth that thawed his body when she smiled at him, and kicked her feet, and put her head on his chest at the end of her nap.

Plus, when Willow was awake, his thoughts didn't stray to Renie as much.

Today marked eight months since he'd seen her, and next week his baby girl would be celebrating her first birthday. He never dreamed they would be doing it without the woman he swore he couldn't live without.

It had also been eight months since Renie had seen her horse. He'd been sure having Pooh stabled at his ranch, would mean she'd come. Another thing he never dreamed—that Renie would go this long without even asking about her horse. Asking would have meant Renie had to talk to him, and he doubted she ever would again.

The woman he thought he knew better than any other person on the planet had turned into someone he no longer recognized. And all because of an innocent baby girl.

October in Monument, Colorado meant that yesterday was a beautiful seventy-degree day, and today the weather report called for snow. The cold front brought ten-degree temperatures with it. He welcomed it. In nothing but his jeans and a T-shirt, the outside of his body was numb. He wished it would numb him straight through, to dull the ache of missing her. He'd gotten used to it, that constant pain no pill took away.

The only time he experienced joy was with Willow, his beautiful baby girl who had the same blue eyes and flaxen hair as Renie. He'd be willing to bet that Willow looked a lot like Renie had when she was a baby. He didn't have any photos to look at though, to find out for sure.

Eight months. It didn't seem possible. Soon, Willow would be walking; she already made her way around the room, holding on to anything that would get her from one place to the next. And Renie wouldn't be here to see it. Why had she left him? He asked himself that question a thousand times a day.

— • —

Previous January

"Damn that Liv Fairchild," he muttered under his breath. Billy slammed the barn door shut behind him, and stomped to the house. Of course, she wasn't Liv Fairchild anymore, now she was Liv Rice, but that didn't change how mad he was at her.

When she came to him and asked whether he wanted to buy her ranch, the answer was obvious. Of course he did. His family's ranch bordered hers, and they'd wanted to buy this land since he was a boy. His family didn't begrudge Liv's; the Pattersons had been leasing grazing rights since they bought the place. And her house, well, it was one of the nicest houses he'd ever seen.

She named a fair price, and he certainly could afford it. It was the side deal she made with him that was the problem. Liv had been boarding horses for years, and she didn't want to let the families down that counted on her, so she made Billy promise to keep the boarding stables open.

How he'd do that, was beyond him. He traveled as a saddle bronc rider on the rodeo circuit, and sometimes he was away for two or three weeks at a time. He told Renie she could keep her horse there for as long as she wanted. She had four years of school to finish before she got her degree and became a large animal vet. He wouldn't have asked her to move Pooh, the fourteen-year-old mare she'd had since she was ten. But taking care of her horse, along with all the others, wasn't something he signed up for.

Liv told him to hire somebody. Plenty of ranch hands worked Patterson Ranch, his parents' place, but he doubted a job this small would be very enticing.

He was almost thirty-four years old, and this was the first time he had a place of his own. It wasn't that he hadn't wanted to before; he just hadn't had any good reason. He was on the road so much, and when he was home, his parents' place was plenty big enough. His room was on the lowest floor of their tri-level house, and he had plenty of privacy, not that he'd ever taken advantage of it.

"You need to move out Billy," Renie said to him. "You kinda seem like a loser, still living with your parents."

He knocked her into the water trough when she'd said it. He thought that might teach her, pain in the ass that she was.

***

"You should hire Blythe," she said, trying to help him come up with a solution for the stables.

"Blythe who?"

"Blythe Cochran." Paige and Mark Cochran were her mother's best friends. She and Blythe had been friends since they were five years old. She wondered why Billy acted as though he didn't know who she was; they'd spent enough Thanksgivings and other holidays together.

"Why would I hire her?"

"Because she's home. She quit school and doesn't have anything to do."

That didn't sound like the best reason he'd ever heard to hire somebody. And the fact that she quit school didn't fill him with confidence. The last thing he needed was to get a phone call while he was out on the road, telling him she was quitting. What the hell would he do then?

"Why'd she quit?"

"She decided she didn't want to be a nurse. You shouldn't look down your nose at her Billy. I quit school too."

"You did? Since when?"

"Well I quit Dartmouth, but I guess I transferred instead of quit. For the same reason though, I realized I would have made a crappy people doc."

Renie had switched fields from biomedical to veterinary medicine last year, in her junior year, and now went to Colorado State University in Fort Collins. It was a two-hour drive from the ranch, so he told her she could stay at the house as much as she wanted. It was the house she grew up in, and with him away so often, they'd almost never bump into each other.

"What about when you bring girls home?" she asked.

"What girls?"

That elicited another "loser" comment out of her. He supposed she was right. Plenty of girls would be happy to come home with him, even if only for a night. He wasn't bragging, it was the nature of being a bronc rider, saddle, or otherwise. Having a one-night stand on the road was one thing; it was different at home.

"You're a hot guy Billy."

"What? God Renie, you can't say that to me."

"What? It's not like I'm interested."

"Jeez, what's wrong with you?"

"I don't see what the issue is, but let's get back to the original subject—you should hire Blythe."

"She know how to take care of horses?"

"No, but..."

Billy figured Renie was at least five times as infuriating as any woman he'd ever met. "Now why would I hire somebody who doesn't have experience with horses?" He walked away at that point.

"Because she needs the job Billy, and she'll learn. In fact, I'll teach her."

"No."

Renie walked over and grabbed his arm.

Whoa, what the hell? It was as though a bolt of lightening hit him and the current surged through his veins. It almost knocked him on his ass.

"Please," she said, in that soft tone she used sometimes when she tried to get her way. It used to make him laugh, and he'd tell her he saw right through her. Today, he had a different reaction. Today, he'd be willing to do anything Renie Fairchild asked.

"What?" she asked.

"Nothing." Billy didn't know what in God's name was going on, but he knew he needed to get away from Renie *right now*. "Listen, I gotta go into town."

"Where are you headed? I'm not doing anything. I'll go with you."

"No. Not tonight. I've…um…got a date."

"You do? With one of these girls you don't plan to bring home?"

She was killing him. She didn't appear as affected by the touch as he had been.

"Whatever Renie. Mind your own damn business."

Renie watched Billy stomp away from her. She spent a lot of time watching him walk away from her. She'd been in love with Billy Patterson her whole life. No one, not a single living person, knew how she felt about him. The only one she ever talked to about him was her horse, which was stabled in the barn Billy now owned.

It didn't seem as though much had changed at the ranch since Billy bought it. In fact, her mom left most of the furniture in the house when she sold it. She and her new husband, Ben, hadn't needed it at their place in Crested Butte.

With Billy home so infrequently, most of the house looked exactly the same as it always had. The master bedroom was the one room Renie was sure was different. She hadn't set foot in it though. It was almost as though the bedroom was the only place in the house Billy lived. It seemed wrong to invade his space.

When her mom decided to sell, she asked Renie first if she wanted to keep it, live there herself, but Renie told her to sell it to Billy.

With four years of school still ahead of her, she didn't have time to take on the ranch.

She thought a lot about whether she'd regret her decision later, after she graduated and started a practice. Even then, she knew she wouldn't be able to live the rest of her life next door to the Patterson family. The heartache of seeing Billy come to visit his parents with the wife he would he eventually marry, and the children they would eventually have, was more than she'd be able to handle. You didn't love someone the way she loved Billy and ever truly move on from it.

Something didn't feel right between them tonight. It almost seemed as though Billy was mad at her.

She'd planned to stay here for the weekend, ride Pooh, and study. She should ask whether it was still okay. Maybe she was making too much of it. Then again, he might be telling the truth about having a date.

She decided to text him. *Can I still stay this weekend?*

He answered within seconds. *Yes.*

Thanks. See you tomorrow.

***

William Prescott Patterson Junior was eleven years older than Irene Louise Fairchild. Her first memory of him was when she was ten, right after her grandfather died, and she got Pooh. She and her mom were out riding in the big meadow over the hill. It was wide open, and a great place to let the horses run. Billy waved them over.

"Who's this Renie?" he rubbed the horse's nose.

"This is Pooh," she said proudly. "She's mine."

"Great name," he answered as he slowly walked around her, running his hand over Pooh's body. "She's sound. You pick her out yourself?"

"Mom helped." See, Billy didn't think Pooh was a boy's name, as her mom did.

"My favorite quote from *Winnie the Pooh* goes like this, 'Some people talk to animals. Not many listen though. That's the problem.' You remember that Renie, talk to her, but remember to listen too. Will you do that?"

Brilliant, she thought. He must be a very good bronc rider if he knew how to listen to horses. From that day on, Renie spent as much time listening to Pooh as she did talking to her.

***

She must've read the same page over at least twenty times when she put the book down and turned off the light. Billy either wasn't coming home tonight, or he planned to get back late enough that she'd already be asleep.

Something happened between them today, and it was the reason he left the way he had. She wondered where he'd gone, but if she thought about it too much, she wouldn't get any sleep at all.

***

Telling Renie to stay at the house had to have been the stupidest thing Billy had ever done. On the other hand, he loved having her there when he was. Hell, he couldn't make up his damn mind what he thought about it.

When she touched him today, he wanted to pull her into his arms and kiss her. Since then it was the only thing he thought about. But, it was more than that. His mind drifted to the other things he wanted to do to Renie Fairchild. He tried to shake it out of his head. Thinking about kissing her was bad enough. More than that was…incestuous—or something.

It might have been a fluke. He'd see her tomorrow, and it would be as though nothing happened today. If it were that cut and dried, he'd be inside his house, not sitting outside in his truck.

He told her he had a date. It was a lie, but at that moment, he had to leave, and the last thing he wanted was take *her* with him.

He ended up at the brewery first, then next door at the movie theatre, and then he went to the bowling alley. All in all, he'd killed about four hours. He drove around for another hour, wasting gas until he decided he was being ridiculous.

Once he got home, he put off going inside. He'd been sitting outside in his truck for twenty minutes, and it was damn cold. It was January after all, and Monument, sitting at 7,000 feet elevation, was colder on average than the surrounding towns and cities.

"Ah, to hell with it." He got out of the truck and went in the back door of the house. One light remained on, in the kitchen. Renie told him she and her mother left that light on whenever someone would be getting home late. He decided it worked for him too. He liked it. It made him feel as though somebody waited for him. He left it on even when he was at the house alone.

* * *

Renie was gone the next morning when he got out of bed. It wasn't unusual for her to be. She was always running off somewhere, meeting up with that friend of hers.

Blythe. That reminded him; he needed to hire somebody to take care of the boarding stables.

He drove to his parents' place and talked to his dad, William Prescott Patterson Senior, whom everybody called Bill. His mom, Dottie, was like a second mother to Liv, and a grandmother to Renie. Which meant Billy was practically Renie's uncle, and for the last twelve hours he'd been fantasizing about what it would be like to kiss his niece. *Yep, he was fucked up all right.*

His dad recommended the same man who ran the stables for Liv last year, after an accident kept her away from the ranch for a couple of months. Steve Sookan was his name, but everyone called him as Sookie. One of their more reliable hands, he'd worked for the Pattersons for a several years.

"What about letting him stay in the house Billy? So he doesn't have to come up from the bunkhouse," his dad suggested.

"Why is he living in the bunkhouse?" Typically it was only used during busy times of the year, like calving season.

"He's going through a divorce. He's trying to get back on his feet."

Billy thought about it for a minute. "I'm not sure Dad."

"Why not?"

He didn't want to tell his dad the real reason he didn't want Sookie staying at the house, but he couldn't come up with another reason off the top of his head.

"I guess it would be okay, but I told Renie she could stay at the house if she wanted to come down and see Pooh on the weekends."

"Sookie's harmless, but I would understand if Renie felt uncomfortable staying there alone with him."

Sookie's reputation with the ladies was the main reason he'd gotten a divorce. Billy didn't want Renie within a hundred feet of the man.

***

"What did he say?"

"It doesn't look good Blythe. He said he didn't want to hire someone who doesn't have any experience with horses."

"I don't care that much about the job. What did he say when you mentioned me? I've been trying to hook up with Billy Patterson for ages. You know that."

"He didn't say anything Blythe. Oh, and he had a date last night. It might be somebody he's serious about."

"Serious? Billy Patterson is serious about someone? That I'd like to see. I'm not talking about forever here Renie. I only want to have some fun. I mean, God, just the thought of him…" Blythe swooned, and rolled her eyes back in her head and made a noise that sounded like an elk during mating season. Renie thought she might be sick to her stomach.

"I wouldn't get your hopes up."

"Let's hang out at your house tonight."

"I told you not to get your hopes up. And, it isn't my house anymore."

"He won't care if you invite me to the house."

Renie told Blythe that she had a midterm she had to study for that night, which was the truth. Not the whole truth, but enough of it.

"What about Sunday? I'll come over for breakfast."

If Blythe Cochran didn't let this go, Renie would kill her.

***

Billy hadn't texted Renie all morning. Before yesterday, he hadn't thought about how often they texted each other. But now that he thought about it, he sent her texts all the time. He told her everything; important stuff, trivial stuff, jokes. He even said good morning and good night to her almost every day. Except today. He hadn't said good morning to her today, he realized as he scrolled back through his texts to her.

Hey, he texted.

Hey, she answered.

What r u doin?

With Blythe.

When will u b back?

Why?

Typical Renie. He wanted to tell her to just answer the damn question.

Because I'm asking.

Planning on bringing a girl home tonight?

He'd never known anyone better at answering a question with a question than Renie Fairchild. Maybe he wouldn't answer her, let her stew for a bit. Or he'd answer yes. But, if he did that, she wouldn't come back to the house, she'd stay at Blythe's or go back up to school. He didn't want that. More than anything he wanted to hang out with her as though everything was normal between them.

Just answer the question.

An hour.

Wanna have dinner with me?

Who's cooking?
You are.
Sure.

* * *

It was one of those relationships. You see them all the time. The girl in love with the hot guy who didn't realize she was alive. She'd do anything to be with him, and he took her for granted. The girl would never tell the guy she was interested in him because then he'd be uncomfortable and stop hanging out with her. That described her and Billy perfectly.

She parked near the barn, and went in to see Pooh before she went in the house. She had things she needed to talk over with her horse before she saw Billy again.

Chapter Two

Liv wished she had the power to turn back the clock, to the time before Billy Patterson broke her daughter's heart. She had important news for Renie, and she wasn't sure how her daughter would react.

Eight months ago Renie showed up unannounced on their doorstep with tear-stained cheeks and a broken heart.

She'd stayed with her and Ben from January to May, and then she left for the summer. Renie was back now, and had been for two weeks, she seemed better than before she left, but she still wasn't herself.

With places gearing up for ski season in Crested Butte, Renie asked Ben if they had any openings at the Goat, the Rice family's bar on Elk Avenue, the main drag in the historic downtown. He was quick to say yes. He wanted her to stay busy, hang out with people her own age, and not slip back into the funk she'd been in last spring.

"I hope you're okay with it," he said to Liv after he'd already agreed to it.

"It's something anyway," Liv answered that day. Renie would turn twenty-four in three months. The girl who was once happy-go-lucky, and on her way to becoming a large animal vet, now had no direction in her life.

If Liv hadn't sold Billy her ranch, or come to live with Ben on his ranch in the East River Valley, maybe Renie's life wouldn't have fallen apart.

— • —

And Then You Dance

Billy didn't remember the last time he was this nervous. Or if he'd ever been this nervous. And it was because of Renie, the person he felt more comfortable around than anyone else.

Half of him hoped that when she got to his house things between them would go back to the way they were two days ago. When she was his buddy. The other half of him hoped he felt *more,* the way he had yesterday.

He took a shower. Then, he spent time picking out what he would wear, as though he had a date. And the thing was, even if he threw on a pair of jeans and a white T-shirt, somehow she'd be on to him, and tease him about it. She was uncanny that way. No one else called him out on his shit the way Renie did.

He should have a couple of beers before she got there. Or a shot of whiskey to calm his nerves. He wasn't even this nervous before riding a bronc.

***

Renie came into the kitchen through the back door. She saw Billy out on the deck leaning on the railing, with his back to her. There were few sights as fine as that one. Billy, in a pair of jeans, the right amount of tight. His T-shirt stretched taut over his shoulders. There he was, short sleeves, no jacket, in ten-degree weather. How long he'd been standing out there?

She closed her eyes and took a deep breath, then another. She wasn't sure what to expect from him, so it would be up to her to set the tone of normalcy between them—make everything okay. It was what she did. Her eyes met his. Billy was still on the deck, but he'd turned around and was watching her. He raised his beer to his mouth and took a long drink. Renie loved how he held the bottle a little away from his mouth, so his lips didn't touch it.

She walked to the wine cooler and then remembered Billy didn't keep wine in the house the way her mom had. She turned back to the refrigerator to get a beer. Alcohol fortification would get her through the next few hours.

"There's wine if you want some," he said, walking into the kitchen.

"There is? Since when?"

"Since I stopped and got it, in case *someone* wanted wine. Does it look any good? It's what they recommended."

She walked back over and opened the door. He'd stocked several whites, several reds, a couple bottles of sparkling and even a rosé.

"You having a party Billy?"

"Nah, I thought since I had this thing I should keep something in it."

Renie went through the bottles, putting the whites on one side, the reds on the other, doing it so it looked as though she was seeing what he had instead of organizing it.

"You have a huge refrigerator over there. Are you feeling compelled to make proper use of that too?" Right now, Renie doubted he had much more than beer. Which reminded her, she had no idea what he thought they'd be having for dinner.

"You got everything figured out, don't ya? Maybe you should quit makin' so many assumptions."

She opened the refrigerator. It still wasn't close to half-full, but he had a lot more in it than beer.

"As I said, looks as though you're having a party. Stocking up for those girls you're inviting over."

"Why are you so fixated on me invitin' girls over? I'm sure the first time you asked me, I told you I didn't have any plans to. You're a little obsessed, aren't you?"

"Well I don't want to show up here unannounced and find you in a compromising position now do I?"

"A compromising position." He rolled his eyes at her. "Right."

"Can't believe a—" she started to say hot, but then thought better of it. "Saddle bronc champion wouldn't have experience with compromising positions." Oh God, why didn't she shut up? She was talking about compromising positions, to Billy. Great. This should end well.

"I have plenty of experience," she heard him mumble as he reached in and pulled out another beer. "I got steaks, shrimp, and chicken. Didn't you say you were gonna make dinner? Whatcha' makin'?"

She wanted to see what else he'd gotten, but he was blocking her view. She bumped his hip with hers to move him out of the way. And there it was again, that little sizzle when she touched him. Like a shock, but stronger.

He moved, but not quite far enough. And instead of looking in the refrigerator, as he had been, he was looking at her.

"What?"

"Nothin'." He walked to the other side of the island and sat on a stool. Still watching her.

The kitchen was Renie's favorite part of the house. It was a cook's kitchen—a gourmet cook. With two convection ovens, a seven-burner Wolf cook top, and big, rough-edged granite counters, it also had all kinds of cool things built in, like the wine cooler.

Renie looked through the refrigerator and found he'd gotten vegetables too.

She pulled out a head of lettuce and raised her eyebrows at him.

"What?"

"This is a vegetable," she answered. "Not a very nutritious one, but still a vegetable. Did you know that when you bought it?"

"You're hysterical. And you should be glad my mama didn't hear you say that to me. She forced me to eat plenty of vegetables when I was a kid."

"Forced you." More eye rolls.

"You gonna make dinner or keep makin' fun of me? If you don't get at it, I'm gonna start cookin' myself, and you don't want that."

"It's time you learned to cook. You've got this amazing kitchen, and then when you invite—"

"Don't say another word about me inviting girls over Renie."

He glared at her, so she gave him an okay sign.

"So who's gonna teach me? You?"

"Sure, tonight will be your first lesson."

Renie made Billy wash the lettuce and then showed him how to chop other vegetables for a salad. He needed to practice chopping and dicing, but it wasn't bad for his first attempt.

A couple of times she put her hand around his on the knife, to show him how to hold it at a better angle. The first time he flinched.

"What?"

"Nothin'. I didn't expect you to do that."

"Billy what's going on with you? It seems as though you're all jacked up on energy drinks or something."

Renie walked to the sink to wash her hands, but more to take a deep breath and get herself settled again.

"What do you want me to do now?"

"Sit down and I'll cook the shrimp. You can watch. Or go out on the deck."

"I'll watch." He pulled the stool closer to the end of the counter. "How come you don't complain about cookin' for me?"

"It isn't all for you. I'm cooking for myself too. Plus I enjoy it. It's something my mom and I did together, as far back as I remember."

"Some of my best memories are sittin' in this kitchen watchin' you and your mama cook."

"We have had good times in this kitchen," she answered. "I miss her."

"I miss her too."

She stopped what she was doing when he said it, and he wondered for a minute if he had said the wrong thing.

"What?"

"Nothing. It's strange. I've lived in this house since I was born, and now I don't anymore. Sometimes I forget."

"You're welcome here anytime," he said quietly.

"Thanks," she said, but there was more to it. She shook her head as if she were shaking a thought away. "I understand what you mean about missing my mom being here. I'd miss Dottie if we were at your parents' place, and she wasn't there."

"See? Exactly."

"It's not the best idea for me to stay here all the time."
"Why not?"
"It's your house now Billy. Not my mom's anymore."
"What does that have to do with anything?"
"Doesn't it feel weird to you?"
"Weird how?" He knew what she was talking about. But, he wanted to know whether she was feeling the same profound changes between them that he felt.

"Never mind," she shrugged.

"Don't make a big deal out of nothin' Renie. I said you could stay here whenever you want, and I meant it. If anything changes, I'll say so." He was lying, and she knew it. Nobody read him as well as she did.

He'd been in Renie's life since she was a little girl. Now that they were both adults, and things were changing between them. Of course, she would handle it better than he would. Even when she was ten, she'd been more mature than he was.

Sometimes he figured that was why they were such good friends. She was at least five years more mature than her age, and he was at least five less mature, so that made them about equal.

Renie dished their shrimp and salad and pulled a stool next to him at the island. He was so happy she was here with him. He wanted her to stay at the house all the time. He wished he could find the right words to tell her so. Every time he tried to think of something, it sounded too much as though he was joking around, or too serious.

"Glad you're here," he murmured.

"Me too."

Two words, so simple, but from her, it made everything feel right.

"You wanna watch a movie after dinner?"

"I have to study."

"You wanna study while I watch a movie after dinner?"

That made her smile.

"Sure, that'd be great."

Renie fell asleep in the big chair next to the fireplace, her book still on her lap. He had to wake her up, or she'd be stiff and sore in the morning. But, he wanted to watch her sleep a little while longer. She leaned over and put her head down on the arm of the chair. A blanket covered her legs, but her shirt had hiked up enough for him to see a little of her skin. He would love to be the arm of that chair, and have her resting against him. He'd reach around and hold her close to him.

Anyone else, he'd carry into his bedroom, and do what he wanted with her. But this was Renie, and if the day came that they took their relationship to a different level, it couldn't be spur of the moment, or in the heat of passion. It was too big a risk for them. Or for him anyway. If she weren't in his life, there would be a big gaping hole that no one else could fill.

She was his best friend. He wondered if she realized that. She shifted, and her eyes opened.

"Movie over?"

"Yep. I was about to wake you up and tell you to go downstairs to bed."

She stood and walked to the stairs, pulling the blanket behind her. She looked like a little girl.

"Night Billy," she said without turning around.

"Night Renie, I had a real nice night."

"Me too," he heard her say as she descended the stairs.

***

Billy was up before she was the next morning. He was sure of it because he went downstairs and peeked in on her. He closed the door behind him, quickly, for two reasons. He didn't want her to wake up and find him stalking her in her sleep. And, if he hadn't, he might have been tempted to crawl in bed with her.

***

Renie rolled over and puffed up her pillow, thinking she'd go back to sleep. Then, she smelled something. It smelled like bacon. Who would be cooking bacon? Had Dottie ridden over this morning and made them breakfast?

Curiosity won out, she had to go upstairs and see what was going on. She threw a sweatshirt over her pajamas, and ran upstairs.

Coffee. Someone made coffee.

Renie rounded the corner and gasped at the sight in front of her. The kitchen was a disaster. Bowls, pots, pans, and utensils covered nearly every surface. A trail of flour wound all the way around the island and over to the back door. She didn't see Billy.

"Boo!" he said, sneaking up behind her.

She jumped. "What happened in here?"

"Whaddaya mean? I'm cooking breakfast."

She walked to the stove, he'd splattered what looked like pancake batter all over it. She had to tread carefully, the look on his face was so…hopeful.

"It smells heavenly." She wasn't lying. "What did you make?"

"Bacon, and pancakes. I was thinking about making eggs too, but I don't know how you like 'em. Which made me feel kinda bad. You've made eggs for me at least a hundred times. I bet you even remember how I like 'em, don't ya?"

"You don't remember because I like eggs lots of different ways." She patted him on the cheek, and he flinched, again. She was getting tired of him flinching every time she touched him. It hurt her feelings. "Billy, is there a reason you don't want me to touch you?"

She got a cup out of the cupboard and poured herself some coffee. He still hadn't answered her, and she was annoyed enough to press him about it.

"We talked about this last night. I told you it might be too weird for me to stay here. If you've decided you agree, all you have to do is say so."

"And I answered you last night. I want you here. I mean Jesus, Renie, look at all this." He waved his hand around in the direction of his mess. "I wanted to make you breakfast."

He looked dejected. Her natural inclination was to rub his back and tell him how much she appreciated it. Or hug him. But since he flinched every time she touched him, she decided against an affectionate response.

"Thank you Billy. When will it be ready?"

"It's ready now, go sit down."

"Stop pouting. You look as though somebody kicked your puppy."

"I suck at this. I wanted to make us breakfast. You cook for me all the time. Now look at the kitchen."

He'd done a good job of making the biggest mess she'd ever seen, but he'd put his heart into it. She leaned over and kissed his cheek.

"This is the nicest thing you've ever done for me Billy. It's sweet, and I'm starving."

That got a grin out of him, and when she kissed his cheek, he didn't flinch.

"I'll even clean the kitchen."

"Nah, I can't let you do that, but I'll let you help."

She had to admit breakfast was good. Nothing was burnt. The pancakes had an odd taste, not bad, just different. She was afraid to ask him what he put in the batter.

"Wanna go for a ride later?" he asked.

"I'd love it. But Billy…I wish you'd stop flinching every time I touch you. It's starting to give me a complex."

What was he supposed to say? *Christ.* Right now, he wanted to lick the bit of syrup off the corner of her mouth, and run his hands over the smooth skin on her legs. Her ridiculously long legs that he could see every bit of because of her impossibly short pajama bottoms.

"Billy, did you hear me?"

"Yeah. So do you want to ride or not?"

"I told you I did, but you haven't answered me. Why are you acting so weird?"

"Just go get dressed," he barked at her.

"Keep talking to me like that, and you're gonna be cleaning the kitchen by yourself cowboy. You might be finished by next weekend."

"I won't be here next weekend." Now he was growling.

She threw her napkin down on the counter and stood. She put her dishes in the sink and went downstairs.

Great. Now he made her mad.

Less than two minutes later she was back upstairs. She was dressed and had her bags with her.

"Where are you going?"

"I'm going home Billy. Everything I say or do makes you mad. Sorry about leaving you to clean up the kitchen, but it's best if I go."

Oh no, no. This wasn't what he wanted to happen. He paced around the kitchen and ran his hand through his hair.

"Jesus Renie, I'm sorry. Look, we do need to talk. I just don't know where to start. The last thing I want you to do is leave though."

She dropped her bags on the floor. She looked as though she was getting ready to cry. Renie almost never cried. He kept making things worse.

"Come on," he said, pulling her by the hand. "Let's ride."

She went to get Pooh out of her stall while he figured out which horse to ride. She was so quiet. It wasn't like her to be so quiet. Under normal circumstances, she'd be giving him hell for how he was acting.

He walked to where she was brushing Pooh.

"Come here," he said and pulled her into a hug. "I'm sorry. I don't know what my problem is. Everything is off kilter this weekend. I can't explain it."

She rested her head on his shoulder. "I hate this. We're never like this. Why are we like this?"

"No idea," he answered, but he was lying again.

They followed the heavily-treed trail until they reached the top of the short incline, in another few feet they'd come to a large meadow. Renie coaxed Pooh into a gallop.

He stayed a few paces back, watching her ride. It was a beautiful thing. She was a perfect rider, a very natural one.

Her long blond hair blew in the wind. It was cold enough today that he could see her breath and her horse's. There was a mist hovering over the trees that made up the Black Forest.

"Let's go see your mom," she shouted out before she took off in that direction.

The best view of his parents' house was from this meadow. The house wasn't as modern as Liv's house—his house now. It had been built in the traditional Colorado-style, with log siding and a tin roof. Each of the three levels had decks off the main rooms; the railings were painted forest green. In the summer, his mom hung baskets filled with colorful flowers off the decks. There were two stone fireplaces, one on each side of the house. Smoke streamed from the one near the kitchen.

Renie climbed off Pooh and had opened the gate to the pasture by the time he rode up to the barn.

"Meet you inside," she said, running in the direction of the back door.

His heart ran right along with her. Why had it taken him so long to realize she took it with her wherever she went?

Renie went in, pulled her gloves off, and hung her jacket on the hook by the back door.

"Dottie? You in here?" she called out.

"Right here sweetheart. I saw you two out riding, so I put milk on the stove to make cocoa. Come in here and warm up by the fire."

Dottie pulled her into a big hug. Nobody gave hugs like Dottie. She held on a little longer than usual and then kissed her cheek. "Everything okay with you honey?"

"I'm okay. But I don't think Billy is," she said, biting her lip. "He's out of sorts."

"Pancakes didn't go so well?"

"No, the pancakes were fine. Wait. How did you...?"

"He called and asked me how to make them. In the time he took to write the directions, I could've ridden over, made them for him, and ridden back home." Dottie laughed. "It seemed important to him."

"He made bacon too."

Dottie raised her eyebrows.

"The kitchen looks as though a war took place in it, and the main weapon used by both sides was flour."

"Oh dear. I can picture it."

"I don't think that's his problem though."

***

Dottie knew what his problem was. Billy figured out the obvious. Renie Fairchild held his heart in the palm of her hand. She'd been waiting for this day.

***

"Hey Mama," he said, coming in the back door and shedding his gloves and jacket as Renie had.

"How'd the pancakes go this morning?"

He glared at her, which made Renie laugh. "Billy I've known you most of my life, and I've never seen you cook anything. Did you think I'd believe you whipped them up all on your own?"

He grumbled something she didn't catch.

"What are you two doing today? Besides cleaning the kitchen?" Dottie winked at Renie.

"I'm beginning to think I made a mistake buying the house next door."

"Oh stop, you love livin' next door to your mama." Dottie patted his cheek.

She was right, he did. He'd loved Liv's house since he was a little boy, and they built it on the open ranch land next to his parents' place.

It had two floors, the main one, where the kitchen, family room, master bedroom, and two other bedrooms were. On that floor there were two big stone fireplaces, both were double-sided. One was between the kitchen and the family room; the other was between the master bedroom and bathroom. It was one of his favorite things about the house.

On the lower level, there were three more bedrooms, and another double-sided fireplace that opened to the deck outside the walkout great room.

The house had three bathrooms on the main floor and another three on the lower level. Billy doubted he'd ever set foot in more than two of them, but he supposed if the time came that he ever had a family, they'd come in handy.

The house sat on one hundred acres that bordered his parents' land. Technically he lived next door to his parents, but there was a lot of open land, and a big, forested hill, between their two houses.

Chapter Three

Renie woke with a start. She'd been dreaming about Billy. Again. She wished she could find the damn off-switch for Billy dreams. She'd give anything not to think about him, not dream about him, yearn for him, ache for him, not miss him so much that her heart hurt the way it did.

She thought by now it would have gotten easier, but it felt the same today as it had earlier this year, when she'd left him in San Antonio, standing in the hospital doorway holding the baby.

It was different during the summer; she'd had a distraction then. Now that she didn't have that distraction *anymore, she felt as though she was right back where she started. A tear ran down her cheek. She didn't bother to brush it away, tears running down her cheeks were as familiar to her as the pain she carried around with her every day.*

"Renie, are you in there?" asked Luke, Ben's ten-year-old son.

"Yep. You can come in," she answered.

Luke opened the door slowly and walked into the dark room.

"Are you crying Renie?"

"Nah."

"I don't believe you."

"You're on to me, aren't you?"

Luke opened the blinds in the bedroom.

"What are you doing?" she covered her eyes against the sunlight that streamed in.

"It's afternoon, time to get up and do something with your day."

"Who are *you*?"

"I'm your worst nightmare," Luke joked, sounding more like his dad than a little boy.

"Go away." She buried her head under her pillow. "I worked at the Goat until two in the morning Luke. I'm tired."

"Let's go ride today Renie."

"No."

Luke got used to her saying no to him. And her getting mad at him every time he asked her to go riding. He also knew that if he pestered her long enough, she'd give in.

He loved it when they went riding because it made her happy, and she smiled. He wanted her to smile all the time, the way she used to. Renie used to be the happiest person he knew. Now sometimes he thought she was the saddest.

Renie stayed in a room on the lowest level of the three in Ben's house. It reminded her of her mother's house, where Billy lived now, but it had another level.

There were two other bedrooms on the bottom floor, where Jake and Luke stayed when they were here, instead of at their mom's. All three bedrooms had their own bathroom attached. There was also a family room on this level, complete with a big screen television, a pool table, foosball, and a ping-pong table.

The main level had another family room, along with the kitchen, dining room, and master bedroom. Her mother used the small bedroom next to the master as an office. The top floor of the house had been converted into a recording studio, conference room, and office for Ben. His band, CB Rice, had *exploded in popularity in the last couple of years. Prior to that, when he wasn't touring, he'd worked at the Goat, and with his brothers on the ranch. He no longer had time to do either.*

— • —

Billy wrote a text to Renie. *Not going this weekend.*
Why not? she answered.
Feeling off.
Why?

He wasn't sure, but things had been off for him for most of the year. At the end of the previous year, he was the saddle bronc champ. This year he considered retiring. He knew it would mentally be worse for him to go out this weekend and have another crappy showing, than it would be for him to stay home and try to get his head on straight. He didn't know where to start; so many things in his life weren't working right.

Are you coming down? Two could play the answer a question with a question game.

Wasn't planning to.

Now what? Should he ask her to? That was part of the reason he wanted to stay home. He wanted to see her. Maybe by Friday she'd change her mind.

She didn't.

***

Billy pulled up to O'Malley's Pub in Palmer Lake, the town northwest of Monument. It would be crowded on a Friday night, and loud. He wanted loud. Maybe it would drown out all the stuff going on inside his head. The stuff about Renie.

Gods somewhere were really fucking with him. If there were any girl alive—any single girl who walked the face of the earth—he shouldn't be attracted to, it would be Renie. And she was all he could think about.

He wanted to get drunk—rip roaring drunk.

Several beers and a few shots of whiskey later, Billy realized was too drunk to drive home. He couldn't think of anyone he could call to come get him. His parents would be sound asleep, not that he'd call them anyway. He was thirty-three years old, not twenty-three. Twenty-three. Renie was twenty-three. All week that'd been happening. No matter what random thought came to mind, something about her followed.

He'd sleep it off in his truck until he sobered up. Wouldn't be the first time.

Renie decided to go to bed. She had no idea what made her drive down here in the first place. And now that she had, he wasn't even home.

Her phone chirped. *Hey,* said the text message.

Hey, she answered.

What r u doin?

Hanging out in your house.

My house?

Yep.

Thought you weren't coming.

Changed my mind.

Renie waited ten minutes for another text from him. She sat there and stared at the phone. Waiting. Nothing. She walked around turning off lights, except the one in the kitchen. She might as well go downstairs and at least try to sleep. Tomorrow she'd drive back up to school. She wouldn't get any studying done staying in Billy's house.

She was halfway down the staircase when her phone chirped again.

Wish I hadn't left tonight.

Oh no. What did he expect her to say? *Why?*

Cuz wish I was home.

Where was he? In jail? *Why don't you come home?*

2 much 2 drink.

Oh for Christ's sake. *Where are you?*

O'Malleys.

On my way.

Renie waited another two or three minutes to leave, in case he told her not to come, but he didn't answer. It would take her at least twenty minutes to get there, he'd better still be there when she did.

Billy was standing next to his truck when she pulled in. There wasn't anywhere for her to park in the crowded lot. She stopped and rolled down her window.

"Lookin' for a ride cowboy?"

Billy didn't answer. He walked toward her car. Even drunk there wasn't anything like watching Billy Patterson swagger. Renie was five ten, and Billy was at least six inches taller. He had dark, almost black hair. His eyes were blue, but pale, not dark blue like hers. By two in the afternoon, dark stubble would start to show on Billy's face.

His jacket was open in the front, and his red plaid True Grit shirt fit tight across his chest, even with the top two buttons undone. His tan suede cowboy hat sat low enough that his eyes were partially covered. He smiled at her, the kind of shit-eating grin that said he'd gotten exactly what he wanted.

His perfectly symmetrical dimples helped him get away with more.

"Hey there cowgirl," Billy said, tipping his hat to her.

Renie looked back and forth. "No cowgirls here."

He climbed in the passenger seat and turned sideways, so he faced her. "Come on Renie, you're a cowgirl, you know you are. You have been since you were a little bit a nuthin' ridin' around on Pooh Bear."

"How much did you have to drink tonight Billy?"

"Not enough to chase the ghosts away Renie." Billy stroked the side of her face.

Oh, no. "What ghosts?" she whispered.

"Your ghosts Renie. You been hauntin' me tonight, you been hauntin' me all week, and no amount of whiskey could get you out of my head."

Billy cupped the back of her neck. "You know what I'm talkin' about Renie?"

She couldn't find her voice to answer. Billy was about to kiss her, but he was very drunk. If he did, and then didn't remember tomorrow, it would kill her.

"Please don't Billy."

"I gotta." He pulled her closer and put his lips on hers.

She gasped, and her lips opened slightly. He must've taken that as a sign. His mouth went from gentle to rough, his tongue attacking hers.

He pulled back, his hand still tight on her neck. "I knew it," he said, his eyes looking deeply into hers.

"What did you know Billy?"

"Fucking amazing. I knew it would be." He leaned forward and nipped her bottom lip, pulling it until her mouth opened to his again.

When she started to get light-headed, Renie pulled back. "Let's get you home," she murmured.

"Home." He threw his hat over the seat. "I live in your house Renie."

"It's your house now," she pulled out of the parking lot on Highway 105 in the direction of home. "It used to be my mom's house."

"I can feel you in it, even when you ain't there. It's your house too Renie. Your ghost hangs out there, hauntin' me."

Yep, he was drunk. She had no idea what he was talking about and doubted he did either. She turned the music up, hoping he'd pass out between here and home. He leaned his head back on the seat; it looked as though he was well on his way.

"Go to sleep Billy," she said.

When she pulled in, she woke him up, and helped him as far as the big sofa in the family room. She wouldn't even try to get him in bed; that would mean she'd have to go in his room. She wasn't ready to be in Billy's bedroom with him.

"Come here," he said, lying on his back, reaching up for her.

"Night Billy," she said and tossed a blanket to him.

"Wait Renie, come back, we need to talk."

We'll talk in the morning if you even remember this, she thought as she went back down the staircase she headed down an hour ago. She wasn't any readier to go to sleep now than she had been then.

***

When he woke up it took him a minute to figure out where he was. He lifted his head to look around and immediately put it back down on the pillow on the sofa. Jesus, how much had he had to drink last night? And how did he get here? He hoped like hell he hadn't driven here.

He didn't remember a thing except his crazy-ass dreams. Renie was in all of them, and he was kissing her. It made him hard thinking about it. He closed his eyes, not ready to get up yet. His head was spinning. Also, when he closed his eyes, the dream about Renie came back to him enough that he felt her lips against his.

He dozed off again, when he woke back up, he pulled his phone out to check the time. One in the afternoon? Shit. He sat up, a little too quickly, and had to wait for a second before he stood. He walked as far as the kitchen and saw his truck keys on the counter. Oh no, he did drive home. What was wrong with him? He knew better. He picked up his keys and saw the note.

Your dad and I went and got your truck. Took care of the horses. Your turn tonight. Renie.

He hadn't dreamt it; she had been here. What about the rest of it? He hoped the memories swirling around in his head were from a dream, and that he hadn't kissed her.

Billy went to the door and didn't see her car.

He walked to the refrigerator and pulled out a beer. He saw a container that hadn't been there the day before. It looked like soup. God love Renie Fairchild, she'd left him something to eat. He heated it up and went to sit back on the sofa, but instead kept going, and went and got into bed.

He set the bowl down on the dresser and pulled out his phone.

Where are you? he texted. He set the phone down and picked up his soup. She still hadn't answered by the time he finished it. He put his head down on the pillow. He'd sleep a little while, then get up and check on the horses.

He shook himself awake and checked to see whether Renie had answered him yet. Nope. It was almost five. If he went out and took care of the horses now, he could go back to sleep after he did.

He walked into the barn. Something didn't feel right. He looked in each of the stalls, and then it hit him, where was Pooh? He didn't remember seeing her out in the pasture. He walked back out to check anyway. No sign of her.

He checked his phone again. Renie still hadn't answered him. Now he was worried. He couldn't very well text her and ask her about her horse, the one that was supposed to be in his care. He called his dad.

"I have a situation over here Dad. I might need your help."

"What's goin' on son?" Billy hit the parent jackpot. There weren't two better people on the face of the earth.

"I think I lost a horse."

His dad started to laugh. "A whole horse?"

"Seriously Dad, I can't find Pooh."

"Renie brought her here."

"Why did she do that? And why didn't she tell me? Shit, she practically gave me a heart attack."

"She wouldn't say, just asked whether it was okay if she did. Then, she told your mama she'd explain later. I hate to ask you this Billy, but did you do something to upset Renie?"

Maybe he hadn't been dreaming after all. And if not, he just made the worst mistake of his life.

***

Renie would have to find somewhere else to board Pooh. Dottie told her she could keep her horse in their barn as long as she needed, but she couldn't impose long. First thing Monday morning she planned to find a place closer to school, and then she'd go down and get her horse. She hoped she didn't run into Billy when she did.

***

"I don't feel right about this son," Bill said.

"Pooh's home is on the other side of this hill Dad. I don't know what Renie's particular problem is, other than I went out and got drunk last night, and then made the mistake of asking her to give me a ride home. I can see her bein' pissed at me, but that isn't a reason to move her horse."

"She seemed determined."

That made Billy laugh. Renie was always determined. "That doesn't sound so unusual Dad."

Bill laughed too. Yep, determined was practically her middle name.

"She's gonna be mad."

"Yep, I know it. But I'll keep you and mom out of it."

He needed to get to the bottom of what Renie was upset about.

Bill put his hand on his son's shoulder. "Why don't you tell me what's really going on?"

"She won't answer me."

"Who won't?"

"Renie. When I got up this morning, she was gone. I've been trying to get in touch with her all day. She won't answer me."

***

Billy texted Renie again, for the fifth time. Still no response out of her. He wanted to wring her damn neck.

"Hey, have you talked to Renie?" He called Liv and asked her.

"Yes, this morning, why? Is everything okay?"

He didn't want to get into what may, or may not, have happened, particularly since he couldn't remember last night very clearly. He also didn't want to tell Liv that Renie moved Pooh to his parents' stable, or that he brought Pooh back to his barn. That would unleash a whole slew of questions he didn't have answers to.

"Everything is fine. I'm trying to reach her and haven't been able to."

"She seemed okay earlier, but I can call her again if you think it's necessary. What's up? Anything I can help with?"

"You've done enough. How you talked me into keeping the stables goin' is beyond me."

"Billy, what does this have to do with Renie?"

"Just ask her to call me."

Three hours later he got a text from her.

What?

Was she kidding? *Call me.*

Fifteen minutes. No response. No call. He called her, but she didn't answer. Now he was pissed.

What the hell Renie? What's your problem?

***

What was *her* problem? If he remembered what happened the night before, he wouldn't be asking her that question.

All her life she wanted Billy Patterson to kiss her, and now that he had, he didn't even remember it.

And what the hell had he been talking about last night? All that stuff about her ghost haunting him? It had to have been the whiskey.

* * *

Renie was about to have the most awkward conversation of her life. She was calling her mom to talk about Billy. She didn't have any choice, there was no one else she trusted enough to tell her deepest darkest secret to.

"Hey Ben," Renie said when her mother's husband answered. The cell coverage at their ranch in Crested Butte was spotty, so Renie usually tried the house phone first. "Is my mom around?"

"Yep, she is, I'll get her. How are you? Everything okay?"

She loved Ben, but she didn't want to talk to him; she wanted to talk to her mom. "Yeah, I'm fine." Ben must've taken the hint because he didn't say anything else.

"Hi sweet girl, how are you?"

"I'm okay. I need to talk to you about Billy."

"I thought you might since he called and asked me whether I had heard from you. What's going on with you two? Is he giving you a hard time about the stables? That isn't your problem, that's between him and me."

"No, that isn't it." Renie had no idea how she would be able to say what she had to say. "Um…"

"Renie just say it. I can hear you're upset by the sound of your voice. What is it?"

"It's about me and Billy."

Silence—the reaction Renie had been expecting.

"Mom, are you there?"

"I'm here. Where are you?"

"At school."

"Are you okay honey?"

Her mother's voice got soft, as it did when she knew Renie was hurting about something. She loved that about her mom, when she got it so easily that Renie didn't have to explain.

"I don't know. Mom, I'm not sure how to say this."

Liv would murder Billy Patterson. If he hurt one hair on her daughter's head, she would have to kill him.

"Just tell me sweetheart. What has Billy done?"

"You know how everybody used to joke that Billy spent most of his life in love with you?"

"We used to joke that Billy had a crush on me when he was a teenager. That's a whole lot different than being in love with me. What's going on Renie?"

"Well someone else has spent their whole life being in love with him."

Liv sat down when her heart went into her throat. How had she not seen this? "Are you that someone Renie?"

"Yes."

"And what's happened?"

Renie told her about Billy's offer to let her stay at the house on the weekends, and then told her what had happened the night before, when Billy kissed her.

"The worst part Mom, is that he doesn't remember it."

Renie was crying, which was completely unlike her.

She hadn't dated much in high school, which worried Liv some, but it also made things easier. She hadn't dated in high school either, and if her daughter had looked to her for advice, she would have been lost.

This was the first time Renie mentioned a specific boy to her, and she was twenty-three years old. Her confession about Billy explained why.

***

Now that Renie wasn't talking to him, Billy realized how much he talked to her. Not talked necessarily, but texted. He doubted there'd been a day in as long as he could remember when they didn't. When he had a good ride, she was the first person he sent a text to. When he was sitting at home, doing nothing, he'd text her to see what she was doing. No matter what, she was always the first person he wanted to talk to. Why hadn't he noticed it before? She comforted him. She was his touchstone. And now she wouldn't answer him.

He knew deep down it hadn't been a dream. He hadn't dreamt it, he kissed her. If he closed his eyes, he could still feel her lips against his. And that's why she wouldn't answer him.

I'm sorry, he texted, not knowing what else to say.

Still no answer.

***

The next morning Liv decided to visit Dottie. She was due for a visit anyway. Ben said he'd fly her over and hang out at Paige and Mark Cochran's who lived between Liv's old ranch and downtown Monument.

Ben was on hiatus from touring while his band, CB Rice, recorded a new album. It was a good time for him to take a couple days break from the studio. They kept the plane he and the band shared with his parents at the airport in Gunnison. Liv could be in Monument in less than two hours.

"You sure you want to do this?" Ben asked her.

"I am. I've never heard Renie talk this way, even if I don't get anywhere with Dottie, I have to see my daughter."

They rented a car at the Centennial airport, and Liv dropped Ben off at the Cochran's.

And Then You Dance

"I could come with you," he offered.

"Thanks, but it would be better if you stayed here." They were spending the night there anyway, unless Liv decided she needed to go see Renie tonight. Fort Collins was a little less than two hours from Monument.

Liv pulled into the long driveway at Patterson Ranch; she could see her old place from there. Billy's truck was parked near the house. She hoped that meant he was there not here.

"Hey-o," she said when she walked in the back door. "Anybody home?"

"Oh my goodness is that a sound for sore ears! Is that my Livvie?" Dottie came out of the kitchen and wrapped Liv in a big hug. *Nobody hugged like Dottie.*

"Hi Dottie," Liv teared up a little being in the kitchen where she'd spent so much time. "I've missed you," she looked around, "and this place."

"I missed you too. And while I surely am happy to see you, I gotta ask, what brings you to my kitchen today?"

Whenever Liv had a problem, of any kind, Dottie was the first person she talked to about it.

"It's about Renie."

Dottie sighed heavily. "I knew that. She was here yesterday. Asked whether we'd keep Pooh here in our barn for a couple of days. Said she wants to move her to a stable in Fort Collins. Closer to her."

Renie hadn't mentioned that during their conversation the night before.

"It has something to do with Billy."

Dottie laughed, "That's obvious darlin'." Dottie patted Liv's hand and stood. "Get you something to drink?"

"What time is it?" Liv asked, looking at her watch, three in the afternoon. "I would love a glass of wine."

Dottie went into the pantry and pulled out a bottle of Zinfandel, Liv's favorite.

Liv told Dottie about her conversation with Renie. "I didn't see this coming, at all."

Dottie didn't say anything. She always said something, so when she didn't, Liv didn't know what to think. "Dottie?"

"I've been watchin' this for a while. Watchin' both of them. There isn't a thing he does in his life without talkin' to Renie about it. And God knows she's had a mad love on him since she was a wee little thing."

"What are you talking about?"

"Oh honey, how could you have not noticed?" Dottie patted her hand again.

"Why didn't you say something to me?" How long had she been completely insensitive to her own daughter?

"Renie's real good at makin' sure everything stays on an even keel. She isn't ever gonna be the one to rock the boat. She's used to hiding her feelings Liv. You know that. "

"But *Billy*? I didn't see it."

"For the longest time, there wasn't anything to see. She was a girl, and he was a man. But in the last couple of years, that's changed. Renie is a woman now. And Billy's noticed."

"She's upset with him right now. She's hurt."

"He's hurtin' too. It's what they both need. He needs it, so he realizes what she means to him. She needs it, so she realizes she can't keep hiding her feelings."

Liv knew talking to Dottie would be the best thing she could do. And it wouldn't have been the same if she had called her instead of coming here.

"So Mama Patterson, what do we do about our kids?"

Dottie laughed and poured Liv another glass of wine. "Not a thing darlin' girl. We let 'em figure it out for themselves."

"You are a wise woman Dottie. I'm thankful every day that you're in my life."

"Who knows Livvie, we might end up official family after all."

Liv's face went white, which made Dottie laugh. She laughed so hard she had to hold her stomach.

"It's gonna happen someday you know. Why not with Billy?" Dottie asked once her giggles had subsided.

"You've had longer to get used to the idea," answered Liv. "Give me a little while to catch up."

***

Renie please. I'm sorry, he wrote again, the next morning. This was killing him, and he didn't know what to do about it.

I brought Pooh home. Maybe that'd get her to respond.

Less than a minute later Billy's phone rang. Yep, that worked.

"I don't want Pooh at your place, Billy. You don't have anyone to take care of her."

"That's all you're gonna say? You aren't going to ask what I'm sorry for?"

"I don't care what you're sorry for, unless it's because you moved my horse."

"I'm here, and when I am, I take good care of her along with the rest of the horses that board here. Also, I hired Sookie. He's gonna stay here whenever I'm out of town."

"I decided to bring her up here anyway."

"Why Renie? Because I kissed you?"

She didn't answer. He wondered for a minute if she hung up, but then he heard her breathing.

"It isn't a reason to move her, but it is a reason for us to talk, which we could've done if you hadn't high-tailed it out of here yesterday. And then refused to answer any of my texts."

"You were drunk."

"I was drunk. Still, not a reason for you to refuse to talk to me."

More silence.

"Look, you gotta give me somethin' here. Are you mad at me because you didn't want me to kiss you, or are you mad at me because you did?"

She hesitated. "I'm not sure."

"What are you doin' right now?"

"Billy—"

"Just answer me. What are you doin' right now?"

"Trying to study."

"Is it workin'?"

"No, not very well."

"You think if we hang up right now, it'll get better?"

"No."

"I'm comin' to your place."

"No, don't do that."

"We gotta resolve this Renie. These have been the two worst days of my life."

"Why?"

"I'll tell you when I get there."

Chapter Four

"Have you talked to her?" Billy asked his mom.

"Livvie, or Renie?" Dottie talked to Liv at least once a week. Billy knew that much.

"Either."

"I talked to Liv a couple of days ago."

"How's she doin'?"

"Which one?"

He gave her exasperated look. "As if my life isn't hard enough Mama, come on."

"Liv is concerned about her. Renie asked Ben about workin' at the Goat for the season." Dottie shook her head.

Willow started babbling through the monitor. She rarely ever cried when she first woke. She babbled. He'd go in to get her, and she'd be standing up in her crib, watching the door, waiting for him. As soon as he walked in she'd babble even more, and reach out for him to pick her up.

"Well, there's my pretty girl," he kissed her forehead, and held her close. "Grandma's here. Let's go see Grandma."

Willow kicked her legs and continued with her unintelligible stream of conversation. He couldn't wait until he understood all that she had to tell him. She was such a chatterbox. Just as Renie used to be. He'd watch her out in the pasture, talking to Pooh a mile a minute. God he missed her.

He held Willow closer, and she opened her mouth on his cheek. A Willow kiss. He loved them.

— • —

It had been a roll of the dice. Billy was pretty sure he'd kissed Renie, but not one hundred percent. It did explain her behavior, which is why he'd decided he hadn't dreamt it.

He hadn't ever visited her at school, but Fort Collins was close to Greeley and he'd competed there enough to know about where he had to get off the highway.

He called Sookie from the road and told him his parents had a house key for him to use until Billy had time to get one made for him.

"You can stay up at the house tonight if you want to. There's a guest room on the main floor, to the left of the kitchen. That'll be yours, and you can stay there as much or as little as you want to."

"Can't tell you how much I appreciate this," Sookie said, and then told him how grateful he was to get out of the bunkhouse. "Whatever you need help with, I'm happy to do it."

As long as Sookie stayed away from Renie, he didn't care what the man did. There was a bigger bedroom downstairs, but it was next to the one she stayed in. Billy didn't want him down there.

***

Billy would be there in about an hour and a half if he left when she thought he did. She looked around her one bedroom apartment, trying to decide if she should try to tidy up, or text him and suggest they meet somewhere.

It would be better to meet somewhere. She wasn't ready to have Billy here, in her space.

Meet me at the hideout, she texted.

No, he answered.

You aren't supposed to be texting and driving.

Not.

How was that even possible?

For a smart girl, you don't know much about technology, do ya?

Meet me at the hideout, she texted again.

No, he answered. Again.

Shit. She really didn't want him here.

An hour later she heard a knock at the door. How had he gotten here so fast?

"Hi," Renie answered. *Damn,* he looked good. He hadn't shaved all day, so the dark stubble was even longer. She wanted to reach out and run her hand over it. He wore his dark blue, plaid True Grit shirt. His Cinch jeans were just the right amount of tight.

"You gonna invite me in to do that or are you gonna feast me with your eyes out here in the hallway?"

She smiled, stepped back, and waved him in.

Her place was small, but it looked like her. The dining room table was stacked high with books and papers, but the kitchen was spotless. The living room, which the dining room infringed on, looked less lived in.

He longed to go and explore the rest of it, see her bedroom. He would've done whatever he wanted to a couple days ago, but now things were different between them.

He looked at her. She studied him, a little smirk on her face, as if she dared him to do it.

"Ah hell," he said and stalked down the hall, opening the first door he came to. Bathroom. He closed the door. There was one other door; it had to be her bedroom. It was, and it wasn't at all what he expected.

It was the only room that looked as though she decorated it in a purposeful way. The rest of her apartment looked like a typical twenty-something's place, a mishmash of randomly-gathered furniture. This was a different story. It looked as though it belonged in Greece. Everything in the room was white, except the bright turquoise and red pillows scattered here and there. The mattress sat on a white platform with a molded headboard that looked as though it was made of clay or stone. On the ledge it formed naturally, was a single vase with three fresh roses, and one picture frame. He walked over and picked up a photo of her and Pooh; she had to have been about eleven or twelve. The man standing next to them, holding the horse's reins, was none other than yours truly.

Renie stood in the doorway, watching him. He set the photo back down and looked around.

"Where do you keep your clothes?"

"In the closet."

Still with the smirk, he wanted to wipe it off her face, but the way he wanted to do it...it might be too soon for him to think about that.

He walked back to her. She didn't move, so he got as close to her as he could, without touching her. He stood in front of her and looked, up and down, the way she had done to him when he got there.

She had on jeans, the same 501s she always wore, and a pink, striped, button-down shirt, with enough buttons undone that from where he stood, he could see the lace on her white bra, and the swell of her breasts. One hand was on her hip; the other hung at her side. Her feet were bare, and her toenails were the lightest shade of pink. Her long blond hair was up off her neck, he preferred it down. Tiny pearl earrings adorned her ears, and her blue eyes didn't blink.

He reached up and took the clip out of her hair, and dropped it on the floor. She started to reach down to pick it up, and he grabbed her arm, stopping her.

He brushed his lips across her cheek, to her ear. "Either let me out of your bedroom Renie, or be prepared to stay in here the rest of the night. With me."

She didn't move, so he took her hand, to pull her into the room with him. She let go, turned, and walked back down the hallway to her living room.

Billy walked into the kitchen and opened the refrigerator. As though he owned the place.

"Whatcha' lookin' for?" she asked.

"Somethin' to eat."

"I told you to meet me at the Hideout."

"Why would I do that? You're a great cook Renie." He pulled out a container, and put it in the microwave.

Was there a more confident man on the planet? If so, she hadn't met him. And she'd been looking. First at Dartmouth, and now here in Fort Collins. She looked and looked for a man to help her forget about Billy Patterson. She hadn't found one yet.

Wherever he was, Billy owned the air. It belonged to him, and he took it. He used as much as he wanted, and figured if you needed any, you'd take it too.

He opened drawers until he found a fork.

"Did you eat?" he asked, as though he suddenly remembered she stood near him.

"It's almost eleven o'clock at night Billy. I ate hours ago."

"I didn't." He set the dish and fork down on the counter. "Wanna know why not?"

No, she didn't. So she shrugged.

"'Cause you had me all wound up Renie."

"You sure you weren't just hung over?"

His eyes flared open wider, and in one long stride he stood in front of her. He pushed her back against the counter.

"No. I wasn't," he said, getting his mouth close to hers, without their lips touching.

She couldn't move; he had her surrounded with his body. If he got any closer, every inch of him would be touching every inch of her.

He shook his head, stepped back, and picked up his food.

"Would you like to sit down while you eat?"

He motioned to her table. "Doesn't look as though there's much room at your table sugar."

Dish still in hand, he looked at the books. "Intense."

"Stuff you'd know in your sleep."

He raised an eyebrow.

"Horses. You know more about them than I do Billy."

"Not all this kinda stuff I don't." He picked up a textbook on anatomy.

"You may not know all the scientific terminology, but everything else?" She sat down on the couch. "I've never met anybody who understands them the way you do. It's because you listen."

He put the dish in the sink. "We gotta talk about the other night."

"You were drunk Billy. I get that."

"And you think that's why I kissed you?"

She shrugged.

He sat down next to her. "Not drunk now." He pulled her into him, and kissed her. At first gentle, probing, his lips brushing back and forth over hers as his tongue gently pushed its way in. His other hand came up and stroked her face, then moved to the back of her neck. His kiss deepened, harder, as his hand slid down to the buttons on her shirt.

She grabbed his wrist, stopping him.

"Let me in," he murmured.

Renie twisted away from him and stood. "I can't do this Billy." She wiped her hand across her mouth.

Billy leaned forward and put his head in his hands. He took a few deep breaths. "Okay. We won't do this, but we have to talk. Have to. You're too important to me not to."

Renie went into the kitchen and opened the refrigerator. Then closed it. She opened up a cupboard and closed it too. She leaned up against the counter.

"Whatever answers you're looking for aren't in there. Come back out here and talk to me."

Renie turned the corner and leaned up against the wall.

"Tell me what you're thinkin'," he pleaded.

"You know me better than that Billy."

"Pretend I'm Pooh."

"There we go," she laughed. "You know me too well,"

"You think I never noticed your little motor mouth runnin' when you were out in the pasture with your horse? I would've given anything to hear what you were talkin' to her about."

You, always you Billy. I've been in love with you forever. And you've never thought of me as anything other than a little sister, or a pest. She closed her eyes at the hurt that pounded in her chest. As much joy as she felt when she saw him, it was always coupled with the pain, the yearning for him. It throbbed in every part of her body. She'd gotten so used to the feeling, it was a part of her being. Yearning for Billy, it's what her body did naturally.

Her eyes stayed closed, she focused on the ache of it. She didn't realize he stood in front of her.

He tucked her hair behind her ear; his hand lingered there. "I wish I could read your mind. I've always wished so."

Thank God he couldn't, she'd never be able to look him in the face again.

"You want me to tell you how I'm feelin' about all this? About you and me…"

Her eyes riveted to his; her brow furrowed. She bit her upper lip. He doubted she realized she did it. She looked terrified.

"Renie, please." His fingers caressed her face.

She leaned her head into his hand. Her eyes closed again.

"Go ahead," he said. "Take a chance, tell me."

She nodded her head back and forth. "I can't," she whispered.

He took her hand. "Come, sit with me."

Renie let him pull her to the couch. Her back was to the arm and she put her feet up, so her legs formed a wall of knee between the two of them. Billy rested his elbow on them.

"Some say, in fact, I've heard you say it yourself, that I've been pitched off one too many broncs," he shook his head and laughed. "And I suppose I act like it often enough. I'm thirty-three years old, and this is the first time I've lived in my own place. I've lived with my parents my whole life."

She nodded.

"Out on the road all the time...let's say there have been women in my life. You know what I'm sayin'?"

She did, or at least she nodded again.

Billy took her feet and pulled them, so her legs stretched over his. He put his arm on top of them.

"The other day, when you touched my arm, you felt it too, didn't you?"

Now, she wouldn't even look at him. She looked across the room.

"Look at me, dammit."

Her head snapped back; her eyes met his.

"Renie, I swear to God, this is the most important conversation I'll ever have with you. You gotta pay attention to me. You're killin' me. Do you even realize it?"

"No, I don't." She whispered again.

"Do you know how ripped up I am about this?"

No response, not even head movement.

"That's why I got drunk the other night. Because when you touched my arm, I felt it throughout my entire body. I almost pulled you into my arms and kissed you then. I wanted to so bad."

She closed her eyes.

"How long have you felt it Renie?"

That made her open her eyes, but she didn't answer him.

"Do you realize that you're the only person I tell everything to? I don't think I go more than a couple of hours without wanting to tell you something."

He did send her some random texts, all day, most days. She assumed he got lonely out on the road. Most of the guys traveled with somebody else. Billy never did. He said it messed with his head too much. He liked to have the time to think, without somebody interrupting him all the time.

When her mom was recovering from her accident, they caravanned to different rodeos they both competed in, but they took their own trucks. Once, after her mother's first rodeo, Renie rode home with Billy. He told her she was the only person he'd ever let ride with him—ever. He also told her he liked having her with him.

"You're my best friend."

It didn't surprise her to hear him say so. It was part of the problem. Billy saw her as his friend. But now the problem changed. Is that what he struggled with?

"We can stay friends Billy."

"Is that what you want?"

She shrugged. "Long history between us. Don't know if we want to mess it up."

"Damn Renie. There's a lot I want to mess up with you, but not our history."

"I don't know what that means Billy. Your friendship means the world to me, it always has. And I suppose you're my best friend too." She grinned. "But if you ever tell Blythe I said so, I'll deny it."

He didn't smile. He was close enough to her that she heard every breath he took. It was her breath he took away, all of it. He stared at her, and she didn't look away.

"How could I have been so blind?"

She was glad he'd been blind. It saved her the awkward conversation. If Billy had told her he didn't "feel that way," about her, it would've destroyed her. It was better believing he didn't know how she felt, so he never pushed her away.

She'd be the friend, the best friend, but always on the inside, so she at least knew how he was feeling.

"How long?"

"Billy, don't."

He got up and went into the kitchen. How long had she felt this thing between them? And how long had he been denying it? Memories started flooding back to him faster than his brain processed them. There she was, in every memory. Sometimes in the background, but always there.

He stood in the kitchen with his hands on the edge of the counter, wondering what in the hell he should do next. He wanted to take her back into that bedroom and never leave.

Renie came around the corner but stopped, and leaned up against it.

"Let's put that last couple of days behind us Billy. We can go back to how it was before."

"I can't do that Renie."

"But…"

She was about to cry again, and in all the years he'd known her, he rarely remembered seeing her cry.

"I can't lose you Billy. You mean too much to me."

"What makes you think you're gonna lose me?"

"I can't be one of your girls Billy—the pack that follows you to rodeos."

"Irene Fairchild, you've never been one of a pack of anything. Not ever. And you never will be."

"You should go home."

"Nope. I'm not goin' anywhere. We gotta work through this."

She bit her lip and shoved her hands in the pockets of her jeans.

"I'm not sayin' anything is gonna happen between us tonight, I'm just sayin' that I'm not goin' home."

If he wanted to reach out, pull her into him, and hold her close. What would she do if he did? She looked scared. He understood her being nervous, but Renie looked scared.

He held his hand out to her, but she didn't budge. He stepped closer. His hand still extended in her direction. "Take my hand."

"Why?"

"'Cause."

"Billy, I can't—"

"Take my hand. That's it. That's all you gotta do."

She took her hand out of her pocket.

"You're gettin' closer." Billy took another step forward.

She put her hand in his and he pulled her into him. She stood with her arms at her sides. He put his arms around her anyway, his head softly leaning against hers.

"Tell me what you're afraid of," he whispered.

"You'll break my heart Billy Patterson."

"Nah, I'd never do that to you Renie."

"You can't guarantee it."

"Never. I promise."

He turned her, so she faced the same direction he did. "We're gonna go to bed now Renie. And I'm gonna sleep with you tonight, but that's all we're gonna do."

Billy went into the bedroom, and Renie went into the bathroom. He took his clothes off, and then decided he better leave his boxer briefs on, at least. Since he promised her nothing would happen between them tonight.

He wondered which side of the bed she slept on. Whichever it was, that's where he wanted to be. He settled on the middle.

She came in wearing a sweatshirt, that he swore used to be his, and flannel pajama bottoms. He could see less of her now than when she was fully dressed. But again, nothing was happening between them tonight.

She saw where he was and shook her head, sliding in next to him.

"You should sleep on top of the covers."

"What? You're crazy, it's freezing in here."

"But—"

"You can trust me Renie. Now, get closer to me." He put his arm around her and scooted her into him.

"Put your head right here," he said, patting his chest. When she did, he took her arm and draped it across his stomach.

"Go to sleep."

It took only a few minutes until she sounded as though she was. It would be a long time before he did the same. He doubted he'd sleep at all tonight. He had a lot of thinking to do. Funny how he usually wanted to be alone when he needed to think on something. Tonight he'd think better with her by his side. That must mean something.

Chapter Five

Renie missed her horse. If she asked her mom, she'd bring Pooh to Crested Butte for her. But she wouldn't ask. She had a very good reason why not.

Billy would take good care of Pooh, better than she would herself. He understood horses, loved them, lived and breathed them. Or at least he used to. Before the baby.

She still didn't want to talk about him, to anyone. If her mom tried to bring him up she'd leave the room. Her mom would get mad at her, but Renie didn't mind making her mom mad. She did mind talking about Billy.

"I'm open to any suggestions you might have," Liv said when Dottie called to check in.

"I haven't come up with anything, if I do, I'll call you."

"How's Willow?"

"As beautiful as the day is long. And Billy's such a good daddy. Have to admit, I wasn't sure he had it in him. Thought that darlin' little girl would be spendin' more time with her grandma than her daddy."

"I'm due for a trip over, I can't wait to see her. I bet she's getting so big."

Liv had been to see Willow, and to check on Pooh, a couple times in the last eight months. Renie didn't ask where she was going, and she didn't volunteer any information. She even took photos of Willow, just in case. But, Renie never mentioned Billy or anything to do with him. She never mentioned Pooh either. It broke Liv's heart as much as anything else.

And Then You Dance

— • —

He checked his phone, almost one in the morning. No wonder she fell asleep so fast. Not to mention the emotional wringer he put her through.

He realized at one point tonight that Renie would be way ahead of him. She saw coming before he did. She was usually at least one step ahead of him, if not more.

He had several things to consider. Their two families were almost one. He was much older than she, and based on her reactions to him tonight, he was more experienced than she too. She was his best friend. Of everything, that was the most important. She was terrified that he would hurt her, which meant she wanted more than friendship with him. If she didn't, she would've said so, and she definitely wouldn't be worried about him hurting her.

He wondered how long it had been that he'd taken Renie Fairchild for granted. Probably since the day he met her. She often looked at him in a way that said she knew exactly what he was thinking; and then she'd laugh at him for it. Nobody called him on his shit better than Renie did. Not even his mom, who called people on their shit all the time.

A couple years ago, Renie's mom broke her neck in an accident while barrel racing. Things changed between them then. Liv had been in a coma, and Renie stayed by her side every minute. And he stayed by Renie's side. As Liv started to recover, he rode with her, encouraged her, got her back in the saddle. Renie had been with them then too.

Wait, he thought, it was before that. The first rodeo Liv competed in, in Woodward, Oklahoma. His parents, Renie,

Paige, and Mark, even Ben, had come to town to see Liv in her first barrel race.

That weekend he danced with Renie. He held her close and realized she wasn't a little girl anymore. She was a woman, and every part of him stood up and took notice. He even remembered the song. They danced to "Free" by Zac Brown Band. It made him wonder what it would be like to hop in a truck and go…travel around the country, just her and him.

The next day when they caravanned home, Renie rode with him. He didn't want anyone riding with him on the road. People on the circuit said he was weird about it, but he didn't care. It was the way he liked it. But, when she rode with him, it was different.

They'd talked, and laughed, and then were quiet, and no matter what, he was comfortable.

Then there was the wedding. Last summer, Ben Rice talked Liv Fairchild into marrying him. It took place in Crested Butte, where Ben lived. His family had owned the Flying R Ranch on the south side of Crested Butte Mountain near East River Valley, since the mid-1800s. Each of Ben's brothers, and their parents, had houses on the ranch. The week of the wedding, he and his parents stayed with Will, Ben's youngest brother and his wife, Maeve. Renie stayed at Ben's with her mom and Ben's two boys, Jake and Luke.

Ben and Liv got married on the porch of his parents' sprawling ranch house. The setting was perfect enough it looked like a movie set.

The house, built of dark wood, had a huge wraparound porch, and a spectacular view of Mount Crested Butte to the east, and the valley to the west. And all around them, the

Rocky Mountains rose majestically out of the earth, as though they were there to witness the wedding. The sun was shining; the sky was a perfect cloud-free Colorado blue. A light breeze blew, but it was warm that day.

Twelve-year-old Jake, and Luke who recently turned ten, walked Liv down the aisle that formed naturally by the stone walkway that wound through the front lawn up to the porch steps. Renie, the maid of honor, stood on those steps looking so beautiful, she took Billy's breath away.

When he closed his eyes, he pictured the soft pink dress she wore. It was sleeveless and rested just above her knees. She was tan from spending all her time outdoors, and her blond hair was loose, blowing in the wind. Her feet were bare. He remembered, that day, realizing Renie was about the sexiest woman he'd ever seen. And the most beautiful.

He watched as her mother made her way to where Ben stood on the porch, right across from Renie. It was almost as though Renie was the parent watching her child marry the love of her life; she looked at her mother with such pride and love.

The ceremony had been short. Liv stood, barefoot herself, one step higher than Ben because he was so much taller than she. And when the ceremony ended, Ben sang to her. He wrote the song, "And Then You Fall," for her. He released it not long after Liv's accident, while she was still in the coma. There wasn't a dry eye at the Rice Ranch that day.

Even when she cried, Renie was beautiful. Her tears made her dark blue eyes sparkle more than they did normally. She cried softly, tears slowing spilling out of her eyes. And she smiled. She smiled through her tears. Picturing her, remembering how she looked took Billy's breath away, as much as it had that day.

The party that followed went on throughout the afternoon and early evening. Ben's band, CB Rice, played for hours. Ben sang off and on, but each time he did, he brought Liv up on stage with him. It was as though he couldn't stand not being able to touch her, even for a few minutes.

Billy danced with Renie most of the night, when he was able to get her away from Jake and Luke, now her stepbrothers. They were still as in love with her as they were the day they met her.

Yep, he'd been in love with Renie then. Why hadn't he realized it? It was so clear to him now.

It was close to midnight when the party started breaking up. Ben and Liv went back to their house. Jake and Luke stayed at their grandparents' house, so did Renie. Billy's parents went back to Will's place on the other side of the ranch, but Billy hadn't been ready to leave.

He and Renie sat on the porch and took in the wonder of the mountain sky that perfect summer night. They stayed there until sunrise, when Bud, Ben's dad, came out to start his day, and offered to take Billy up to Will's house.

It hadn't occurred to Billy to kiss Renie that night. Now he wished he had.

***

Billy turned so more of his body came in contact with Renie's. He wanted nothing more than to hold her tight. He woke her. He hadn't meant to.

"Billy?"

"Yeah Renie?"

"Are we gonna be okay?"

"We're gonna be way better than that."

***

When Billy woke up later, the sun streamed through the thin white window coverings. It had to be mid-morning at least. Renie was still sound asleep.

They'd moved in the night, so they faced each other. Her lips were so close to his; he felt her breath on his cheek. He had to brush his lips across hers. She woke with a start, and a gasp.

That had done it. His mouth descended on hers as his hand came up to fist in her hair, holding her still, so she had no choice but to kiss him back. He tucked his other arm under her body and pulled her closer into him. He wrapped a leg over hers, so she had no choice but to press against him.

Renie put her hands on his chest and pushed back from him. He looked into her eyes, trying to figure out what she was thinking.

His hand moved to the curve of her back, down to her bottom, and pulled her back into him.

God he wished her eyes could speak. Everything he needed to hear was in them, they were telling him, but he couldn't grasp what they were saying.

She pushed away from him again and sat up. She pulled her sweatshirt over her head. Her hands moved to her waist, and she pushed off her pajama bottoms.

Billy lost every bit of air in his lungs. He closed his eyes and opened them again. He was dizzy, delirious almost, as he took in the sight before him, of her naked.

"I knew it," he said.

"What did you know Billy?" she smiled.

"*Fucking amazing.* I knew you would be."

She was cold; it was cold in her bedroom. He didn't want to cover her with the comforter; he had no choice but to cover her with himself. He slipped off his boxers and pushed his thigh between hers, forcing his way in closer to her.

"Wait," she whispered.

He leaned over to where his jeans lay on the floor. He reached into the pocket and found a condom. A miracle he had one with him. She watched him open the packet and put it on. Every move he made, her eyes followed.

He kissed her again, first her lips, then down her neck, taking a turn with each breast, while his hands reached down to where they would soon come together.

Slowly, very slowly, he slid into her, and stopped. He pushed back from her. His hands went to each side of her face and held her, looking into her eyes, his questioning, their bodies still joined.

She leaned forward and brought her lips to his. Her mouth pulled at his. She kissed him so hard, his body reacted instinctively, moving into her of its own accord. He pushed into her. She breathed in deeply, but made no other sound. His hands caressed her face as their lips stayed joined in the same way their bodies were.

There would be no holding back; he had no control over his body's reaction to her. He wanted to go slow, be gentle and make this, her first time, perfect for her. His pace quickened. He moved harder into her, and then, when he couldn't wait a moment longer, she cried out. Her fingers dug in where her hands pulled at his shoulders. He had to see her face.

"Open your eyes," he said softly. "Look at me."

He pulled her on top of him. His body refused to leave the snug comfort of hers. "Renie—"

"Shh." She ran her fingertips over his lips.

He closed his eyes for a moment, to steady himself, before he thought about what they had done. He'd promised her he wouldn't hurt her. He hoped and prayed he hadn't.

She'd been waiting for this moment, this day, all her life, or at least the last couple of years, when she allowed herself to fantasize about the first time she and Billy had sex. And now here he was, underneath her. Every time she went to move away from him, to move her body enough that their bodies were no longer joined, he held her still.

He wanted to talk, she knew he did, the same way she understood everything else about Billy's subtle nuances. But she wasn't ready to, or even to listen to what he had to say. Instead, she wanted to linger, savor this time with him. No matter what happened between them, it wouldn't be this way ever again, because this was her first time, not just with Billy, but with anyone.

She'd wanted it to be with Billy, but she never considered it would happen. Now that it had, she was so glad she waited. Anyone else, no matter whom it had been, wouldn't have been Billy. He was all that mattered to her.

"Do you have to be anywhere?" he asked.

"Not until this afternoon."

"How are you?"

"Fine. How are you?"

"Gotta be a smart ass, don't ya?"

Renie put her hands on either side of Billy's head and raised herself up so she could see the look on his face.

"I'm okay Billy."

"I wish you would've told me."

"Why? Would it have changed anything?"

Yeah, it would have. That's why she didn't tell him. He would've wanted to talk about it. He might have even told her they shouldn't. Or they should wait. He would have made a big deal out of it, as he had about making her breakfast. He would've planned for it to be special…and he would've over-thought it.

If anyone knew him, to his core, she did. She would've already known the things he was just figuring out himself.

"It would have. Which is why you didn't tell me."

He brought his head up at the same time his hand gripped the back of her neck, and kissed her.

***

Billy didn't want to leave. He wanted to spend another night with her. She had class until nine, then she had to study she told him. He didn't care. She came to his house and studied all the time. He never bothered her. He wouldn't bother her here either.

Are you hungry? He texted her at eight. If she were, he'd get take-out and have it ready for her when she got back to the apartment.

She answered. *Are you still here?*

Yep.

Why?

Because I want to be, he thought, but he wouldn't answer her. And he wouldn't get into a text argument with her. He was staying, and that was the end of it. He looked through her kitchen until he found the drawer with the takeout menus. She thought she knew him so well, but he knew her too, better than she thought he did.

All these years Renie thought he hadn't been paying attention. He got that now. But he had been. Who didn't pay attention to their best friend? He recognized the meaning behind every look. He knew what her texts meant, even if they consisted of one word. He was able to fill in enough blanks to finish her thoughts.

He hadn't noticed until now how often she'd kept him at a distance, under her terms. Renie came to him, when she wanted to. She stayed, when she wanted to. She put up with his shit, when she wanted to.

Billy wondered why Renie hadn't invited him up here before. They could've hung out, gone to the places she liked to go. He would've been happy to sleep on her couch. But, she hadn't ever invited him up, and he hadn't ever invited himself, until last night.

He decided on Thai food. They had a favorite Thai place they went to in Colorado Springs sometimes. He'd get her favorites.

When Renie unlocked the door to her apartment, she was met with the overwhelming aroma of Tom Ka Gai. If she hadn't already loved Billy most of her life, she would have fallen in love with him right then.

It was ten degrees outside, and she walked a mile from her class to her apartment. She was frozen to her core and chicken-coconut soup would thaw her out better than anything.

"I'm glad you're still here."

"Because you're happy to see me?" He helped her take off her jacket, leaned in, and kissed her. "Or because I have dinner waiting?"

"Both, I guess."

"You guess." He wound his hand around her neck and pulled her closer to kiss her again. Her nose was like an ice cube, so he kissed it too.

"Come and eat," he said. He pointed to the sofa, and when she sat down, he threw a blanket over her. "Get warm, I'll bring the soup to you."

"Who are you and what have you done with Billy Patterson?"

"I never do anything for you. Is that what you're trying to say?" She was right. She did a lot more for him than he did for her.

"What have you been doing since I left?"

"Nothin' much. Had some calls to make. Took a little nap. Tried on some of your clothes."

She smirked.

"So you are listening to me? You look a million miles away. Whatcha' thinkin' about pretty girl?"

She had been lost in thought, wondering how long he planned to stay, how things would be between them now. It would've been easier if he'd been gone when she got home tonight. It would've given her time to process this drastic change in their relationship. That was precisely why he hadn't left. He didn't want her to make any decisions without him there.

"You and me," she answered.

"And?"

She didn't know what to say. She had no idea how to do this. She'd dated, but no one long enough to get serious enough to sleep with them. Which meant she'd never been in a relationship.

He watched her, waiting for her to say something. She took another spoonful of soup. And he smiled. Billy Patterson had the best smile. Those dimples, his soft blue eyes…Renie imagined he got away with an awful lot in life by playing his smile card, as he did right now.

She took another spoonful of soup, and smiled back.

"I don't know whether I love you because you're such a brat, or despite it."

She stopped smiling.

"Oh come on Renie. You know I love you. You love me too. Don't ya? Doesn't matter that things have changed for us in the between-the-sheets department. That's not what I'm talkin' about."

He was right. They did love each other; they'd been part of each other's lives forever.

"You're right."

"So…come on, tell me what you're thinkin'."

"I can't do that Billy."

"You always make me go first. Okay. I will. *Again.*"

She set her empty bowl down on the coffee table.

"You want more soup first? Or are you ready for Pad Thai?"

"I can wait. I want to hear what you have to say first."

Billy stood and took her bowl to the kitchen. Now that he'd offered to go first, he had no idea what he would say. He knew how he felt; he didn't know how to put it into words.

When he came back out of the kitchen, her eyes were closed. He'd give anything to be able to read her thoughts. He'd spent most of his life wondering what Renie Fairchild was thinking. Now he knew why.

"I've never done this before either."

She opened her eyes and raised her eyebrows.

"The girlfriend thing, I mean."

"Girlfriend?"

"Relationship? Is that better?"

"Not ever?"

"Come on. If I had, you would've known about it. I would've talked to you about it." He was glad he never had. But then, there hadn't been any women in his life worth talking about.

When he was on the road, plenty of women were interested in keeping him company. But, he almost never slept with a woman more than once. There had been a few here and there, girls who followed the riders from rodeo to rodeo, but they never lasted longer than a week. He wouldn't let them travel with him, and when they gave him shit about it; he walked away and never looked back.

"Maybe I had more important things to deal with, more important things to be doin'. You don't win a national championship if you're not focused."

She still wasn't talking.

"I want this with you," he said softly, almost a whisper. It wasn't like him to be quiet, or still. Billy rarely stopped moving, but he sat next to her, so still.

It spilled over to her. It was that way between them. They shared feelings.

"Do you want it Renie?"

She did. It's what she'd always wanted. But now that it was a possibility, a reality, she wasn't sure she could do it. What if it didn't work out between them? Then what?

"*Fuck Renie, answer me.*"

She jumped at his drastic change in tone. "I don't know."

Billy got up and started to pace. "Why the hell not?"

"What happens Billy if it doesn't work? We *have* to take that into consideration."

He sat back down and pulled her into him. "Tell you what, we'll be ourselves, be the way we've always been, but let's see where bein' intimate takes us."

"I have to think about it Billy, without you here."

"Nah, if I'm not here you'll get weird about it. Like you did with Pooh."

"What do you mean?"

"You moved her. What the hell was that all about? You think I was gonna let you get away with doin' something like that?" He laughed and shook his head.

"No, I guess not," she laughed too.

"I'm goin' home in the morning, which means I'm gonna sleep here with you tonight. And when you come down this weekend, you're gonna sleep with me."

"What if I don't come down?"

"Then, I'll come back here."

"Don't you need to get back out on the road Billy?"

"Not ready yet."

Renie fidgeted on the sofa, moving further away from him. "Wanna talk about it?"

"Not really." He ran his hand through his hair. "Yeah, I guess I do. My heart isn't in it. I can't explain it any better than that."

"Hmm."

"What's that mean? You got an opinion, which you always do, don't be shy about tellin' me what it is."

"The best thing would be for you to get back out there. The longer you don't, the easier it'll get for you to convince yourself you're done."

"What about us?"

"You can't use 'us' as an excuse Billy. Get back out there. Ride. Compete. It's what you do."

"Don't wanna."

"Get over it Billy. Turn your attitude around."

"What about us?" He asked for the second time.

"Again, we aren't an 'us.' Get back out on the road and do what you do. I'll be here when you get back."

"Come with me."

She'd been to many rodeos Billy competed in, but not because she was there for him, or with him. He asked her to go once, the year he won the national finals in Las Vegas. But, he hadn't really invited her; she and her mom went more as part of the family.

"I can't Billy. I've got too much work to do here. I have labs due, and I have to study. This gets harder every year. And as much as you have to focus, so do I."

Billy abruptly stood and pulled her up with him. "I want your body next to mine Renie, and I want it now."

"Billy—"

"Now Renie. Don't argue with me."

He kissed her lightly. "I want you," he whispered. He put his hands on the small of her back and pulled her closer to him, his tongue licking over her lips, her breasts pushed into his body. He shifted to bring her pelvis into his.

She made a sound, a whimper, and kissed him back. Her hands came up and ran over his chest. She was so tender, so loving. It almost brought him to tears. She had so much love within her for him it spilled out through her lips, her hands, her pores. Renie breathed love for him.

"I want to be inside you," he murmured. His lust for her overwhelmed him. He put his arm behind her knees and carried her into the bedroom.

He set her gently down on the bed, and before she moved away from him, he unbuttoned her shirt. His hands moved to her wrists and undid the buttons there. Lifting her, he pulled her arms out of it. She had a turtleneck on. His hands reached under it, but instead of pushing it up and over her head, his hands found her breasts instead. Her nipples were hard, through the sheer fabric of her bra. He pulled at it, and put his hands on her skin.

Renie put her hand against his cheek, her fingers trailed down to his neck, inside his collar, and over his collarbone, over the scar there. He'd broken it, nine years ago. She remembered. She remembered everything about him.

His hands still on her breasts, he stared at her. She closed her eyes. And then she smiled. Billy moved to take her turtleneck off. He'd run out of patience. He wanted her naked against him.

He reached around and unfastened her bra; she shimmied out of it. His lips found hers, and he kissed her as he kneed her legs apart. His mouth left hers and traveled to her neck and then her shoulders. He licked over her collarbone, as she had run her fingers over his. His lips found her nipple, and he sucked it in. She gasped and arched against him.

He groaned as he switched to the other breast, teasing her with his tongue. Her hands moved to her jeans, and she started to unfasten them. His hands stopped her.

"I want to do it," he said, lifting himself away from her. His hands finished what they stopped hers from doing, dragging her jeans down her long legs. He slid down further and put her legs over his shoulders. Her hands went to his hair as he rested his head against her. He nuzzled her, breathing in deeply and groaned again.

Renie lay there, still, almost holding her breath.

His mouth trailed kisses over her, "I want you to fall apart for me Renie. I want to watch you fall apart." She gripped the sheets and did as he asked her to.

Renie continued to watch him as he stood and took off his clothes. He reached behind her where she saw he left a box of condoms on her headboard, right next to the picture of them. It brought a smile to her face.

"Stocked up today," he said as he ripped one open.

"I want you," she murmured.

Billy's jaw locked, his shoulders tensed and his gaze went from heated to scorching. He drove into her hard and fast while she continued to watch his determined face. She saw everything in his face. Billy loved her.

When they came together, it emptied her mind of any thoughts other than how it felt to be this close, this inseparable from him. She held onto him, refusing to release her hold. His gaze came to hers as he held her as tightly as she held him.

She'd be tired the next morning, but he couldn't stop himself from waking her throughout the night. He'd drift off, but then her body next to his would wake him again. He couldn't sleep through his body's pull to her. He wanted to kiss her everywhere. When he trailed kisses down her side, from the soft skin under her arm, down her waist, to her hips, she giggled. When his lips moved across her pelvis, she groaned. He loved the sound of her—giggling, groaning, screaming in pleasure. He wanted all her sounds, all her love, all her everything.

Renie made him promise he'd go out on the road the next weekend. As much as he didn't want to, he knew she was right. He needed to get back out there and figure out why his heart wasn't in saddle bronc riding anymore. Was it winning the championship? Had once been enough, and now the fire was out? He didn't care about competing. He'd been competing all his life, and now he didn't care. He couldn't understand it himself, how could he explain it to her or anyone else.

Something pulled at him, telling him it was time to move on to the next chapter of his life, he just didn't know what it was.

His second night in Rapid City, South Dakota, at the end of a less than impressive ride, Billy found out what the universe had in store for him.

Chapter Six

"I've been thinking about what you said."
"About Pooh?"
"Yeah. You're right. I'm sure Renie misses her like crazy. Too damn stubborn, always has been," he mumbled.
This went way beyond stubborn, thought Dottie.

Billy looked out at the meadow, where he'd spent most of his life watching Renie Fairchild ride her horse. He'd give anything to see that sight again. He wiped a tear away. He knew his mom saw it, but he was beyond caring whether anyone knew he cried. He cried a lot about his broken life.
"What about Willow?"
"What about her?"
"Will you take her with you?"
"Do you think I should?"
"Let me think on it."
Billy knew it might be a day or two before she'd get back to him. She liked to think things through; she wasn't impulsive like him and his dad.

Two days later Dottie walked into his kitchen. Willow was in her high chair, and Billy was trying to get her to eat scrambled eggs, which she was not in the mood for.
"Hey Mama," he said, getting up to kiss her cheek.
"How's my beautiful girl?"
Willow reached out her hands for Dottie who picked her up.

"Leave her with me and your daddy."

"You don't think I should take her?"

"I don't, and neither does Liv."

"I wish I understood."

"Me too. We all do. No one could've predicted this reaction from her."

Billy paced back and forth in the kitchen. Pooh tied them together. He knew she'd have to come and get her horse eventually, or send someone to do it for her. If he did this, and she wouldn't see him, he'd be cutting that tie himself.

"You have to prepare yourself Billy. In case it doesn't go the way you want it to."

"I already know how it's gonna go." She'll refuse to see me. *There he went again, getting choked up. He reached his hands out for Willow who was all too happy to come see her daddy.*

— • —

"Billy Patterson?" the old man said.

"That's me. What can I do for you?" Billy answered, turning toward him. He was struck by the serious expression on the man's face.

"It's about my granddaughter," he said. His voice faltered. "And my great-granddaughter."

Billy wasn't sure what to say. Was the man looking for an autograph? It had been a few months since anyone had sought him out for one.

"Son," he said, putting his hand on Billy's shoulder. "I have something I need to talk to you about. Can we go somewhere more private?"

There was something about the way the man spoke that made Billy pay attention.

"Sure," he said. "Come with me."

Billy was familiar with these grounds. There was a break room off the main barn he doubted anyone would be using. It would give them privacy to talk.

He opened the door and switched on the lights. "Have a seat," he said, motioning to the table in the middle of the room.

The man moved slowly. He reached in his back pocket and took out his wallet. He pulled out a photo and handed it to Billy. "This is the only picture I have of Roxanne with her baby." A tear slid down his cheek as he said it.

Billy recognized the girl in the photo. Roxanne—yeah, he remembered her. He'd hooked up with her a couple of times. Sweet girl. Billy got a feeling of dread in the pit of his stomach.

The man swiped his hand across his cheek, brushing the tears away. He took a deep breath.

"Roxanne was in a car accident two months ago on her way home from the store." The man paused. "She said she'd be gone a few minutes. But my wife, she doesn't believe in anybody ever leaving the house, even for a few minutes, without a kiss goodbye."

The man was openly crying now, trying to catch his breath to continue. Billy put his hand firmly on the man's shoulder.

"She would've told you, eventually. I'm sorry she didn't get the chance to do it herself."

The conversation had taken a turn Billy didn't understand.

"Willow is a sweet baby, but my wife and I are in our eighties. It'll break both our hearts, but we want what's best for this little girl. Roxanne's mom died when she was a little girl herself, and we raised her. Never knew who her daddy was. I guess that's why she was so set on making sure that when the time was right, Willow would know you. I believe she was working up the courage to tell you."

Billy stood and walked to the other side of the room. Was this man trying to tell him that Roxanne believed he was her baby's father?

"Roxanne?" he ventured, wishing he didn't have to ask the question.

"She didn't make it," the man barely managed to answer before his shoulders hunched over, and he cried again.

Billy paced, not knowing what to say. He studied the photo. Why did Roxanne believe he was the baby's father? They'd been careful; he was sure of it. He was always careful.

Renie…no, he couldn't think about her, although his hand was on his phone, longing to call her. It was his first instinct. But, he needed to deal with this news on his own.

The old man was watching him. "I guess you want proof."

Billy didn't want to be an asshole. The man was telling him his granddaughter passed away. He couldn't bring himself to doubt what the man was telling him, as much as that was how he was feeling.

"Listen…" Billy started to say, not knowing what he'd say next.

The man reached into his jacket pocket and drew out a letter. The return address on the envelope appeared to be from a law firm.

"I understand you might have questions. You call me when you're ready to ask 'em. It tells you in the letter how to reach me."

Billy wanted to stop the man when he rose and walked out of the room, but he couldn't bring himself to.

He sat down in the chair the man vacated and stared at the envelope.

An hour later, he hadn't moved. Every time he went to open the letter, he tossed it back down on the table instead.

This was the fourth rodeo in the last six weeks he registered to compete in, and the first one he'd shown up for. He wondered if the man had gone to the other three looking for him.

He put his head in his hands. He longed to call Renie. She'd help him figure out what he was supposed to do next. There was something telling him not to.

Instead, he got in his truck and started the seven-hour drive home. It would take him close to five to get to Fort Collins. He'd decide then whether to stop and talk to her about it.

It was one in the morning when he drove by her exit. It wouldn't be right to wake her up over this. He decided to drive home and talk to her in the morning. He still hadn't opened the envelope.

***

Renie logged onto Twitter and saw on RodeoChat that Billy hadn't placed either Friday or Saturday night. He'd probably head home early Sunday morning. And when he got there, she'd be waiting for him. It's what she would've done anyway, before things had changed between them.

She loved her horse, no question, but if it hadn't been for Billy, she wouldn't go and see her as often as she did. Pooh was the excuse for her visit, Billy was the reason.

When she got to the house a little after nine, Sookie was sitting at the kitchen counter reading the newspaper. She knew Sookie; he'd worked for her mom last year. She sat and talked to him for a few minutes, and then went downstairs to the room she usually stayed in. The one that had been hers all her life. If Sookie hadn't been there, she might have gone in and crawled into Billy's bed. Probably not, but she might have.

***

Billy got home just after 2:00 AM and saw Renie's car, and Sookie's truck. God, if there were ever a time he regretted telling Sookie he could stay at the house, it was now.

What was she doing here anyway? He hadn't texted her last night, and she hadn't texted him either. He bet she worried about him, since she hadn't heard from him. He often texted after he rode. And he would've, if Roxanne's grandfather hadn't gotten there when he had. After that conversation, he hadn't known what to say to her, so he didn't say anything.

He went inside and went straight downstairs to her room, instead of to his. As selfish as it was to wake her, he needed her. He took off his clothes as quietly as he could, eased into the double bed, and wrapped himself around her.

She murmured, turned so her body faced his, but didn't wake. And he didn't go to sleep.

It was after seven when she finally woke. Billy thought he'd go crazy waiting for her to.

"Hi," she said, her voice heavy with sleep.

"Hi," he answered.

"I didn't expect you until later this morning. When did you get in?"

"Couple hours ago."

She opened her eyes wider. "How come you came home in the middle of the night Billy?"

He hesitated and ran his hand over his face. "Listen, I got somethin' I have to talk to you about Renie. It's important."

That made her sit up. Without realizing she did it, she pulled the sheet closer to her, almost up to her chin. She was wearing that sweatshirt again, the one that used to be his. It wasn't as though she were covering anything up with the sheet. Her reaction was purely instinctual. She knew by the tone of his voice that whatever it was he needed to talk to her about would hurt.

"Come here first."

"No, Billy," she started to get out of bed, but he held her where she was.

There was that fear again, the fear he saw in her eyes last weekend. She was afraid he was about to hurt her. And he was.

He had the envelope close enough that he could reach it. He sat up and pulled her into him, so he had one arm around her, holding her tighter than he should.

"A man came to see me last night after I rode. He brought this letter with him. I haven't opened it yet, but I know what's in it."

"What?" she whispered.

"He came to tell me that his granddaughter was killed in an accident."

He meant to keep talking, to tell her the rest, but the look in her eyes was ripping him to pieces. He pulled her closer, tighter, and she rested her head in the crook of his shoulder.

"She has a baby. A baby she believed is mine."

Renie gasped.

"I don't know what to think," he continued.

"Are you going to open it?"

"At some point, I guess I'm gonna have to."

"Do it now Billy."

"Do you want me to go upstairs and open it?"

"No, you can open it here."

He was her best friend after all. And she knew him. He wasn't irresponsible. Even if things hadn't changed between them, even if he weren't in her bed right now, she'd still believe that about him. Billy might be a bit of a cad, but that didn't make him irresponsible.

He tore the end off and reached in for the letter.

"Do you want me to read it for you?"

"Would you?"

For him, she'd do anything. Didn't he realize that? Her own instincts kicked in, and the most powerful thing she was feeling was the need to protect him.

She read it out loud, so he could hear it. She wanted to rip this bandage off fast, for both their sakes.

It said that before she died, Roxanne had told her grandparents that Billy Patterson was the father of her child. She hadn't told him she was pregnant, or that she'd had a baby. She'd told her grandparents that she planned to. But, the letter went on to say, she died before she was able to.

The lawyer representing the family, and the baby, wrote that a paternity test would be arranged at Billy's earliest convenience. It also stated that Roxanne's grandparents wanted Billy, the baby's father, to become her sole guardian. They were too elderly to raise a baby.

"Do you have any reason to confirm or deny this Billy?" She was trying to be as straightforward with him as she could be.

"I slept with her," he answered. "But not without protection Renie, I wouldn't…"

It felt as though a rock landed in the middle of her chest. This wasn't news to her. Even though Billy didn't talk to her about having sex when he was out on the road, she knew he had. She didn't want to think about it, talk about it, or acknowledge it, but she knew it.

"I know you wouldn't Billy. But, obviously there was a reason Roxanne thought you were her baby's father."

"I don't know what to do." He was having a hard time looking at her. She sensed his discomfort.

"Do what they ask. Take the paternity test. There isn't anything you can figure out until you know for sure you're the father."

"God Renie. I mean…*God*."

"I know." She felt the same way. "You should tell your parents right away. You can't handle the burden of this on your own Billy. I know you can't. You'll need their support."

"What about you?"

"What about me?"

"Does this change things between us?"

"I'm your friend Billy. I'll stick by you. You know that."

"What about us? You and me? What about that?"
"I don't know."

He knew it would change things. He'd held out hope it wouldn't, but he'd known it would. How could it not?
"Her name is Willow."
"That's a beautiful name Billy."

He had to call the Johnsons. That was their name. Earl and Sophie Johnson. They lived in Texas, which was where he'd met Roxanne. He felt like a shit realizing that Mr. Johnson had come to South Dakota to track him down. He felt like a shit about it all. He especially felt like a shit that deep down he hoped the baby wasn't his, although something was telling him she was.
"Let's go see your mom and dad."
"Now?"
"Yeah Billy, now. You need all the support you can get with this."
"Can we stay here a little bit longer?"
"Okay, but..."
Billy tried to kiss her, but she moved away from him.
"Renie?"
"Give me a minute, okay Billy?"
"A minute?"
"Don't do this now. I can't do this now." She wriggled out of his arms, grabbed her clothes, and walked out of the bedroom.

When she left the room, he felt as though his chest was closing in on itself. He wanted to race after her, turn her around and kiss every bit of air out of her. He went upstairs and got in the shower instead.

In two weeks, his entire life had changed. He realized that Renie Fairchild was the love of his life. And somehow he knew Roxanne had been telling the truth; Willow was his baby. The love of his life and a baby. And it couldn't have happened in a more fucked up way.

When he came out of the bedroom, Renie was sitting at the kitchen counter.

"Ready?" she said to him.

"You'll go with me?"

"Of course I will."

"Still my best friend, but not my lover?"

"Let's take this one step at a time. First, you need to find out if the baby is yours."

"And if she is? Then what?"

"Don't push me Billy."

He wanted to hold his hands up in surrender, but he knew she'd take it the wrong way if he did. Instead, he did the other thing he knew she wouldn't want him to do. He pulled her into a hug, and he held her as tightly as he could.

He put his head next to hers, his face in her hair. "I need you Renie."

She didn't answer him.

***

"Well," Dottie looked at Billy, then at her husband before she met Renie's eyes. She wasn't sure what to say. The baby, if it were Billy's, was something they'd welcome with open arms, and handle as a family. That part she wasn't worried about. Dottie was worried most about what she knew her son was worried most about. Renie. It would've been different if Billy had gotten this news even six months from now. They would've had some time together under their belts.

She doubted Renie thought anyone noticed, but she was sitting on her hands. Dottie had known Renie since she was a baby; she'd watched her grow up. Dottie said she knew when Renie was worried about something because she bit her nails. That was when Renie started sitting on her hands instead.

Billy reached over and pulled her arm, then took her hand in his. He knew too, thought Dottie.

"The best thing would be for me to go to Texas," Billy said, looking between his mom and dad. "If they expedite it, they can have the results back from the lab in twenty-four hours. I'll stay until they do."

"And then what?" Bill asked his son.

Billy looked at Dottie.

"I'll go with you honey," she said matter-of-factly. "We'll figure it out as we go."

Both Dottie and Billy looked at Renie.

"What?"

Dottie stood up and put her arms around Renie. She looked at her son and husband and moved her eyes in the direction of the other room. They both got up and left the kitchen. Dottie didn't let go of Renie.

"How are you doin'?"

"It doesn't matter."

"It's all that matters sweet girl." Dottie kissed the top of her head. "It's all that matters to him."

"It shouldn't be. He's got a daughter to think about now. He won't have time for…"

"For you? You don't think so? Oh Renie, when are you gonna realize that Billy loves you? He loves you more than anything."

"I can't do this," she answered, barely a whisper.

Renie pushed away from Dottie, put on her coat, and walked out of the Patterson's kitchen, hoping Dottie wouldn't try to keep her from leaving. Hoping more Dottie wouldn't tell Billy she left.

She walked through the woods back to Billy's, grabbed her keys, and drove to Fort Collins.

Her and Billy…what? What about her and Billy? Was God trying to tell her something? And if he were, what was it? Did this happen so she could help him through it? Or was it a sign that she and Billy shouldn't have crossed the line they had in the last couple of weeks?

She was south of Denver when she called her mom.

"Hey Mom," she said when Liv answered the phone. "I need to take a few days off from school. I'd like to come to Crested Butte. Okay?"

"You don't ever have to ask Renie. This is your home as much as it's mine. You know that."

"Thanks Mom. And thank Ben for me too. I'll be there tomorrow afternoon some time."

"Are you sure you want to drive here alone? Ben could come and get you."

"No, I want to drive. I'll see you tomorrow." Renie hung up before either of two things happened, she told her mom what was going on with Billy, or she started to cry.

If she wanted to, she could cry the whole way there tomorrow, alone, with no one to see her, or judge her for her tears.

***

"What's up?" asked Ben when Liv hung up.

"Renie's coming to visit. Tomorrow."

"But tomorrow's Monday."

"I know."

"Think somethin's goin' on with her and Cowboy Patterson?"

"That would be my guess."

"Come here and let me hold you baby."

Liv sat down next to Ben and let him pull her into him. This whole thing with Billy and her daughter was peculiar. There was no better word for it. Her *drama-less* daughter who had the world by the tail, was suddenly an insecure twenty-three-year-old woman.

She smiled.

"What?" Ben asked.

"Renie might be normal after all."

Ben threw his head back and laughed. It was one of Liv's favorite things about him, the way he laughed with abandon. "I love you Liv."

"I love you too Ben."

Chapter Seven

Renie looked at the time on her phone, 12:30 AM. She used to check her phone to see if Billy sent her a text. It had been a long time since there'd been one.

It had taken him a while to give up, but he had.

She fell asleep not long after she got in bed a couple of hours ago, but then she dreamt about him, and it woke her up.

This time they danced. She loved to dance with him. When she was a little girl, Billy would twirl her around the dance floor, either by holding her around the waist, or letting her legs swing as he twirled her in circles. Sometimes she'd stand on his feet while he two-stepped her across the floor.

When she got older, he held her close, even before he realized she'd grown up. She remembered the first time it changed between them, at a rodeo in Oklahoma. Her mom competed in her first barrel race that weekend, and when Billy took her in his arms, she knew he held her as a woman, not a little girl. It had been one of the best nights of her life.

Sleep would not come soon; instead, she'd toss and turn trying to drive thoughts of Billy out of her head. She didn't know why she bothered; it almost never worked.

Billy was up too, walking the floor with Willow. No matter what he did, he couldn't get her settled down. He thought about calling his mama, but it was the middle of the night, and he was Willow's daddy; he needed to figure it out on his own.

He worried she was fussy because she sensed his unease. But, she was chewing on his shoulder; she was teething. He hated to give her sugar in the middle of the night, but he had cherry ice-pops in the freezer. Maybe if he gave her a little bit it would numb her teeth and she'd sleep, and then he could too.

— • —

Renie left at five. She'd be in Crested Butte before noon that way. She called Billy last night after she got back to Fort Collins. She could hear the hurt in his voice when he answered the phone.

"Hi," he said.

"I'm sorry I left that way Billy. But I had to."

"It's okay."

"It isn't okay. I know it isn't. But…I don't know what else to say."

"This isn't your problem. It's my problem."

"That isn't fair Billy."

"I got this Renie. Whatever happens, it's my responsibility. Me. It's on me. I understand that."

"Give me some time."

"You know where to find me. I'm not goin' anywhere."

"I'm going to see my mom for a few days."

"Sounds like a good idea."

"I still want you to talk to me Billy."

"Just try to stop me."

She swore she could feel him smile through the phone. "I'll call you from the road."

"I'll call you first." His voice caught, and he took a deep breath. "I can't imagine my life without you in it. Please don't give up on me because of this. Please don't stop bein' a part of my life."

"I won't Billy."

He wished he believed her.

* * *

A little before seven her phone rang.

"Mornin'." Billy said when she answered.

"Mornin' yourself. Just wake up?" The sleep she could hear in his voice made her wish she was snuggled up next to him.

"Yeah. Where are you?"

"Larkspur." She was an exit north of Monument.

"Pull that car off the highway, come over, and crawl in bed with me."

She didn't answer him.

"Come let me love on you Renie. Please."

"I can't Billy. I'm on my way to Crested Butte. I have to keep going."

"No, you don't. Come see me. Please Renie."

It was as though her car had a mind of its own, and it wanted to go see Billy.

"Did you get off the highway Renie?"

"You know I did."

"Ah, that's my girl. You wanna know what I'm gonna do to you when you get here?"

"What are you gonna do to me Billy?"

"I'm gonna go so slow Renie. Takin' off your clothes, lettin' your hair down, 'cause I know you got it tied up, don't ya?"

He didn't wait for her to answer. "Then, I'm gonna lay you down and run my lips all over that sweet body. You still there darlin'?"

"I'm here," she breathed.

"Then, I'm gonna cover your body with mine, sink into you nice and slow. I'll watch your face as you close your eyes and throw your head back, makin' those love noises that drive me wild."

If he kept this up, she wouldn't be able to keep driving. "I'm hanging up now Billy. I'll be there in a minute."

"Hurry sweet girl," she heard him say right before she ended the call.

Billy met her at the back door. He was shirtless, the first two buttons of his 501 jeans were undone, and his feet were bare. He lifted her up and held her against the wall. His mouth found her neck as she wrapped her legs around his waist.

"God Renie, I need you so much." He reached up and took the clip out of her hair, and then started to pull her jacket off her shoulders. He remembered they weren't alone in the house. He turned her around and grasped her bottom, carrying her with him.

He couldn't help himself; he needed his lips touching hers. He pulled back and looked into her eyes. "Thank you Renie."

"Don't thank me Billy." She closed her eyes.

"No, don't do that, look at me."

She opened her eyes.

"I needed this. I needed you. I needed to connect with you. So, thank you. I don't know what I would've done if I didn't get to see you this mornin'."

He laid her down on the bed and started to pull her clothes off. When she tried to help, he stopped her hands. "No, let me. I need to do this Renie."

She rested her hands at her sides and watched him as his eyes lingered over each part of her body as he uncovered it. When she was naked, he tangled one hand in her hair while he ran the other over her body. "Renie, I…"

She reached up and put her hand over his mouth. "Shh. Just love me Billy. Please."

"But—"

"Shh," she said again before she lifted up to take his mouth with hers.

It was nine before she got back on the road, and that was after begging Billy to let her go. She almost wished she'd let Ben fly over to get her.

Her phone rang again.

"Hey," she answered, without looking to see who was calling. She assumed it was Billy.

"Hi honey," said her mom. "How far are you?"

"I'm not even to the Springs yet."

"Have you listened to the weather? Monarch Pass is closed."

No, she hadn't. She'd been too wrapped up in Billy to think about the weather.

"Oh no."

"I'm glad I reached you before you got further. Ben will come get you."

"It's okay Mom. I can wait until the weather clears up. I'll head home. I mean, to Billy's."

"See whether he can give you a ride up to the airport."

Renie didn't want to tell her mom that Billy and Dottie were leaving for Texas, or why. She didn't know when or how they were getting there. She could drive herself to the airport and leave her car there.

"I'll call you when he's leaving."

"Are you flying over with him?"

"Not this time honey. Ben is flying over with his dad. I'll call you when I know more."

She called Billy. "I miss you too much. I'm coming back."

"Wait. What? You're comin' back? Really? Shit. That's great!"

"Monarch Pass is closed."

"You are such a brat."

"I'm still coming back, so you better retract that insult Patterson."

"I'll be waitin' here in bed for you. Ready and willin', by the way."

"When are you leaving?"

"Our flight's this afternoon baby." His voice got soft to match the tone of hers. "I'm so sorry about this."

"Don't Billy, don't be sorry."

"Aw, don't cry honey. God, just hurry back here. But Renie, be safe, okay."

"I will. I'll be there in a minute."

She was crying, and he didn't have any idea what to do about it. His life was one big Charlie Foxtrot. He *wasn't* riding, he *was* in love with Renie Fairchild, and he *might* be a daddy. Shit.

He was lost in thought when he heard the back door open. God he was happy she was back. He wished more than anything that he could take her to Texas with him. With Renie by his side, he could face anything life threw in his direction.

"You lit a fire," she said as she took off her coat and tossed it on the chair.

He sat up and looked her in the eye. "I love you Renie."

She climbed on the bed and snuggled up against him.

"No, wait, that isn't supposed to make you cry." Why was she crying again?

"It's okay," she said. "I'm glad you love me Billy."

"You are?"

"Yeah."

"Does that mean we're gonna make it through all this."

"I'm not sure what it means, but I guess so. One way or another."

"Oh no, it's gonna be one way darlin', and that's with you and me sharin' sheets on a regular basis."

At noon, Renie's phone rang. It was her mom.

"Hey Mom, Ben on his way?"

"No honey, they've been at the airport waiting for the weather to clear. It doesn't look as though it's getting any better. I'm so sorry sweetheart. We'll have to wait until tomorrow."

"It's okay," she answered, knowing her disappointment hung heavily on her words. "We'll talk in the morning then. Bye Mom."

"Bye sweetheart. I'll see you tomorrow."

"What's up?"

"Weather. They can't fly out today."

"I'm sorry. I know you wanted to see your mom. I feel as though it's my fault that I talked you into stoppin' here."

"You saved me. I might have been stuck on the pass if I hadn't stopped."

"Thanks for makin' me feel better about it. I wish you could…"

"What?"

"*I know* I'm a selfish prick. *You know* I'm a selfish prick. I can't imagine doing anything this big without you with me."

"You've done lots of big things without me."

"But this doesn't feel like me Renie. This feels like us. Whatever I find out in Texas affects us. Both of us. Us together."

"Billy—"

"Please Renie. Please go with me."

She put her head on his chest, right above his heart. "Okay."

He held her tight and closed his eyes, saying a silent prayer of thanks.

"Dottie still needs to go with us Billy. I can't go with you if Dottie doesn't go."

"My mama will still go with us darlin'. Don't worry."

He knew he should tell her she didn't have to go, but now that he'd talked her into it, he didn't want to risk saying anything that might change her mind. It wasn't just that he wanted her with him; he needed her with him.

It cost him a fortune to get her ticket, and theirs, at the last minute, but he would've paid ten times more to have her with him.

Renie sat next to him. Dottie sat across the aisle.

"I didn't realize we were flying first-class Billy."

He often flew first-class and even if he didn't, he would've this trip. He was about to ask his mother and the love of his life to help him bring his baby girl home. He didn't need a paternity test, he felt it in his bones; he was Willow's father.

He closed his eyes, wishing he could sleep, but knew he wouldn't.

He lifted the armrest that was between the two of them and brought Renie closer to him. "Sleep darlin'. Get some rest." He knew she was asleep before he finished his sentence. He doubted she'd gotten any more sleep than he had the last couple of days.

Dottie looked across the aisle at her son. The worry and tension that had been so evident on his face yesterday had softened. She knew he was still feeling it, but having Renie with them made such a difference.

His life had changed so drastically in the last few days. He'd gone from a carefree cowboy to a man ready to accept that he'd found the love of his life standing right in front of him. Now he was facing the biggest responsibility of his life. Billy knew the baby was his; she felt it as much as he did. He'd accepted it the minute Earl Johnson told him, in South Dakota.

***

The Johnsons suggested they meet at the hospital the next day, which was a few minutes away from the airport in San Antonio. Billy had gone the afternoon before and given the lab what they needed to run the test.

They were waiting in the lobby when he walked in with Renie and his mother. Sophie Johnson was holding the baby.

And Then You Dance

Dottie knew as soon as she looked at her, it didn't matter what any lab or doctor told her. That baby was a Patterson.

Renie saw it too. Billy saw it in her face. He watched her, afraid to look away, afraid he'd miss something. Her look went from shock to…something he didn't have words for. But when he looked at Willow, he hoped Renie was feeling the same thing he was. It was indescribable.

Sophie Johnson couldn't take her eyes off Billy. After he came back from South Dakota, her husband told her Billy was the baby's father. He'd known it the minute he looked in the boy's eyes. Willow was the spitting image of her daddy, including her pale blue eyes. Roxanne had big, brown eyes. Willow had his dimples too.

"Here," said Mrs. Johnson. "You hold your girl."

Billy hesitated, not sure what to do. Willow started kicking her legs, leaning toward him.

"Hold tight Billy," said Dottie, smiling through her tears. "She's a squirmer…like you."

"Why don't you have a seat son?" Earl Johnson motioned. "Your mama's right. Willow's a squirmer."

Billy could hear him, understood what he was saying, but he couldn't move. He and Willow stared at each other, as though they were looking in a mirror. He was sure that any minute his heart was would burst right open. When he did look away, it was at Renie. He had no idea what the expression on her face meant.

It was as though all the air left her body when Billy took the baby in his arms. And she watched him fall in love. In that moment, she realized she would never hold his heart the way she hoped she would. She'd dreamed of this day for the two of them, but in her dreams they were falling in love together with *their* baby. Not the baby Billy had with somebody else.

What was she thinking coming with him? She wasn't any part of the scene playing out in front of her. She was a bystander, and not an innocent one. She was a damaged bystander, witnessing the cause of the worst pain she could imagine.

When Dottie rested her hand on Renie's back, she flinched, as though the touch burned her.

"Renie?" Billy was walking toward her, with the baby.

"Billy—" Her voice caught in a sob. "I can't. I can't do this."

She felt the walls closing in on her. She couldn't breathe. All she knew was she had to get away from *this*...Billy and his baby, as fast as she could.

She turned and ran out of the hospital. She jumped into the cab parked outside the entrance. "Take me to the airport," she said. "Hurry." The cab sped away.

She couldn't bring herself to look back to see Billy, standing outside the door, baby in his arms.

Chapter Eight

Pooh was in the trailer, and Billy was almost ready to leave. He was waiting until Willow woke up and had breakfast before he did. There hadn't been a day since he brought her home that he wasn't there when she woke. He didn't want today to be the first. He hoped instead it would be tomorrow. That would mean he would still be in Crested Butte, and if he were, it would mean Renie had agreed to see him. If she hadn't, there'd be no reason for him to stay.

He'd never wanted anything more in his life than he wanted Renie to talk to him again. He didn't care if she didn't love him anymore. He'd accept it, although he'd still love her for the rest of his life. It wouldn't be fair for him to ask the same of her. She was young; she deserved to have all the fun someone her age should have. She shouldn't be tied down, taking care of someone else's baby.

If he knew she was doing that, having fun, dating, staying out too late, laughing…the way he knew she loved to, he'd be happy.

He never meant to break her heart. Never. He was as shocked as anyone to find out his one night stand had resulted in a baby. He still didn't know how it had. He'd always been so careful. But now it didn't matter. Willow was part of his life, the biggest part of it. And he wouldn't trade her for anything. Not even Renie.

— • —

When Renie got out of the cab, Liv almost didn't recognize her. She looked as though she'd been crying for hours and the expression on her face...Liv didn't think she'd ever seen her look that way.

She was walking toward the front door, but it wasn't the person Liv knew as her daughter. This girl had no life in her; she was beaten down in a way that made Liv's heart break.

"Renie? Are you okay? What are you doing here?"

"I don't want to talk right now Mom. Is that okay?" When Renie started to cry, then sob, Liv didn't know what to do other than put her arms around her and hold her tight.

"I'd like to go lie down."

"Go ahead honey. We'll talk after you rest."

Renie went downstairs and closed the door behind her.

Ben was in the kitchen waiting when Liv turned around.

"What happened?"

"I don't have any idea."

"Can you call Billy? Or Dottie?"

"I'll try. But Ben, I cannot imagine what could have happened. I've never seen her this way." Liv started to cry.

Ben led her into the bedroom. "Come here."

Liv couldn't stop crying herself. Renie's heart was broken; there could be no other explanation for her behavior. But, Liv had known Billy Patterson a long time, and she couldn't imagine anything he could do that would break Renie so completely. As much as she wanted to know what happened, she couldn't bring herself to make the call to find out.

***

Dottie told Billy that she'd be back in a few minutes to help with the baby, she needed to go home and grab a couple of things. When she walked in the back door, Bill was sitting at the kitchen table waiting for her.

"How is he?"

"Devastated."

"She just left?"

Dottie let her husband hug her, the way she usually hugged everybody else. She needed his comfort.

"She's twenty-three years old Bill. It's hard to remember she's so young. She's usually the wisest old soul in the room. When it comes to Billy, she's a young woman in love, and she was completely unprepared for this."

Dottie let go. "I need to get back up there, but I want you to do somethin' for me. It won't be easy, but I need you to call Liv, and tell her what's happened. I can't. Billy needs help with that beautiful little baby. Come up to the house after you talk to Liv, and meet your granddaughter."

"Okay, honey. I'll call Livvie. Don't you worry, this will all work out eventually."

Dottie patted Bill's cheek. "So certain everything will work out. It's one of the reasons I fell in love with you Bill Patterson."

***

Ben picked up Liv's phone when it rang and looked at the screen.

"It's Dottie," he said, handing it to her.

"Hi Dottie," she answered.

"No Livvie, not Dottie. Bill here."

"Oh. Hi Bill. Is everything okay with Dottie?" Bill never called her.

"Dottie's fine, but there are things I need to tell you Livvie. Have you talked to Renie? Do you know anything of what's happened?"

"I tried to talk to her, but she wouldn't talk back. So no, I don't know anything."

Fifteen minutes later Liv ended the call. She'd done nothing but listen, so Ben still didn't know what was happening. When she told him, he put his head in his hands. "Jesus," was all he said.

Every time Liv went to check on Renie, she was still asleep. She came upstairs a little after noon.

Liv stood and pulled her into a hug.

"Did you talk to Dottie?"

"I did honey."

"Good. Now you know. We don't have to talk about it."

"We don't? I think we should."

Renie pulled away from her and walked to the window that looked out at the ranch.

"I don't ever want to talk about Billy Patterson again Mom. Not ever."

"Okay Renie. I understand that you're upset about this, but the Pattersons are family. You and Billy will get past this."

Renie didn't even look at Liv. She went straight back down the stairs to the bedroom, and closed the door. This time she locked it. Liv didn't see her again until the next afternoon.

By that point, she was so worried she asked Ben to see whether he could get the door unlocked so she could check on her.

"I heard noises in the bathroom a few minutes ago," Ben told her. "She's fine. Well maybe not fine, but we don't have to break into her room yet."

Liv went downstairs and knocked on the door. "Renie? Can I come in?"

No answer.

"Please honey. Let me in. We don't have to talk about… anything."

"You can come in Mom. It's open."

Liv sat down on the bed and pulled her daughter closer to her. "I'm so sorry baby."

Renie put her arms around Liv and cried. And cried. She cried so hard that Liv started crying too.

Her breathing evened out, and Liv knew she'd fallen back to sleep. It was for the best. After she got more rest, maybe she'd be ready to talk about it.

A week later, nothing had changed with Renie. She still didn't want to talk about Billy. She didn't seem worried about school either, but Liv was.

"Honey, I'm not sure how to say this. I want you to know you can stay as long as you want to, but do you think you should get back to school?"

"No."

No? That was it? "Have you been in touch with any of your professors?"

"No."

Liv thought she might pull her hair out. "Renie, you are not a child. You have a responsibility to contact your professors and let them know when you'll be back."

Renie didn't answer her. She got up from the table, went downstairs and closed the bedroom door.

Ben was around the corner, listening. "Want me to talk to her?"

"You better, but not right now. Maybe the next time she decides to come out of exile."

"She doesn't know what she wants to do yet." Ben told her. "This is worse than we originally thought Liv."

"What do you mean?"

"We should try to get her to talk to someone."

Ben had been in rehab a year before he met Liv, to quit drinking. There was a therapist he knew in town that he thought Renie should meet with.

"She's sinking deeper into depression Liv. I'm worried about her."

He asked Liv to let him be the one to talk to her about it. Renie was against it, in fact, she was furious with him, but Ben insisted. As hard as it was for Liv to let him handle it, she did, and Ben got Renie to go. He went with her, and then a few days later, he went with her again.

"Renie we need to talk about school; you need to decide what you want to do."

"I'm not going back."

"You're sure."

"Positive."

This wasn't the first time Renie had taken a break from school. She took a semester off when Liv broke her neck in her accident.

"You can start up again in the summer and still hold your place in the vet program this fall."

"No Mom. I'm not going back. Ever."

"Don't be ridiculous—"

She was up and gone before Liv finished her sentence.

"I don't even know her," Liv cried to Ben later.

"I told you the other day, this is much worse than a breakup Liv. Renie has sunk into depression."

"She's never…"

"Renie has done a fan-freaking-tastic job of hiding her feelings for years Liv. *Years.* She has spent her entire life in love with Billy Patterson. I didn't see it, not that I would, but you didn't either. Now she's decided that her life will never be what she imagined it to be, she can't see past that. She has no idea what the rest of her life will look like, and she's not ready to try."

"I don't know how to help her."

"She has to work through this on her own, for herself. All we can do now is be available to her when she needs us. That, and I'm coming down hard on her to keep talking to the therapist. That I'll be an asshole about, because I feel strong she needs it."

***

Renie picked up her phone and looked. She knew she shouldn't. She had to stop looking. She had to stop caring whether Billy was trying to reach her or not. She had to stop caring about Billy.

She knew everyone thought she was selfish, but she couldn't help it. She couldn't become the caregiver of Billy's dead girlfriend's baby. The girlfriend he said he never had. *Fucking liar.*

She didn't believe for one minute she'd been someone who hadn't mattered, another one-night stand. Or that he'd been careful. The truth was, she hadn't known him as well as she thought.

She'd wanted forever with Billy. She'd wanted him to love her the way she loved him. Now, she knew that was impossible. He loved that baby—more than he loved her. She felt it that day in the hospital. And when he looked at her so expectantly, hoping she'd embrace this child the same way he was, she wanted to throw up.

She was finished being Billy Patterson's doormat. She'd spent her whole life being everything he needed, whenever he needed it. God, she'd even slept with him.

The hardest thing for her to accept was how completely clueless she'd been…*her whole life.* She looked in the mirror and had no idea who she was. She'd let Billy define her for so long; she didn't know who she was without him. She was nothing. She had nothing.

The therapist asked her whether she'd considered taking her life. "What life?" she answered. She didn't have one to take. Her life as she knew it, was over.

***

"Do you want to keep your apartment Renie?" her mom asked while they ate breakfast.

"No."

"Then you need to do something about it." Liv walked out of the room before Renie could respond.

"What the hell?" she said to Ben who sat across from her.

"She's getting sick of your shit Renie."

Renie stared at him.

"You've been treating her as though this is her fault, and she doesn't deserve it. She has nothing to do with what happened between you and Patterson. She's been patient with you, more patient than I would've been. But now she's done. She has her own life to live."

"What does that mean?"

"It means you need to start taking responsibility for your life. You wanna quit school? Fine. Nobody's gonna try to talk you out of it. Even if it is the stupidest thing I've ever heard." When she started to speak, Ben held up his hand. "She's going back out on the road in April Renie. Have you thought about that? Or are you just thinking about yourself?"

"I'm not going back to school Ben."

"Fine. You wanna quit, quit. But you've got an apartment your mom is paying the rent on, and the utilities. She's not gonna do that forever, and she's not gonna take care of it for you."

"What am I supposed to do?"

"Ask. Us. To. Help. You."

Renie went in search of her mom.

"I'm sorry," she said when she found her. "Can you and Ben take me to Fort Collins? I'll pack up the apartment and go see the registrar at school, let them know I won't be starting the vet program this year."

"That's a start."

"What else Mom?"

"Your car? Your horse? You have other responsibilities Renie. You can't turn your back on them."

Renie started to cry, hard and crawled onto the bed.

"*I...can't...Mom,*" she said through her sobs. "*Please don't make me.*"

Liv got her calmed down and told her she and Ben would figure something out. She'd have Paige or Mark go get her car. They'd decide what to do about Pooh later.

Paige and Mark were her best friends, but putting them in the middle of this thing between Billy and her daughter by asking them to go get Renie's horse was more than Liv could ask even of them.

She called Billy the next morning, while Renie was still asleep.

"Hi Billy."

"Hi Liv. How's Renie?" He sounded awful. He probably wasn't sleeping, but Liv didn't know whether that was because he was suddenly a single father of a baby, or if he were as heartbroken as Renie was.

"Not good Billy. Ben convinced her to see a therapist, but..."

"God Livvie, I'm so sorry," his voice broke when he said it.

"I know you are Billy, but I'm not sure what for. I don't understand this reaction from Renie. I don't understand much about my daughter right now. It's as though she's become a different person. She certainly isn't the girl I thought I knew all these years."

She shouldn't be saying this to Billy, but he knew Renie as well as she did, or thought she did. He was at as much of a loss as she was. Or more. At least Renie was talking to her.

"I've tried calling her, but she won't answer or call me back. I've texted her, sent her emails, and nothing. *Nothing.*" His voice broke again.

"She's quitting school."

"What? Why?"

"I don't know. I'm telling you, I cannot understand any of the decisions she's making.

"We're driving to Fort Collins in the next few days to pack up her apartment. And Billy, I'll ask Paige to come get her car. I hope you understand I can't force her—"

"I'll drive it to their house." The reservation in his voice hung like thick sludge.

"I'm so sorry Billy."

"Don't be. I did this. I destroyed any chance of a life for Renie and me. And so you know, it's what I wanted. I wanted her in my life, forever."

"I don't know what to say," Liv took a deep breath, "I hope she comes around Billy, I really do, but I'm not seeing any signs of it yet."

"What about Pooh?"

"I talked to her about us coming to get her, but…she fell apart when I did. It's too much right now."

Chapter Nine

He asked his mother to please not tell Liv he was coming. If he had any chance of seeing Renie, his arrival had to be a complete surprise.

The drive from Monument to Crested Butte was the longest five hours of his life. He tried to imagine what he'd do if he saw her. And he tried to imagine what he'd do if he didn't.

What would Liv and Ben do? Would they invite him in, put Renie in the position of having to see him, talk to him, deal with him? He hoped not. If they did, he'd refuse. That wouldn't be fair to her. She had to decide on her own that she wanted to see him. He wouldn't force himself on her.

If she refused, he'd get Pooh settled, ask Liv to give her the letter he spent most of the night before writing to her, get in his truck, and drive home. The thought of it was enough to bring him to tears.

His arms started to ache; he missed Willow. He didn't have a cell signal where he was, but when he did, he'd call and see whether she would babble at him over the phone. His daughter saved his life. If it weren't for her, he'd never have survived this rift between him and Renie. But then again, if it weren't for her, there wouldn't be a rift in the first place. It broke his heart.

— • —

Renie asked her mother to pack her bedroom. She couldn't bear to set foot in it. Going into her apartment reduced her to tears. Ben took control, telling her and Liv to go get them coffee while he got started. She told him she thought she'd be better off with a sedative, and he laughed. She *almost* did—it was progress. She couldn't even remember the last time she'd smiled.

"This will go quick," her mom said when they came back. "You handle the kitchen."

The kitchen, the dining room, the living room…there wasn't a room in her apartment that she didn't see Billy standing in when she closed her eyes.

"Don't think, just pack," said Ben, squeezing her shoulder. "Let's get this done, and get the hell out of here."

It took them two hours to finish. Renie needed to stop at the registrar's office on campus, and once she had, she'd never have to set foot in Fort Collins again. It wasn't as though Billy had even spent much time with her here. But, it was the first place they'd made love. That was the part she couldn't allow herself to think about. If she did, it made her physically ill.

It wasn't just here in Fort Collins; it was everywhere they'd ever been together. She even avoided Ben's parents' house. She doubted she'd be able to much longer, but for now no one had pushed her. No one pushed her to do much of anything. And going there, to Bud and Ginny's house wouldn't be as bad. They weren't lovers the night they spent there looking at the stars, after her mom and Ben's wedding.

Mark, bless his heart, offered to drive Renie's car to Crested Butte for her. Paige came with him and they spent a few days at the ranch.

"How's Blythe?" Renie asked Paige.

"She's okay sweetie. She doesn't understand why you're so distant though." Paige put her arm around Renie's shoulders.

"Don't shut everyone out honey, there are a lot of people who love you. If you need to push Billy out, no one will argue with you about it, but everyone else…you need us."

Renie started to cry and couldn't speak. She walked away and a moment later, they heard the bedroom door close.

"That's what she does. She goes downstairs, and we have no idea when we might see her again."

"It's so unlike her."

"Paige—she's my daughter, and I swear, I almost don't recognize her. I don't know who this person is. I want my happy, smiling, life-loving, warm, sweet, caring, unselfish, smart, brave daughter back dammit."

"Blythe is upset too. She feels as though Renie's been lying to her. She said she's been trying to get Renie to fix her up with Billy for the last couple of years, and she never said a word about being interested in him herself. Blythe feels terrible about it."

"Renie spent most of her life hiding how she felt about him. Makes you wonder now, doesn't it?"

"Wonder what?"

"How much else has she been hiding? When I say I don't recognize her, I mean it. Renie's heart is broken over Billy, but my heart is broken over her."

Liv broke down just as Ben and Mark came in the back door.

"Oh jeez," said Mark. "We need to get the hell out of here. Come on, we're goin' to the Goat." He pulled Liv up out of her chair. "Let's go."

Liv had to admit it was a good idea, getting away from the house, away from Renie. She hadn't realized how long it had been since she'd done something other than worry about her daughter.

She knew Ben's boys felt it, and not just because she and Ben worried, they were worried themselves. Luke made it his mission to get Renie to go riding with him whenever he was at the house. Liv would look out and see her daughter smile at him, and she wanted to hug that little boy to her and never let him go. It was the only time she'd seen her daughter smile in the last few weeks.

Jake was distant. Liv tried to talk to him about it, but he told her he didn't know what to say, or what to do. He didn't get it, that's what he said. Neither did she. No one did.

The four friends stayed all evening, eventually closing the Goat. Ben played and sang, Mark told raunchy jokes, Liv and Paige laughed.

"I've missed you so much," Liv said to Paige.

"Likewise. Your husband has a plane; we shouldn't let so much time pass between visits."

"Agreed."

"I wish I could tell you what to do about Renie."

That made Liv laugh. Paige often told her what to do about the things she saw as problems in Liv's life. She missed that. She surely wished Paige had the answer for this one.

***

The house had gotten so quiet; Renie came upstairs to see what was going on. Jake was sitting in the family room, staring into space.

"Where is everybody?" she asked.

"Out."

"Oh." Renie started to go back downstairs.

"Luke is at my grandparents' house. I wanted to stay here. They said I could."

"Where's everybody else?"

"Somewhere in town. Probably the Goat."

"Oh," she said again. She started to turn around.

"Wanna know why I didn't go?"

"Okay. Why didn't you want to go?"

"Because I didn't want you to be here alone."

She walked toward the stairs.

"Don't go back to your room." Jake shouted at her. "I'm so sick of you just hanging out in there, not talking to any of us. And you look like shit, by the way."

"Wow. Thanks Jake."

"Ya know, you used to be my favorite."

"Your favorite what?"

"Person. In the whole world."

Renie sat down on the couch next to him. "I'm sorry. I'm a mess right now. It doesn't have anything to do with you."

"It has to do with all of us. We have to live with you. Sometimes I don't even want to come here."

Oh God that cut deep. Jake didn't want to come home because of her. She put her head in the pillow and cried.

He put his hand on her back. She knew how hard that was for him to do. He was shy, especially around her. It had taken a lot for him to tell her how he was feeling, and more to try to comfort her.

"I mean it Jake. I'm sorry. I don't mean to be such a pain in the ass."

"Then stop being one."

She laughed. "I wish I knew how."

"Go back to the way you were before."

"I don't think I'll ever be able to go back to the way I was before." *I was in love then. I won't ever be again.*

"Then don't go back to how you were, just stop being how you are now."

"And how do you suggest I do that?"

"Go outside, that would help. Get some fresh air. Read a book. Watch TV. Do *something*."

She thought for a minute about what he was suggesting. "You sound very grown up Jake."

"It's what you would say to me if I were acting the way you are. Back when you were *normal*."

"You're all right for a little brother, you know that?" She hugged him, which she was sure was making him as uncomfortable as everything he said made her.

The next morning Renie was upstairs by nine, and had breakfast with everyone. Her eyes met Jake's, and he gave her the briefest of smiles. She didn't miss the raised eyebrows between Paige and her mom. Or between her mom and Ben.

"Decided to break out of the vampire phase huh?" said Mark. "And look, it's daylight, and you haven't *melted*."

Renie didn't answer him, but she did smile, even if it were for a split second.

"Jake and I are going for a hike today," she said, looking at him. "Right?"

Jake nodded.

"I wanna go," said Luke.

"We might go for a long one, can you keep up?"

"Of course I can. Can you?"

Liv was almost too afraid to hope this might be the start of a change in her daughter. The conversation taking place between her and the boys almost sounded like the old Renie coming back.

Two days later, when Paige and Mark went home, and the boys went back to their mom's, Renie went back into her vampire phase, as Mark called it.

***

Billy was more tired than he had been in his entire life. Willow, almost four months old, was a good baby. She slept a lot, she was happy most of the time, but she was a *baby*, and she required his undivided attention. He wasn't sure how people did it. How did they have babies and *work*? He couldn't get anything done. He couldn't take care of the horses; thank God he'd hired Sookie, who'd taken to staying in the bunkhouse again. Billy guessed Sookie didn't like Willow's two in the morning wake up calls.

He hadn't been on a horse in the month since he brought her home with him. His body ached from the lack of exercise, but it was nothing compared to the ache in his heart.

He missed Renie every minute of every day. But, he gave up calling her. The day he brought Willow home, the day Renie left him standing in the doorway of the hospital, he'd called her twenty-seven times. He texted her even more than that.

Every day the number of calls and texts diminished, but his need to talk to her didn't. He wanted to pull his hair out, but there was little he could do about it. He wasn't about to drop his baby on his parents while he went to fix things between him and Renie. He hoped that after a few days, she'd come around on her own. After the second weekend went by, with no word from her, no visit to Pooh, he started to realize she might never come around.

His mom came up to the house every morning to check on them. In the first few days, he didn't know what he would've done without her. She taught him how to change Willow's diaper, told him what to feed her, even gave her a bath, which Willow loved.

The second morning she came armed with books. A lot of books. "You'll need to read these, so you know what to expect." She gave him books about a baby's first year, first aid, childhood illnesses, single parenting. If Billy hadn't been overwhelmed enough before, now he was doubly so.

"I'm so tired Mama, I don't know how I'm gonna read a book."

"Guess you're startin' to have a lot more respect for the mothers in this world then aren't you?"

"God yes. I don't know why anyone would have a second baby once they knew what having the first one was like. Is that why I don't have any brothers or sisters?"

"You were a handful, no doubt about that, but your daddy and I would have done it again, if we could've. God had other plans for us. I never got pregnant again."

"I'm sorry Mama, I didn't mean to make you feel bad. I'm so exhausted I don't know what I'm sayin' half the time." He rubbed his hands over his face, and his eyes filled with tears.

Dottie put her arms around him and held him tight.

"I don't know why I'm so emotional. I cry as much as Willow does. But don't get me wrong, I'm not feeling sorry for myself."

"You're tired, you're overwhelmed…it's natural for you to be emotional."

"That isn't all it is. You know that."

"You haven't heard anything from her?"

"Nothing. She won't answer me."

"You need to give her time."

Here he was, a month later and nothing had changed. How much more time did she need?

He called Liv, but she didn't know what to tell him.

***

"What are you gonna do with the rest of your life?" Ben asked Renie.

"The rest of my life? First thing in the morning Ben? I haven't even had a cup of coffee yet."

"You've moped around here for a couple of months now. You quit school, which again, was the stupidest thing you've ever done."

"Leave me alone Ben." Renie started to walk toward the stairs.

"You go into that bedroom, and I'm taking the door off the hinges."

"*What?* Jesus, what is your problem this morning?"

"You have to do something with your life Renie. Figure it out. Quit feeling so fucking sorry for yourself. He has a baby, big damn deal. I had a baby before I was ready for it too. By accident. I was less prepared for it than Billy was, if you can imagine that. But I dealt with it."

"Well I *didn't* have a baby. So I *don't* need to deal with it."

"Get it together Renie. I don't want to be an asshole, but I will be. Your mom has a lot on her plate, she doesn't need this shit from you."

It took her a week, but at the end of it, she had a plan. She'd be leaving by the middle of May, to work at Black Mountain Ranch.

"What do you mean?" Liv asked her.

"I'm getting out of your hair, at least for a little while."

"I don't think that's what Ben wanted. He's worried about you, that's all."

"No, he's right. I'm making everyone miserable being here. And you're gonna be gone, competing. It's until September, unless I figure something else out by then. And I'll be making money, so I can pay…for…you know."

Liv wanted to tell Renie she could come with her, help her while she traveled the rodeo circuit. Last December Liv came in fourth place at the nationals. She was determined to do better this year. She and Ben had a plan, and if it came to fruition, she'd retire after the finals this year and never race again.

But Liv knew there'd be no way Renie would want to set foot on rodeo grounds. It would remind her too much of Billy.

Maybe this was the right thing for her daughter then. There was a chance that working a dude ranch for the summer would make Renie miss her horse enough, her old life enough, that she'd find her way back.

***

Hard work. Mind-numbingly hard work. That was what she was after. She'd never been shy of it. She'd applied as a wrangler, and she knew she'd be expected to work her ass off.

She'd be one of a group responsible for maintaining the health of the horses and upkeep of the barn. In addition to that, she'd lead trail rides, go on cattle drives, even ferry guests back and forth from white water rafting trips in Glenwood Springs.

She'd also be expected to participate in evening activities with the guests, to dance and have fun, and make sure everyone there had the best time possible. It meant shutting off her emotions, setting them aside, trying to act normal, even if it were the furthest thing from how she felt.

No one there would know a thing about Billy Patterson, or her broken heart. No one would look at her with pity or wonder what she was thinking about, if she were thinking about him. She would be, but no one would know it.

***

On the fifteenth day of May, Renie climbed in her car after hugging and kissing her mom, Ben and the boys goodbye, and started the four and a half hour drive to what she hoped would be a new life.

Chapter Ten

He never would've believed he could go eight months without talking to Renie. Hell, he hadn't been able to go eight hours without talking to her. Or at least texting her.

He took pictures of Willow with his phone every day. And each time he did, the first person he wanted to send them to was Renie. Instead, he kept them to himself, believing that one day he'd show them to her. One day she'd want to see them.

He wished he could figure out why Renie reacted the way she had. Everyone who knew her was surprised by it. She was great with kids. Lots of kids who had boarded horses came to the ranch. She rode with them. She even talked about giving riding lessons, before school got to be too much work for her to consider it.

But, where Willow was concerned, it was an entirely different story. Renie had gone from being his best friend, the love of his life, to being someone he didn't know, all because of his baby girl. He wished he could figure out why.

A couple more hours...he prayed he would see her again.

— • —

When Renie drove through the gates of Black Mountain Ranch, she felt a sense of peace wash over her. No one, not a single person, here knew her, and it felt liberating.

She wanted to ride, and dance, and sing...and be happy. She wanted to forget Billy Patterson existed, and be a girl who got to be a wrangler for one summer of her life.

When the cowboy tipped his hat and offered to carry her bags to her cabin, she was happy to accept his offer—

although part of getting the job here for the summer included proving she could lift and carry at least seventy-five pounds of tack, or potatoes or firewood—whatever they threw at her. She'd be able to, no problem. And meanwhile she'd let the handsome cowboy help her all he wanted to.

"What's your name cowgirl?" he asked.

"Irene Fairchild." It was the name she'd put on the application, and for the next four months, it would be the name she went by. If anyone called her Renie, she was prepared to ignore them.

"What's yours?"

"Jace Rice."

"Rice? My mom married a man named Ben Rice."

"Yep. Ben's my cousin, second or third, somethin' like that. We aren't close," he laughed.

She was glad to hear it. Sometimes the world was too damn small. The next thing she knew she'd meet somebody related to Billy. And if she did, she'd be in her car and on her way home faster than you could say, "Patterson."

"When's the last time you saw Ben?"

"I was about eight or nine years old."

That made her laugh.

"You have a mighty pretty smile."

"Why thank you Jace. I hope to be smiling around you a lot while I'm here this summer."

Jace blushed and put her bags on her bed for her. "Meet up with you later, after you get settled in. You should also check in up at the office before it gets too late."

"Thank you Jace, I'll see you later."

Yep, Jace Rice was just the kind of man she was looking for. He didn't look anything like Billy, but he did look mighty fine. He had broad shoulders, like a bull rider. His ash blonde hair was closely clipped, but he let his beard grow in, so it was the perfect amount of stubble. His green eyes drew her in, especially the way they met hers and didn't back away from the challenge of her stare. This was a man who was confident, maybe even more confident than Billy.

She wished she could stop comparing every man she met to Billy. It was time to let a man show her who he was without being measured against the Billy Patterson yardstick. She figured Jace was more than up for the challenge.

"We have free time in the evenings until next week, when the first guests start arriving for the season. Once they get here, we're on the clock almost twenty-four hours a day, except when we're sleepin' of course." He winked at her. "And Sundays, we have Sunday nights off, as long as the ranch is ready for the new guests who arrive on Monday."

She'd read most of this in the new employee packet they'd sent her. She doubted he was telling her all this as the human resources greeter. Jace was interested in her, she knew he was.

"There's dancin' later too. After dinner." He shifted the cowboy hat he held in this right hand to his left. His right hand took hers, and he spun her around into him, then back out again. "Looks as though you know how to dance."

"It was a prerequisite for getting hired," she laughed.

"Yep."

"Is it your job to make sure all the new cowgirls can dance?"

"Nope, not all of 'em. Just you." He brought her hand up to his lips, turned it over, and kissed her palm.

Oh yeah, this would be a good summer Renie decided.

Jace didn't disappoint on the dance floor later that night. By the time he walked her back to her cabin, her face hurt from smiling. It had been way too long since she smiled that much. It hurt, but it felt good too.

He didn't try to kiss her good night, which she found comfort in since it was her first night here. She'd have to try to get the lay of the land tomorrow, and make sure there wasn't a hot cowboy welcoming committee for all the new girls when they arrived. She had no desire to be someone's conquest. She planned to be the one taking the prisoners, not the other way around.

"Will I see you tomorrow morning at breakfast?"

"Nope, sorry to say I won't be able to join you. I'll be out rustling cattle in the mornin'. But, I'd surely like to dance with you again tomorrow night after dinner."

"I'd like that Jace. Very much."

He tipped his hat, said good night, and walked in the direction of a group of cabins cloistered further up in the woods.

"It's gonna be a *good* summer," she heard him say to the trees.

***

At the end of her first week at the ranch, Renie knew she was in over her head. She wasn't cut out for the long days and hard work she'd craved before she got here. Of course, she'd never admit it. She'd pull her weight the same as everyone else, but at the end of the night she was happy to be able to fall into bed and let sleep overtake her, sometimes before she got her boots off.

Other than her constant physical exhaustion, coming here to work was the best decision she could've made. The

And Then You Dance

ranch catered to families mostly, but had a few weeks during the summer that were for adults only. She loved hanging out with the little kids, teaching them how ride. When they'd take the horses through the river, and they'd swim with the riders on their backs, the looks on people's faces when they did it the first time was priceless. The ranch was all about making the best memories they could for the people who paid to come and stay. She loved being a part of it all.

Jace continued to flirt with her, but when guests around, he played it completely cool. Part of the fantasy of spending a week at a dude ranch was falling in love with one of the wranglers. The cowboys played their part, but never took it further than a dance with a guest. There was a fine line they all walked, to not mix fantasy and reality.

Sunday nights, when the guests went home, the wranglers came out to play. They still walked a fine line when it came to romancing fellow employees. It was frowned upon, although Renie was sure not all the cowboys and cowgirls slept alone every night as she did.

She was assigned white water rafting duty the next week, which meant she'd be away from the ranch for a couple days, staying in a hotel in Glenwood Springs instead. While the guests were at the river, she'd have time to herself during the day, unless she chose to go rafting with them.

When she walked up to the van Tuesday morning, she was surprised to see Jace already comfortable in the driver's seat.

"What's up? Schedule change?"

"Signed myself up for it."

"So should I stay here?"

"No way cowgirl, you're the reason I'm goin' along."

The way he smiled at her made Renie's toes curl.

It took them an hour to drive from McCoy to Glenwood Springs. Once they dropped the guests off at the rafting company, Jace and Renie had ranch business to take care of in town, including picking up supplies. Then, they'd be free until the next afternoon when the rafters got back from their overnight trip.

Jace talked her into going to the hot springs.

"Gotta take advantage of it while we can. Don't know about you, but my muscles could use a good, long soak in some hot mineral water."

Nothing sounded better to her, except she hadn't brought a swimsuit with her.

"They sell 'em at the hot springs," Jace told her. She wondered how many other female wranglers he'd brought here that hadn't remembered their suit.

"What was that?" he asked her.

"What?"

"Sometimes your face gets this little pinch in it, as though you bit into somethin' sour."

"It does?"

He tweaked her nose. "Yeah, it does. So what were you thinkin' about just then?"

"How this body hasn't been in a bathing suit since last summer and I'm not sure I want to try one on."

Jace started to say something but then stopped himself.

"What?"

"I don't think you're gonna like what I have to say, so I think it would be best if I kept my mouth shut."

"What? You can't do that. God, are you agreeing with me?"

"Huh? What're you talkin' about now?"

"You don't want to see me in a bathing suit?"

How she thought he meant he didn't want to see her in a bathing suit when that was all he wanted…that or nothing, was beyond him. Jace couldn't help himself, this conversation was going nowhere fast. He put his hand on the back of her neck before she had time to scoot away from him, as she usually did, and kissed her, hard on the mouth.

Once he started he couldn't stop. For two weeks he'd wanted to do that, to kiss her. Two long weeks. He was done waiting.

Oh. She hadn't expected this. Well she had, but not right now. And wow, he was a good kisser. She could kiss him all day long.

"Sorry, I couldn't help it."

"What? Don't be sorry. God."

He laughed. "What does that mean?"

"You are, um, a good kisser."

He laughed again. "You are too Irene." He ran his fingers down the side of her face. "Such a formal name for such an informal girl. Where'd you get it? Are you named after somebody?"

"My grandmother, on my father's side. Her name was Alice Irene, but no one ever called her Alice. At least that's the story I've been told. I never met her."

"Got a nickname? Somethin' people call you when they don't want to be so formal?"

"Nope. I'm not a nickname kind of girl."

"So tell me more about your family. I know your mom is married to my cousin. Are your parents divorced?"

"Nope. My father died before I was born."

"You're kidding?"

"Not something I'd kid about."

"Sorry, I didn't mean it that way. How'd he die?"

"Fighter pilot, died in the Gulf War."

"Wow. Gosh. I'm sorry. That must've been hard for you."

"Since it was before I was born, it wasn't something that I ever thought much about. My mom and my grandparents told me stories about him, and I've seen photos. But no, it wasn't hard."

He leaned in to kiss her again. "I've been wanting to do that since the day you drove into the ranch."

"I thought you might be part of the welcoming committee."

"Never helped any of the other wranglers with their bags, before or since."

"Come on, don't you try to play me Jace Rice."

"I'm serious. There's somethin' about you Irene. You know dating is frowned upon at the ranch."

"I got that impression. I also got the impression that not everyone follows the rules."

He laughed. "No, not everyone does. As long as the parties involved are discreet, management looks the other way."

"How much practice do you have being discreet?"

"You're somethin' else," he laughed. "I can't decide whether you're the least confident, or most confident girl I've ever met." He stopped smiling. "But I do know I want to get to know you better."

Renie found a reasonably modest bathing suit at the hot springs and Jace was right; her muscles needed the time she spent in the warm water. The other thing they needed was a good long massage, so she booked one for later that afternoon. Jace thought that was a good idea, so he did too.

"We could get a couple's massage."

She rolled her eyes at him.

"What? I was serious."

"I don't think so cowboy."

He pushed her up against the wall in the hallway outside the locker rooms and brushed his lips under her ear. "Come on Irene, let's make good use of our hours away from the ranch."

Oh it would be so easy to let herself go, give into Jace, so easy. And why not? What was stopping her? Billy. Ha! Wasn't that the reason she'd decided to work at the ranch in the first place? To forget all about him. Jace would certainly help that along. It was time she moved on, in every way. Billy Patterson was the only man she'd ever slept with, it was time to change that.

"You know, you're right."

He didn't wait for her to change her mind. He went back into the salon office and changed their appointment from two individual massages to two for a couple.

Although they had rooms at the Ramada Inn on Sixth Street, which the ranch paid for, they decided to book a room at the Colorado Hotel. It was connected to the hot springs. They'd get the massage in their room that way.

Renie wondered for a few minutes if this was a bad idea, but reminded herself again, this was the reason she was here. She was the one who was going to live her life, on her terms, Billy Patterson be damned.

Renie looked at the clock, it was almost seven, and she was starving. And spending time with Jace Rice had definitely been the best way she could think of to work up an appetite. She bit his shoulder.

"Ow. You tryin' to tell me something girl?"

"I'm hungry. Feed me."

He raised his eyebrows at her.

"Later cowboy…where's the best place to eat in this town?"

"Depends on what you're in the mood for, but Juicy Lucy's Steakhouse is one of my favorites."

"Sounds perfect."

"Might be a wait on a Saturday night, but we can take a walk along the river if there is."

She smiled. She liked him. Jace was easy to be around, and as good in bed as he was a kisser. She hadn't thought about Billy, before now, all afternoon. It was some kind of record.

"Whatcha' thinkin' about?"

"You."

"Ah that makes me happy since you have such a sweet smile on your face."

"You put it there."

There was a wait, so they walked along the river and Jace asked her questions about herself. They both loved to ski, in fact, Jace had thought about going pro a few years back. A torn ACL took him out of competition, but it had healed, and he was thinking about getting back into it.

He'd also been thinking about getting back on some bulls. It had been a while, longer than he intended for it to be. But, he felt like he was ready to try bull-riding again.

Renie told him about her mom, and how she didn't start barrel racing until she was forty. "If anyone has shown me it's never too late to chase your dream, it's my mom. And barrel racing isn't for the faint of heart." She told him about her accident too.

"You know, now that you're telling me the story, I remember hearing about this. CB Rice was on tour, and there was an uproar about her being in a coma when she wasn't."

"Yep, that's the story, but it's way more complicated than that. She was in a coma, and then when she came out of it she was paralyzed. She made all of us who knew keep it a secret from Ben."

Billy had been at her side through all of it. He'd been her rock. She closed her eyes against the memory, but it made it worse. She could see his face when she closed her eyes.

"It was a rough time, for everyone. Ben included."

Jace put his arm around her shoulders and kissed her forehead. "Sorry I brought it up."

"It's okay. She's fine now, in fact, she's back at it, competing again."

"You sound proud of her."

"I am, but..."

"But?"

"I'm not sure she's proud of me."

Renie wasn't sure what made her tell Jace about quitting school, although she stopped short of telling him exactly why she had. She told him that her heart wasn't in it any longer and with as hard as it was, and how expensive it was, she thought it better not to waste the money or time.

"You seem as though you'd be a natural. I've watched you around the horses. You're good with them. Think you might go back to it someday?"

"At this point, no. But again, with my mom as inspiration, who knows?"

The buzzer went off in his pocket letting them know their table was ready. "I've enjoyed this time with you Irene. It's gonna be hard to go back tomorrow and act like I'm not crazy about you."

She smiled, and he pulled her close again. "Damn, I like your smile cowgirl."

Chapter Eleven

Renie had been sending Billy checks every month for Pooh's care. He never cashed them. She wondered if he got them, but she thought he must. And if he didn't, did he really think she wouldn't send money to feed and care for her horse? She knew she had the address right; it had been her address for the first twenty-two years of her life.

Renie saw the truck coming down the long dirt road toward Ben's place on the Rice family ranch. It wasn't until she realized it was pulling a horse trailer that she got a feeling of dread in the pit of her stomach. Was Billy in that truck? And was Pooh in the trailer?

Was this really the end of them? Once Pooh was here with her, there'd never be a reason for Renie to go back to Monument. There'd never be a reason for her and Billy to talk again.

"Mom?" Renie called out. She went into the kitchen, to get a better view of the truck, and who was in it.

No one answered. She was here alone. And the truck was close enough for her to see the person driving. It was Billy.

— • —

If Renie thought she was sore when they left for Glenwood Springs, she was more so now. Although for an entirely different reason.

She and Jace were on their way to pick up the ranch guests from their rafting trip. Soon, he wouldn't be able to caress her cheek or pull her in close for a kiss. She wouldn't be able to stand behind him and wrap her arms around his waist, or run her lips across the strong muscles on his back. At least in public. She wondered how long it would be before the two of them could get away on their own again.

Jace pulled the van over at a scenic lookout and turned it off. Renie looked around trying to figure out why he'd stopped.

"Come here girl. I need to kiss you a little while longer." She groaned as she let him take her in his arms. "I need more of you."

"I feel the same way."

"What're we gonna do?"

"I guess we'll learn how to be discreet," she smirked.

"I'm not sure how you pulled off getting a cabin on your own girl, but I'm sure glad you did."

That night after the dancing was over and the guests retired for the night, Jace snuck into Renie's cabin, as he did every night for the rest of the summer.

***

Billy couldn't stand it any longer. It had been almost three months to the day since Renie walked out of the hospital in San Antonio, and out of his life.

Willow was six months old. She slept longer at night, which made life easier. On the other hand, she was crawling. Billy had to watch her every second, or she'd get into something. Dottie came up to the house and helped him baby-proof it. He loved the fireplaces in Liv's house—his house, as he had to keep reminding himself it was. But now that he had a baby girl, he cursed them. There wasn't a way he could figure out, besides putting pillows on the hearths and corners of every one of them, to keep Willow from bumping her head.

If he weren't dreaming about Willow getting hurt on something he'd overlooked, he was dreaming about Renie. Both caused him equal amounts of pain when he did. When he woke up this morning, Renie was on his mind. He still hadn't heard a word from her, although he hadn't expected to.

He called Liv who was out on the rodeo circuit.

"Hey-o Billy," she answered.

"Hey Livvie. How goes chasin' the cans?"

"Great, but we sure miss you out here. No matter where I am people come and ask me when you'll be back."

"What do you tell them?"

"I don't tell them anything Billy. It isn't up to me to tell them why you aren't here."

"Appreciate that Livvie."

Billy figured everyone knew about Willow anyway. The rodeo world was a small one.

"I'm calling to ask you about Renie."

"I know."

"How is she?"

"She's doing a bit better. At least I think she is. I haven't talked to her in a few days."

"How long you been out?"

"A couple of days. Renie left two weeks ago. She's working at Black Mountain Ranch this summer."

"Where? Isn't that a dude ranch?"

"It is."

"She'll be there all summer?"

"Yes Billy. She will be."

It was May. She'd be gone until at least September.

"I gotta go Livvie. I'm sorry."

"It's okay Billy. I understand."

He needed to sit down, catch his breath, and figure out how in the hell he'd last another four months without any chance of seeing her.

***

Knowing the thing between her and Jace would end when summer did, made it easy between them. They stayed so busy at the ranch, they barely had time for each other anyway. There wasn't time for them to disagree. They didn't have any relationship "issues." They worked hard all day, sometimes they saw each other, and sometimes they didn't.

Jace would seek her out at dinner, sometimes he'd sit next to her, sometimes he wouldn't. He tried to get at least one dance in with her a night, sometimes it wasn't possible. Jace was a good-looking cowboy, and there was usually a line of ranch guests waiting to dance with him. Some were not willing to give him up at the end of a song.

It didn't make Renie jealous; it made her laugh. She was in the same boat. She did a lot of dancing with guests herself. Her favorite dance partners were the little boys who reminded her of Jake and Luke. She missed her stepbrothers so much. And her mom. She even missed Ben.

It made her realize that she hadn't been allowing herself to miss anyone. Missing someone reminded her of the person she missed the most. But at some point in the last couple of weeks, she'd been able to think about other people in her life, people outside the fences of Black Mountain Ranch, and she missed them.

She called her mom that night right before dinner.

"Hi Mama," she said when her mother answered her cell phone.

"Renie! Oh my goodness. It is so good to hear your voice. How are you?"

"I'm good. I miss you."

"I miss you too honey."

"Where are you?"

"I'm in Lewisburg, Ohio, of all places."

"How's it going?"

"Second in the money for the region."

"Woohoo!" Renie shouted out.

"I can't tell you how good it is to hear you 'woohooing.'"

"It feels good to be doing it."

"Are you having a good time?"

"I am Mom. It's the best thing I could've done for myself. Don't get me wrong though, it's hard work."

They talked for a few more minutes about the ranch, Jake and Luke, and Ben's album, which he'd almost finished recording. Liv told her that Paige had been traveling with her from time to time, and Mark was sitting in on a few tracks on Ben's record. They even talked about Will and Matt, Ben's brothers, and his parents. They ran out of people to talk about, but the air hung heavily on the phone connection.

"Dottie and Bill asked me to tell you they miss you the next time I talked to you."

"I miss them too. You can tell them that."

Her mom didn't say anything else and Renie didn't ask. "Okay, I better go, they're ringing the dinner bell. I love you Mom."

"I love you too honey."

Renie hung up and looked up at the stars. "Damn you Billy Patterson, you're not getting back in. Not ever," she said, feeling as though she wanted to shake her fists at the sky.

"Who's Billy Patterson?" Jace said, walking up behind her.

"Jace, you scared me," she turned to look at him.

"Come on Irene, tell me. Who is he?"

"Nobody important."

"Don't lie to me."

"I'm not lying. He's not important."

"You talk in your sleep you know."

She did? This was the first he mentioned it.

"I've been wondering who Billy was. Now at least there's a last name to go with the first one."

"He's someone from my past. Not someone I want to talk about, or even think about."

"They say dreams are the manifestation of unresolved emotion."

"Maybe they are, sometimes. But in this case Billy is someone I grew up with. He isn't in my life anymore."

"What happened to him?"

"What part of 'I don't want to talk about him,' aren't you hearing Jace?"

He turned around to make sure no one was watching them and took her arm, drawing her away from the front porch and out of the light.

"Okay, I got it. Now come here."

As much as she knew she shouldn't, she let Jace kiss her. She needed it so badly, the feel of him to wash away the memories of Billy that still crept in too often.

He held her for a while, and she rested her cheek against his shoulder. "Thanks."

"What for?"

"Not pressing the issue."

"Come on, let's go eat. Somebody's gonna come looking for us." He squeezed her hand before he dropped it and followed her into the dining hall.

Renie tried to avoid talking to Jace about anything that could lead to questions about Billy. She changed the subject so fast sometimes that even her head spun.

"I'm not going to ask about him again," he said as he climbed into bed with her a couple weeks later.

"What do you mean?"

"Billy. You've been dancin' around every topic that you think might lead to him, and it's exhaustin' me. I'm not gonna ask you about him. You'll talk about him when you're ready."

"I don't think I'll ever be ready Jace. And it isn't even that, it's more that there isn't anything to talk about."

She looked straight at him, waiting for him to raise his eyebrows, or do something else to indicate he didn't believe her. That's what Billy would've done. But Jace didn't. When he said he wouldn't ask about him, he meant it. When he said he was tired of dancing around it, he meant that too.

"Thanks Jace," she said as she kissed him.

"It's okay, I get it."

She believed he did get it. Once again, he was so easy going. Billy was never easy going. When he wanted to talk about something, he wouldn't relent until they did.

"Stop comparing me to him."

That startled her. "What does that mean?"

"I can see you doing it. I'm watchin' the wheels spin. You're thinkin' about him right now. You don't want to talk about him that's one thing, but thinkin' about him when you're in bed with me? That won't fly with me Irene."

Jace moved over her and gently pinned her arms above her head. "Do you understand me? When you're with me this way, you think about me."

She looked into his eyes and nodded her head enough that he knew she understood.

In early August Jace and Renie had another opportunity to go to Glenwood Springs on a rafting excursion. She couldn't wait to spend time with him without pretending there was nothing between them, without looking over her shoulder every time he smiled at her to make sure no one was looking.

They decided to repeat what they did the last time and booked a couple's massage in their room at the Colorado Hotel. And then, they went and ate at Juicy Lucy's.

"Tate talked to me about you the other day," Jace said during dinner.

Tate was the ranch manager. Renie doubted it had been a good conversation.

"Uh oh. What did he say? And why are you telling me about it now?"

"It wasn't that bad. Mainly he wanted to know what our plans were at the end of the summer."

"Plans?"

"Yeah, where I'm going. Where you're going. That kind of thing."

"I hadn't thought about it much, other than going home I guess."

"Home to Crested Butte?"

"That's the only home I have anymore."

Jace's family lived in Aspen. He and his brother had a condo there, although both of them were gone most of the summer. He was there during the winter though. Last year Jace helped train a group of competitive skiers, he told her. This winter he planned to spend more time at the rodeo than he did on the ski slopes.

"It's a nice drive over Kebler Pass, especially in the fall. Maybe we can make a couple of trips back and forth."

Renie wasn't sure what to say. This was the first time Jace mentioned anything about seeing each other once summer ended, and the ranch closed for the season.

"Yeah, maybe."

"You don't sound too sure about it."

"No, that sounds nice."

"Again, missing the enthusiasm factor. Does this have anything to do with the mysterious Billy?"

It had been a few weeks since they'd last talked about Billy. She wondered if she were still talking in her sleep, but that wasn't a question she'd ever ask him. She still dreamt about Billy. All the time. She'd hoped Jace would never bring him up again, but it looked as though her luck had run out.

"It doesn't have anything to do with him."

"Aha, so it does have to do with something."

"You're twisting my words. I haven't thought that far ahead. I haven't wanted to."

"Why not?"

She smiled. "Because I'm enjoying my summer so much. That's why."

He smiled too. "Me too. But Irene, I would like to see you again after the summer is over."

The last week at the ranch, which was the last week of September, was hard on everyone. Friendships formed every summer and even if a lot of them came back the next year, it would never be the same again. Different guests, new personalities among the wranglers, there was beauty in it, but there was a sadness too.

Jace had a great attitude, as he did about most things. Nothing much rattled the man. He went back and forth, season to season, doing what he loved. In the summer, he was a wrangler; in the winter he was a skier. Between he hiked fourteeners or traveled somewhere exotic. Money didn't seem to be much of an issue for Jace, although he rarely talked about it.

"Come to Aspen for a couple days before you head home. Let me show you around," he said a few days before they were scheduled to leave.

No one was waiting for her at home. Her mom was still out on the rodeo circuit and Ben was with her, which meant the boys wouldn't be coming to the house. So why not?

"Sure," she answered, as though it was the easiest thing in the world.

"Wow."

"What?"

He laughed. "I didn't expect you to say yes so quickly."

"Want to rescind your offer?"

"No way! I was wondering what else I could ask you while you're so agreeable."

That was funny, she thought. She was usually agreeable to anything Jace suggested. She wondered if he saw it differently.

He tweaked her nose. "There's that sour face again."

A week later Renie followed Jace out of the ranch and was glad she was going to Aspen with him. It made the end of their summer so much easier. She was afraid she might have cried if she'd had to say goodbye to him along with everyone else.

The thing between Jace and Renie wasn't a very well-kept secret. Consequently, Renie hadn't gotten very close to the other wranglers. She was friendly, she liked everyone well enough, but there wasn't anyone else she'd keep in touch with after she left.

Two hours later they pulled up behind Jace's condo. It was at the base of the mountain.

"Nice digs," she said getting out of the car. "Am I okay parked here?"

"For now, I'll put your car in the garage later. I have a parking permit on mine, so it can stay on the street."

"You don't have to do that—"

"Not a big deal Irene."

Nothing was for him. She forgot that. He had to be the most easy going man she'd ever known.

"How do you do it?"

"What?"

"Nothing ever bothers you. I'm not sure it's normal."

"Plenty of things bother me."

"Name one."

He let out a deep breath. "It bothers me to hear the name Billy every night. That bothers me a lot."

"Every night? You can't be serious."

"There hasn't been a night I've slept with you that you haven't woken me up talking about him. Most of it's gibberish, but his name is clear as a bell, every time you say it." He paused and ran his hand through his hair. "The other thing that bothers me is that when you're awake you refuse to talk about him."

Renie put her arms around him and squeezed him hard. "I'm sorry. It's my subconscious. There isn't anything to talk about. That's why I don't."

"Bullshit."

That took her by surprise. "Maybe it would be better if I went home."

"No way. You started this conversation by saying nothing ever bothers me. I'm telling you there is something that does. It isn't a reason for you to take off. Stay instead. Talk to me about it. Tell me about him for God's sake. Clearly you aren't together, or you wouldn't have spent the summer sharin' sheets with me. And you wouldn't be here now."

Sharin' sheets, Billy used that expression. It was the only other time she'd heard it.

"Come inside. Let me show you my house." He pulled her with him. When they got to the front door, he turned around and smiled at her. "I know how much you hate confrontation, so I'll drop it for now. You'll tell me about him when you're ready to."

She hated confrontation? Yeah, she supposed he was right about that. How had they gone from casual sleeping buddies to him knowing so much about her once they left the ranch?

His condo was beautiful. The view of the mountain was incredible, but it was equally impressive inside. It definitely didn't look like a place two brothers shared. It had to have been professionally decorated.

She walked around studying the different pieces of artwork that were perfectly placed throughout the condo. She realized that the paintings all bore the same signature, which she couldn't make out.

"My brother. It's his work."

"What? It's...amazing. He's very talented."

"He is. The sculpture is his too. He gets bored with one medium and moves on to another one. Eventually, he makes his way back around again."

"What's his name?"

"Tucker. We're twins, by the way."

"Where is he now?"

"Spain."

"Oh, okay." He was so matter-of-fact about everything. She smiled.

"What?"

"Nothing." She started to laugh.

"What? Come on, tell me. What's funny?"

"It's that nothing flusters you thing again. Notice I said 'flusters,' not 'bothers.'"

He laughed too, and put his arms around her. "I like you Irene."

"I like you too Jace." It was nice to *like* him, and not think about it being more than that.

That night he took her to Belly Up to see one of his favorite bands play. And before they went to Matsuhisa for dinner.

He hadn't asked whether she liked sushi or not. She liked that about him—his confidence. That was a deal breaker for her. After Billy, she couldn't have dealt with anyone who lacked self-confidence. Jace had confidence in spades.

The next day they went up Independence Pass and hiked to the top. The view was breathtaking, and she said so.

"This is nothing," Jace answered. "We're at 12,000 feet. Wait until I get you on top of a fourteener."

He'd been doing that more and more, talking about things they'd do together in the future. Renie hadn't planned to continue this little fling past September. Jace clearly had other ideas.

That night he took her to the White House Tavern. It was a casual place, but historic. Jace knew everyone there. He introduced her as his summer wrangling partner and winked at her every time he did. He wasn't shy about putting his arm around her, or nuzzling her hair, even kissing her. It was so different for them, not having to hide that they were together from people. It made it feel more like a relationship.

"I don't suppose you'd want to go to Spain with me?" he said sheepishly the next morning.

"Wait. What? Spain?"

He laughed. "Remember I told you Tucker is in Spain?"

"Yes."

"My whole family is. They're expecting me."

"I'll have to draw the line at Spain," she laughed.

"I figured you would, but thought I'd give it a try anyway."

She walked to the window and looked out at the mountain. "I've never skied here. I'd like to some time."

"Is that your way of asking when I'll be back?"

She turned around, and he was smiling. She didn't want to hurt his feelings, but that wasn't what she'd been thinking at all. "Sure," she answered instead.

"Okay sourface. That wasn't your way of asking, but I'll tell you anyway. I'll be back for Thanksgiving."

Sourface? She was beginning to think it was time for a Jace-break. He was becoming all too familiar, and Renie wasn't sure she was ready to go in the direction Jace seemed headed in.

"When are you leaving?"

"Friday."

Today was Wednesday. Maybe she should think about leaving today, to give him time to get ready for his trip.

"Stay with me another night?" he asked, as though he read her mind.

"Sure," she answered.

"I'm beginning to dislike that word," he said, but he was still smiling.

They stayed in that night, and the next morning they said goodbye as though they'd be seeing each other in a few days.

It was a long drive from Aspen to Crested Butte, but a beautiful one. The aspens were in their full glory on Kebler Pass. Renie stopped several times to take photos.

The further she got away from Aspen, and Jace, the more her chest started to hurt. She tried to push it away, but nothing was working. As she drove down the mountain road and into Crested Butte, all she could think about was Billy.

Chapter Twelve

Billy pulled up in front of Ben's ranch house and turned off the truck. He took several deep breaths and said a prayer that Renie was here, and that she'd want to see him.

He looked at the house. It didn't look as though anyone were home, but it was a big house, they could be anywhere in it. He saw something move in one of the front windows, and by the long blonde hair, he knew it was Renie. Would she come out? Or if he went to the front door and knocked, would she pretend she wasn't home?

There was one way to find out. He got out of the truck and walked back to the trailer to check on Pooh first. She was fine. Now or never, he thought as he turned and walked up the porch steps toward the front door.

— • —

Her mom and Ben still weren't home. She didn't even know what state they were in. Trying to keep up with rodeo schedules was hard enough, but for all Renie knew, Ben could be out on tour by now.

She had no idea; she hadn't shown much interest in anyone's life but her own.

She checked the refrigerator to see whether she needed to run to the store for milk or any other essentials. It appeared as though it were well-stocked.

She texted her mom. *When will you be home?*

Half hour, Liv answered.

They must not be traveling; they must've gone to town for something.

The boys?
With us.
Oh good, she was looking forward to seeing them.

Jake and Luke came running through the front door a few minutes later.

"Renie's here!" Luke shouted, jumping on her and almost knocking her down.

"I guess you missed me."

He stood back and took a long look at her. "Yep, I've missed you."

She squinted her eyes at him. "What was that all about?"

"I missed happy Renie. The other one I can do without."

"Always a gentleman aren't you pard'ner," Ben said, coming up to hug her.

Jake looked at her from a few feet away.

"You can hug me too ya know," she said as he stood in front of her. "Holy crap, how much have you grown in the last couple of months?"

Jake was as tall as she was, if not a little taller. He hadn't been much past her shoulder when she left.

Liv ran toward her much in the same way Luke had.

"I've missed you sweet girl," she said, hugging Renie so hard she could barely breathe.

"I've missed you too Mom."

The boys wanted to hear all about her time at the ranch. Jake wanted to know how old he had to be before you could get a job there.

"How about a good long ride tomorrow?" Renie offered. "I'll tell you all about it then."

Ben got up and motioned to the boys. "Let's make tracks out to the barn and get our chores done." He winked at Liv. "Give the girls time to catch up."

"Thanks honey."

He grabbed her hand and leaned down to kiss her on his way out the door.

"You two are so happy."

"We are. We're very happy."

"I met someone this summer."

Liv sat up a little straighter. "Yeah?"

"Yeah. It's nothing serious."

"But important enough to bring him up. Tell me about him. What's his name? Where's he from?"

"His name is Jace. Jace Rice. Oh damn, I forgot to mention him to Ben. Jace said they were cousins, but he hadn't seen Ben since they were kids."

"How old is he?"

Renie laughed. "He's my age Mom. Or a couple years older. He's not as old as Ben."

"Not as old as Ben." Liv rolled her eyes.

"Anyway, his family lives in Aspen. He's a twin."

"And?"

"That's about it."

"When do we get to meet him?"

"He's in Spain. He won't be back until the end of November. And even then…I'm not sure we'll see each other again."

Liv hated to ruin the moment between them, but she had to ask. "What about Billy?"

"What about him?"

"Have you talked to him?"

"You know I haven't."

"I don't know that at all. You and Billy have been friends all your life. Don't you think it's time you made up?"

"Made up? What do we have to make up?" Renie shook her head. "Billy wasn't who I thought he was. I don't have anything to say to him."

"That's a little harsh don't you think? He's raising that little girl all on his own. I'm proud of him."

Renie stood. "Good for you Mom. You are entitled to feel however you want to. And so am I. I wouldn't ask you not to be friends with him, or Dottie and Bill. You need to show me the same respect."

"Are you disappearing again because I brought up Billy?"

Renie sighed. "No. I'm not. I'm done spending all my time thinking about Billy Patterson. I'm having a glass of wine, and then I thought I'd show you photos of the ranch."

"Sounds great. I'd love to see your photos."

"Can I get you a glass of wine?"

"No thanks, I'll have a glass of water."

When Ben and the boys came back inside, Liv and Renie were huddled together looking at pictures on her phone.

"Here's one of him," she said.

"Hey Ben, Renie met one of your cousins at the ranch. Jace, do you remember him?"

Ben sat down on the chair next to him. He looked at Jake. "I bet Jace was Jake's age the last time I saw him. He might have been younger than that. Wow." He shook his head. "How is he? Was Tucker there too?"

Renie told them about visiting their place in Aspen and seeing Tucker's art, and then told them Jace was in Spain with his family. She didn't miss the looks going back and forth between Ben and her mom.

"Are we allowed to ask about the other one?"

"No Ben, we're not," answered Liv.

He held his hands up. "Never much liked Cowboy Patterson anyway," he mumbled. "Get you more wine?"

"Sure." Renie got up and followed him into the kitchen to fill her own glass.

"He calls your mom sometimes."

"I figured he did."

"And she talks to Dottie and Bill."

"I wouldn't expect it to be any other way."

***

Billy checked the Black Mountain Ranch website to confirm they'd closed for the season. As he scrolled through the pages, he did his best not to look at the photos, but he couldn't help himself. Renie was in several of them. And she looked happy.

There were photos of her on horseback, dancing, and on cattle drives. The most precious one was of her sitting off to the side of what appeared to be a chuck wagon dinner. She had a daisy in her hand, and she was looking away from the camera. He looked closer at the photo. The cowboy standing behind her was looking at her in a way that Billy would've been if he'd been there.

He didn't like it one bit. But what did he expect? That she was pining away for him the way he was for her? Of

And Then You Dance

course she wouldn't be. She hadn't given any indication in seven months that she missed him, or even thought about him.

He heard the back door open and shut the computer down.

"There's my girl!" He walked toward his mom and took Willow out of her arms.

"Dada," she said, putting her head on his shoulder.

"She's tired. Didn't sleep a wink all afternoon."

"You ready for a nap baby girl?"

Willow rubbed her face on his chest, a telltale sign.

"Let's go snuggle for a bit."

Billy walked toward her bedroom.

"I'll stay for a few minutes, if you want to talk," his mother said.

"Got somethin' to tell me?"

When she nodded her head, Billy doubted it was good news.

"She's home."

"I know."

"What about Pooh?"

"She knows where her horse is."

"Uh huh."

"What do you want me to do?"

"Take Pooh to Crested Butte."

"Mama—"

"It's the right thing to do. Renie Fairchild will do anything to avoid confrontation Billy. You of all people should know that. Don't force this. If you care about her, you'll make it easier for her."

"Even if I break my own heart in the process?"

***

"So Jace? Should we be planning a family reunion?"

"Let's not get too far ahead of ourselves."

"My daddy would surely love to see them. Jace's daddy is his cousin. Our grandfathers were brothers. My grandfather came to Crested Butte. Jace's granddad went to Aspen."

"Again Ben, let's not start making plans."

"Did you say he's in Spain?"

"Yeah. He'll be back around Thanksgiving."

"Thanksgiving?"

"Back off Ben. I'm not kidding."

Liv came into the kitchen and put her arms around Ben's waist. "Causing problems cowboy?"

"Nah. Matchmaking. That's what I'm doin'. Right Renie?"

Renie smiled and walked toward the stairs. "I'm happy to be home."

"I'm happy to have you here sweet girl. It's nice to see you smile."

"Thanks Mom. And thanks Ben, for letting me stay here."

"Your home too. Always and forever."

Renie threw herself across her bed and rolled onto her back. She wasn't sure she was ready to declare open season on her relationship with Jace. If you could call it that. He'd made it clear he wanted to continue what they started during the summer, but she wasn't sure she did.

Billy. There he was, in the back of her mind. And as much as she told her mom that she was done spending all her time thinking about him, she was lying. Since she'd been home she'd rarely thought about anything but him.

Ben climbed into bed next to Liv and wiggled his arm under her to pull her closer to him. "What do you think she's gonna do?"

"I don't know. She still refuses to talk about Billy. If she were as 'done' with him as she says she is, she wouldn't be so sensitive about him."

"What about her horse? Do you think I should go get her? Would that make it easier on everybody?"

Liv kissed his cheek. "That's sweet of you to offer." She put her head down on his chest. "Let's give it a little while longer. Her horse, her responsibility. Also her only remaining tie to Billy, besides our lifelong friendship with the Pattersons."

"You're thinking Pooh is still there on purpose."

"Very much so."

"Maybe I should stay out of it."

"Usually best when you're dealing with affairs of someone else's heart."

Chapter Thirteen

Billy stood at the front door, willing himself to knock, praying Renie would answer.

Renie didn't know what to do. She knew he saw her in the window. And he had her horse. She couldn't leave him standing out there. Why wasn't anyone else home? *Oh God, she didn't know what to do.*

She looked awful. She worked late last night, and stayed in bed reading most of the day. She'd showered last night when she got home, but hadn't this morning, she had serious bed head.

She heard his boots on the porch, and her heart started to pound. She got so dizzy that she had to grab the closest chair, or she thought she might pass out. *This must be what a panic attack feels like.*

He knocked on the door.

She took a deep breath and opened it. "Hi Billy."

Billy thought he was ready for this, to see her, but he wasn't. A rush of emotions overtook him, and he thought for a minute he might cry. "Hi Renie."

"Come in." She walked in the opposite direction and sat down on a stool near the kitchen.

How was she so calm? He was ready to pass out, and she was so calm. But, then he saw it; she was sitting on her hands. She wasn't calm at all. Thank God.

"You didn't cash my checks."

"No. I didn't."

"Why not?"

He couldn't answer that. They were on his dresser, every single one of them. He didn't have a reason not to put them in the bank, he just hadn't.

"I don't know, to tell you the truth."

"So that isn't why you're delivering my horse."

"Renie—"

She got up and grabbed a jacket off the hook by the door. It was huge on her. It must be someone else's. She put her feet inside a pair of boots, also not hers, but sitting near the door.

He followed her out to the trailer. By the time he caught up to her, she was inside of it, hugging her horse.

He backed away. She was talking to Pooh, rubbing her nose, arms around her neck, and she was crying. He didn't want to intrude. He understood how much she loved that horse, how hard it must've been to stay away all this time.

"I missed you so much," he heard her say between her cries.

A few minutes later she led the horse out of the trailer.

"Thank you Billy, for bringing her."

"You're welcome. I would've brought her sooner, if I'd known you wanted me to."

"Thank you," she said again. She was walking toward the barn. He got Pooh's tack and followed.

"Is anyone else home?" he asked once they were inside the barn.

"I don't think so," she answered. She got Pooh settled in the stall next to Micah, and started putting her tack away.

"I'll get her some water," Billy said, looking around for a spigot.

"Over there," she pointed.

Billy filled a bucket, but stood where he was for a minute. Renie was talking to her horse again. He'd give her some time.

She came out of the stall looking for him, so he started walking toward her. He got closer and realized she was crying. She was breaking his heart, but she'd been breaking his heart for months. He thought he'd be anesthetized to it by now, but he wasn't.

He set the bucket down and put his arms around her. She didn't move, except when her body involuntarily did with her sobs.

He didn't know what to say, so he didn't say anything. He didn't know what to do either, so he didn't do anything except hold her. She wiped her nose on his jacket, which made him smile. Then, her hands came up, and she put them on his arms. He was afraid she would push him away, but she didn't. She rested them at first, and then she held on to him, tight. She turned her head and rested it against his heart.

When she looked up at him, he couldn't move. He stared into her eyes, neither of them blinked. When she moved her hands higher, to his shoulders, he pulled the rest of her body in closer to his. When she reached up and her lips met his, he was sure he was either dreaming, or he'd died and gone to heaven.

He let her take the lead, so afraid that any move he made would bring this dream to an end. How often had he had this dream? He'd be in her arms, kissing her, or making love to her. His heart would soar, and then he'd wake up to that familiar and excruciating realization that once again he'd been dreaming.

When she reached around and fisted her hand in his hair, pulling it, he couldn't hold back any longer. He kissed her back with all the passion she was giving him.

He heard her cry muffled by his mouth. He tightened his grip on her and she didn't try to back away. He refused to stop kissing her, even if she pulled away, which she hadn't, he wouldn't stop.

He'd never been kissed like this. She was ravaging his mouth, pulling at his hair, her fingernails digging into his scalp. He lifted her, and she wrapped her legs around his waist. He backed her up, so she was up against the side of the barn. When she started to pull him down into the hay, he let go, but followed her.

She was pulling at her jacket, trying to get it off. He didn't know whether to help her, or take his own jacket off. She let him know, taking his hands and putting them on her waist, pushing them toward the hem of her sweatshirt. He pushed it up and over her head. She didn't have anything on under it.

"Wait," she said, and he froze.

No, no, no. The dream was ending, and he was about to wake up. Renie grabbed her sweatshirt and pulled it back over her head. Billy watched her, not knowing what to do.

She was torn. She wanted Billy more than anything. She couldn't think past the way her body was throbbing. But not like this. Not in the barn. What should they do? Should they go inside? She had no idea where her mom and Ben were.

The last thing she wanted was for them to walk in, particularly if they had the boys with them.

Think, think. What should they do?

Billy hadn't moved. The look on his face...it was breaking her heart, but she didn't know what to say. Even if she did, she wasn't sure she could speak.

"I don't know where my mom is," she said, as though that explained anything.

"Okay," he answered.

"Not here," she managed.

He didn't answer. He grabbed her hand.

Billy made arrangements on his way into town for a place to stay. He knew whatever happened with Renie, he wouldn't be in any shape to drive home. That's where they'd go.

"Wait," she said again.

Oh God no, please don't say no. Please God.

"Let me get my jacket and shoes. And lock the door."

Thank God. He grabbed the back of the pickup, holding on for dear life, praying all the while that she'd come back out that door and not change her mind.

He thought about taking the trailer off the back of the truck, but was afraid his hands wouldn't work well enough for him to do it quickly. He was all about quickly, at least until they got where they were going. Then, he'd be all about making his time with Renie last forever.

She was taking too long. Where was she? He started to pace, but close enough to the truck that he could grab hold of it if he needed to. When she came out of the front door, she had a bag with her, and she had on a jacket that looked as though it fit better.

He opened the passenger door, and she climbed into the seat, but grabbed his coat as she did, pulling him to her. She kissed him again, so hard it almost hurt. He wanted to close his eyes and concentrate on how she felt, but he was too afraid. He needed to see her so he was sure this wasn't a dream.

He couldn't speak, he almost couldn't breathe.

She pulled away from him. "Let's go."

He walked around the pickup, holding on the whole way, to steady himself. He hoped he could drive. When he got in the truck, Renie slid over and sat next to him. Somehow he managed to get the truck in gear using his left hand because he had to have his right arm wrapped around her.

He pulled up behind a house in town, and parked in the alley, out of the way of the other garages. He got out, and she followed him. The key was supposed to be in a lock box on the back door. He reached in and pulled the code out of his pocket, hoping his hands would be steady enough to punch it in. It popped open on the first try. Renie grabbed the key and opened the back door.

Oh no! He didn't have any condoms.

"Renie," he found his voice. "I'm so sorry, I don't have any—"

"It's okay," she said.

He didn't want to think about why it was okay. He couldn't let himself think about why it was okay. Why was it okay?

"No." That was his voice. He'd said it. He'd said no.

"What do you mean?"

"Renie, I can't."

"You can't what?"

"I need to go get condoms."

"No, it's okay, I grabbed these from Ben's nightstand."

He started to laugh. Why was that the funniest thing he'd ever heard? He couldn't stop laughing. His body was misinterpreting the schizophrenic emotions he was experiencing, and now he was laughing.

Renie was laughing too. She pulled the stream of condoms, several packets connected together, out of her pocket, and they laughed harder.

He stopped laughing and stalked toward her. She became as serious as he was, her body leaned into his. She reached up and kissed him. He picked up her and started carrying her, but realized he didn't know where he was going.

He walked throughout the downstairs, her in his arms. Each door they came to, she'd reach down and open. They found a bedroom.

He set her down, wanting to rip every bit of clothing off her body, but she was way ahead of him, pulling it off faster than he could've torn it.

She was naked, standing in front of him. "Billy?"

He hadn't even started taking his clothes off, so she helped him. Once he was as naked as she was, she ripped open a condom packet and handed it to him. Again, he hoped his hands worked.

She was on the bed, watching him as he came toward her. He couldn't wait. He needed to be inside her, nothing else mattered.

She reached for him, pushed him onto his back, and straddled him, letting him know she wanted the same thing he did. He let her take the lead. She came above him and slowly took him deep inside her. She put her hands on his chest, and he reached up and put his on the sides of her face.

He wanted to tell her he loved her, so badly, but he was afraid, again, if he spoke, something would change. That he'd ruin it. That she'd stop. That he'd wake up.

He grabbed her hips and set his own rhythm. They both cried out as they came together.

Renie stayed where she was, but put her head down on his chest. He could feel her tears. He wrapped his arms around her and held her as tightly as he could, as her body was wracked with sobs.

***

When Ben pulled up to the house, he noticed the barn door was partway open. He looked at Liv, and she shrugged her shoulders. She didn't remember leaving it open.

"I'll go," she said, "I need to check on Micah anyway."

"I'll go with you."

When they went inside, they saw Pooh in the stall next to Micah's. The two seemed very content being back together.

Liv wanted to run to the house, but Ben held her hand, keeping her pace slower than she would've liked.

"Renie?" she shouted out when she went in the front door.

Ben released her hand, and she ran to the stairs. When she got to the bottom, Renie's door was open, and she wasn't inside. Ben was standing behind her.

"Well, what do you think?" he asked.

"I'll call Dottie."

Dottie confirmed that Billy had left that morning, to bring Pooh to Renie. He'd made her promise not to say anything to Liv and as hard as it was, Dottie kept that promise.

"She's not here."

"I haven't heard anything from him. At the very least, I'd expect him to call and want me to put Willow on the phone. She doesn't talk, but she babbles at him enough that it makes him happy."

"So he hasn't called?"

"Nope. I've had the phone right here next to me all day. We heard from him about three hours ago, but he wasn't to Crested Butte yet."

"I don't know what to think."

"Let's hope for the best for the time being. If I hear anything, you'll be the first to know," Dottie reassured her.

"Likewise," Liv agreed.

After she hung up Ben said, "Decided not to tell her yet?"

"Oh! No, I forgot. Plus it might be too soon. I'd rather wait."

"People will notice you're not on the circuit."

"I'll think of something to tell them. But if Dottie asks, I'll tell her the truth."

"Come on little mama," he said, rubbing her belly. "Let's go cuddle."

Liv hoped this new development with Billy meant it would be easier to tell Renie she would soon be a big sister.

***

They made love three more times, but they hadn't talked yet. Every time he thought he wouldn't be able to do it again, his body disagreed. He didn't think it had anything to do with not having sex for eight months, but everything to do with being with Renie. His body had craved hers for so long.

She was sleeping, splayed across him. He needed to get out of bed. He should check in with his mom, see how Willow was, but again, he didn't want to do anything that would break this spell between them. If he had to ignore the world for a while to have a few more hours, even a few more minutes with Renie, he would.

She stirred. She looked up at him, and then put her head back down.

"I dream about you every night," she said.

"I dream about you too."

"I'm afraid I'm dreaming now."

"Me too."

"I don't think you have to use the bathroom when you're dreaming." She got up and padded out of the bedroom. He followed, going in the opposite direction, looking for another one.

***

Ben opened the drawer of the nightstand looking for the television remote. He started to laugh, which woke Liv, who had been dozing.

"What?"

"I'd say she's with him." He kept laughing.

"Why?"

"The packs of condoms, the ones we haven't made use of in months, are gone."

"Are you sure you still had them in there?"

"Absolutely sure. I was thinking about throwing them away the other day."

"Do you think Renie took them?"

"I'd bet on it."

***

When he came out, she was in the kitchen.

"Not much food in here," she said, opening and closing cupboard doors.

"Vacation rental."

"I'm hungry."

"Where do you want to go?"

"Nowhere."

"Me either."

"But I have to eat."

"I don't suppose there's any fast food in Crested Butte."

"None."

"Think we could force ourselves to leave long enough to go get take-out?"

"We could get pizza delivered."

"Perfect," he said, opening drawers looking for a phone book, or menus. "Here we go. How about the Secret Stash? Are they any good?"

"The best." Renie grabbed the menu and went in search of her phone. She knew what he liked. It was a good sign that she remembered. Or maybe she didn't care, and was ordering what she wanted. Either way was fine with him.

"We have twenty-five minutes," she shouted from the bedroom. "Get your butt in here Patterson."

He needed nourishment, and soon, but he probably had another round in him, as long as he knew food was on the way.

"Are they bringing us anything to drink?" he asked on his way.

Billy grabbed his pants and wallet when he heard the knock at the door.

"That'll be $85.72," the deliveryman said. Billy saw there was another bag sitting behind him.

"You sure you got the right address?"

The man looked at his notes. "Renie Fairchild. I guess you don't look like a Renie. What did you order?"

"Nope, that's us, and I have no idea what she ordered."

"Is it just the two of you?"

"Nah, we have friends coming over," Billy lied.

He handed the man a hundred and a twenty, and thanked him. He brought one bag and set it on the kitchen counter and went back for the second. Renie was rummaging through the first by the time he turned back around.

"I'm starving," she said, taking boxes out of the bag.

"I guess. What did you order anyway?"

"Pizza, wings, stuffed mushrooms, garlic bread, fries, salad. Oh and did he bring beer? I told him there'd be an extra big tip in it for him if he brought us a twelve-pack. So I hope you tipped him big."

"It so happens I did. You put the order in your name, so I wanted to do you proud."

She looked at him and smiled. "I love you Billy Patterson."

He almost dropped the second bag as he reached out to grab the counter. She took the air out of his lungs.

"I'm sorry."

"What? No. God, Renie. Don't be sorry. It surprised me."

"I do though. I love you."

"I love you too." Somehow he knew that wasn't the end of it. There was more she wanted to say.

"Let's eat," she said instead.

Chapter Fourteen

Liv wished she'd hear something from her. Anything. She wanted to know Renie was okay, but she didn't want to call her.

"Maybe I'll text her. That way she doesn't have to answer, you know, right away."

Ben threw his head back in that way he did, and laughed. "Whatever makes you feel better baby." He put his arms around her. "She's a grown up ya know."

"I know. But—"

"But she's with Billy. I get it. I'm as worried as you are. I mean, I hope she's still with Billy."

Liv slugged him. "Why did you have to say *that*? Now I'm more worried than I was before."

***

"You seem different," he said.

"What do you mean? Different how?"

"I don't know. I mean, I've been in hell for the last eight months. You seem kinda…fine."

She set her plate down and looked right at him. "Don't misjudge me Billy. I can assure you I've been to hell and back again these last few months."

"See? That's what I mean. You're so…good at saying what you're thinking."

"I guess you're right. I used to be afraid to tell you what I thought or how I was feeling."

"Really? Well that makes me feel like shit. So what's different?"

"I don't know exactly. I grew up."

"Are you sure it isn't that you don't care what I think?"

"It's that too, at least a little."

He looked wounded.

"If you didn't want the answer to the question Billy, you shouldn't have asked it."

"Damn Renie, I don't know how best to handle this."

"Me either."

"I've never been so afraid of the words 'we should talk,' in my life."

"We should though."

"I need you to tell me what you're thinking and feeling first Renie. If you can't do that, I'm not sure we're gonna get much talking done."

"No, I can." She stood up and got her cell phone out. "I should call my mom first though. I need her to check on Pooh, which I'm sure she has already. She's probably completely freaking out."

He wanted to laugh, but he couldn't. He was *sure* Liv was freaking out, but he couldn't get past what she said, that she was going to talk. He wasn't sure he wanted to hear whatever it was she had to say. He also needed to call his mother, and check on his baby girl. He was afraid of that too. What if that made Renie freak out?

"I need to call home too Renie," he said, grabbing her wrist so she'd look at him. "I need to check on Willow."

"I know you do Billy." She walked into the other room while she punched the speed dial on her phone.

"Hi Mom," Renie said when her mom answered the phone.

"Hi."

"I'm with Billy."

"I'm glad to hear it. Everything okay?"

"It's okay for now anyway."

"Do you need anything?"

"Pooh's in the barn."

"Yes I know. I went and said hello. She looks good. And Micah's happy."

"Good. Um, I'm not sure when I'll be back."

"Okay. That's fine. Text me so I don't worry."

"It won't be tonight."

"I figured that Renie," she laughed. "You're welcome to bring him around here in the morning. Well I guess you have to since he has to bring you home."

"Yep, he has to bring me home," Renie said wistfully. "Okay gotta go Mom. Bye."

"Bye Renie. I love you."

"Love you too."

"That'd be great Mom, thanks. Yep, talk to you later," she heard Billy say when she walked back in the room.

"Willow's sleeping. She's gonna call me when she's awake."

Renie didn't know what to say. They had a lot of talking to do. About the changes in her life as much as the changes in his. It wouldn't be easy for her to tell Billy about Jace. And listening to Billy talk about his baby? She wasn't sure she could bear it.

"Do you have a picture of her?"

"Come here and I'll show you some."

And Then You Dance

Billy held his phone out to her. "Swipe your finger if you want to see more. There are hundreds," he laughed.

Renie swiped her finger several times. He couldn't read her expression.

"She's beautiful," Renie whispered. "She looks so much like you."

"You're gonna think this is crazy but..."

"But what?"

"God, Renie," he put his arms around her and kissed her neck. "I think she looks like you. Maybe it's because you're the two people I love most in the world, so when I look at her, I see love, and love is you."

Her eyes filled with tears, and she set the phone in his hand.

"She's growin' up so fast. She'll be a year old in a few weeks."

She took his phone back and started looking at more photos. There were a lot of photos of the two of them together. "You're good with her."

"She's my life." This was the hardest part, he knew it was. He could pretend she wasn't, but she was. And if Renie couldn't live with that, there wasn't any hope for them.

"I know she is." She was going back through the pictures again, slower this time. "I can tell."

"You left me because of her."

"I left you because of you. I left you because of me. I wasn't sure I could handle it. No, that's not right. I *knew* I couldn't handle it."

"What about now? You still feelin' the same way?"

It took her so damn long to answer him he thought he would jump out of his skin.

"I don't know. You said it yourself. I'm different."

He knew she was different; there were specific things about her that were different. But, it seemed as though it was more, things he couldn't see.

"I've spent more time with myself. I've gotten to know myself better. Part of that was seeing myself through someone else's eyes."

There it was, the knife in his heart that he'd been waiting for. There was someone else.

"Whose eyes?"

"That's not important."

"If it wasn't important, you wouldn't have said it."

"A friend. Someone I met this summer. I went to work at a dude ranch. I'm sure Dottie told you."

"She did, and I thought it was great. Was it fun?"

"Fun? It was a lot of hard work is what it was."

"I bet ya had some fun though, didn't ya?"

Yeah, she had. She had fun. And she worked hard. And she didn't spend every minute of every day thinking about Billy Patterson, as she had every day of her life before she went to the ranch.

"I didn't spend all my time thinking about you."

"No? I guess that's good, right?"

"Right. It's what I needed Billy. I needed to get away from you for a while."

"I know you did. I wish it hadn't been so far away from me. I missed you so damn much."

"I missed you too Billy. You already know that." She stood and walked to the other side of the room. She turned and leaned back against the wall. "I'm not ready to be anyone's mama Billy."

"Maybe you could get to know her a little bit, instead of thinkin' you need to be her mama."

"Isn't that what you want though? Tell me the truth Billy. If you could have anything you wanted, would you pack me up and take me home with you? Marry me and keep me in your bed? Make me your baby's mama?"

At one time, that might have been true. Back when he had no idea how to take care of a baby, or what it meant to be somebody's father. It would've been real easy to lean on Renie that way. But, he was different now too. He didn't let his own mother take care of Willow very often, just on rare occasions. He was careful about not taking advantage of his parents. In fact, he'd be willing to bet his parents would say they didn't get enough time alone with their granddaughter.

"No, that wouldn't be what I wanted, even if I could have things my way."

"I'm sorry Billy, but I don't believe you."

"Then let me prove it to you."

"How will you do that?"

"I'm not sure exactly. But I can tell you this, when I'm with my daughter, I'm a different person. I've grown up too. As hard as it was to be away from you, as much as I missed you, I have to admit, it was a good thing for me too." He got up and came over to where she stood.

"I leaned on you too much."

"You did Billy. And you took me for granted."

"Yes, I did. That was something I realized even before I found out about Willow." He pulled her back to the bed.

"When I came up to your apartment, I realized it. I expected you to be there for me."

"I can't go back to that Billy."

"I don't want that Renie. I really don't. I know you don't believe me. But, I do want *you*."

"So what do we do?"

"I have no idea." He laughed a little. "I prepared more for how I would handle it if you refused to talk to me. I didn't plan what I'd do if you did talk to me. And I didn't plan for *this* at all."

"Me either," she said, kissing her way from his neck up to his lips.

"I need you so much. My body wants to stay connected to yours all the time. All the damn time. I love you so fucking much."

It was his turn to take over, he wanted her, and he needed to show her how much. He grabbed her panties and yanked them off. He pushed her back against the pillows and pulled her sweatshirt over her head. He ran his lips over her body, trying hard not to miss a single inch of her skin. He went slowly, torturing her with his hands and his tongue.

This was how he wanted her, writhing beneath him, begging him for more. By the time he was finished, Renie would be begging him to love her.

He woke up and saw it was getting light out. He quickly grabbed his phone, hoping he hadn't missed a call from his mother last night. He and Renie were so wrapped up in each other; he forgot he had a phone. They'd taken their time, and she begged for him, but he did as much begging for her.

There wasn't a call. Willow must have slept through the night, or if she did wake up, his mother decided it was too late to call. Since it was a little before seven, he'd wait to see whether she called. If she hadn't in an hour, he'd call her. No way Willow would sleep past eight.

He looked at Renie who was still sound asleep. Whenever he looked at Willow, he wondered how his heart would ever have room to love anyone else. But now looking at Renie, he realized he had love enough for both of them.

He still wondered about the comment she made about seeing herself through someone else's eyes. There was something telling him that whoever it was, was more than a friend.

Renie rolled over and groaned, so he kissed the back of her neck.

"No, don't you start that Billy Patterson. I'm not gonna be able to walk today as it is. And I really want to ride Pooh."

"I'd love to go ridin' with you pretty girl. You think your mama will let me ride Micah?"

"Not a chance in hell, but Ben will let you ride his horse."

"Ben has a horse?"

"Give me a break Billy. Ben has a *ranch*. And it's bigger than yours."

He started to tickle her. "Now that was just plain mean. You don't compare the size of a man's ranch Renie Fairchild."

"Let's go ride cowboy."

"Not yet cowgirl," he said, kissing his way down the back of her body.

Billy's phone rang.

"Answer it."

"I'll call her back."

"Answer it," Renie said again, rolling away from him.

"Ah, shit."

Billy grabbed the phone. "Hey Mama."

He got up and walked out of the bedroom. Renie went in and turned on the shower. She wasn't ready to hear the conversations he had with Willow, or about Willow. She wasn't ready for anything to do with Willow.

It ate her up that she felt the way she did. She loved kids, so why the problem with this one particular?

Billy opened the bathroom door a few minutes later. "Can I come in?"

"Sure," she reached out and grabbed a towel. "I'm finished if you want to come in when I get out."

"I was thinking more about joining you—finishing what we started."

"I don't think so Billy." Renie was out of the shower and drying off, but the water was still running. Billy reached in and turned it off.

He put his hands over hers on the towel. "Come on now."

"No, I don't feel like it anymore."

"You're poutin' darlin'." He leaned forward and grabbed her lower lip between his teeth. She breathed in deeply and let the towel fall to the floor. Billy pushed off his boxer briefs, reached behind her and turned the shower back on.

"I'm gonna get you dirty then all clean again baby."

She couldn't resist him. He was so damn sexy, and persuasive. She let him move her back under the water. But she couldn't get Willow's image out of her head. She turned him around, so his back was to the stream of water and got back out of the shower.

"Renie, what're you doin'?"

"I'm done Billy."

He didn't like the sound of that. Done with what? He finished up as quickly as he could. When he came out of the bathroom, he found her sitting in the kitchen, eating a piece of cold pizza.

"Still poutin'?"

"Don't Billy."

"Find any coffee?"

"Yeah, I made some," she answered, pointing toward the French Press sitting on the counter.

"I want you to meet her. That's it. She's a lot less scary in person."

"What's that supposed to mean?"

"It means that I believe you're more afraid of the idea of her, and once you meet her, you'll feel different."

He was right. But, it didn't change anything. "Can you take me home now? I mean to Ben's."

"Of course I can. You gonna invite me in when we get there, or are you gonna make me give you a kiss goodbye on the front porch?"

"Are you going home?" *Already?*

"I could be talked into staying, if you'll come back here with me after we've seen your mom and Ben."

That felt better. He was willing to stay at least another day, before she had to give him back to the other woman in his life.

We're headed back, Renie texted her mom.
Have you eaten? she answered.
No.
Ben's making breakfast.
Billy's with me.
I know.

"You're invited for breakfast," Renie said, putting her phone in her pocket.

Billy looked out the window and shook his head. "I'm nervous."

"I am too."

"Why are you nervous?"

"Why are you?"

"I love that about you."

"What?"

"How you answer a question with a question."

"I don't do that."

"You *always* do that."

"Do I sometimes get a look on my face like I've eaten something sour?"

Billy laughed. "Yep, you do that too."

"What else do I do?"

"Let's see. You sit on your hands when you're nervous." He looked at her, and she realized she'd tucked her hands under her legs. She quickly took them out, but stuck them in her pockets.

"You talk in your sleep."

Uh oh. "What do I talk about?"

"Not much I can decipher. Although I've always been able to understand it when you say my name." Billy took her hand. He brought it up to his lips and kissed across her knuckles.

"I love how it sounds when you're all sleepy, and you moan a little. Makes me hard as a rock when I hear it," he grinned.

"What else?"

"That you do?"

"Yeah."

They weren't all the way to Ben's house, but Billy pulled the truck over anyway.

"You're not very good at sharing."

"Are you saying that because it suits your purpose, or am I really not good at sharing?"

"Let's see. You're an only child. And an only grandchild, by the way, even though your grandparents have been gone a long time. You've never had siblings to share with, or even cousins. You've had your mama's undivided attention. In fact, before she met Ben, you were the only thing in her life, except the ranch, and taking care of the horses."

"I've heard enough."

"You care more about the people you love than anyone I've ever known. You can coax a smile out of an unhappy person with that quick wit of yours.

"I've watched you charm the most miserable people into cracking a smile. I've seen you calm a horse that's skittish because they're in a new barn, and nothing is familiar to them. I watched you care for your mama even when she was doin' her best to act as mean and nasty as she could be."

"Anything else?"

"You love me with your whole heart and soul, and as scared as you are of this, you can't help yourself, you're gonna figure out how to make this work."

It was her turn to look out the window, but he could see the tear slide down her cheek.

"Talk to me baby."

"You're right about me."

"Which part?"

"I'm not good at sharing."

When they walked in the house, it was as though Billy was walking into her mom's house back at the ranch in Monument. He shrugged off his jacket, hung it on the hook by the door, and was in the kitchen hugging her mom before Renie had her boots off.

He picked her up and swung her around. "I missed you so much Livvie. Almost as much as I missed your daughter."

Ben looked as though he wanted to throttle Billy. Was he upset with him, or had he just never liked him? Renie remembered that before Ben and her mom got back together, he thought there was something between Billy and her mom. But now he knew otherwise, so what was that look on his face all about? He turned and caught her looking at him. His face changed completely as he gave her one of his Ben smiles. Dottie hugged. Ben smiled.

"I missed you too cowboy," Liv said, when Billy set her back on her feet. She looked a little green and held onto the counter for a minute.

"Mom? Are you okay?"

Liv held up a hand and started to answer, but hurried off in the direction of the bathroom before she could.

"Is she okay?" she looked at Ben.

"She's okay."

"But she's sick. Why are you making her cook breakfast?"

Ben pulled her into a hug. "I don't make your mom do anything Renie. You know that. She's fine."

Liv came out of the bathroom, but she didn't look fine to Renie. She saw Billy catch Ben's eye, and she didn't miss the smile that passed between them.

"Honey, maybe you should come with me." Liv was reaching out for her hand.

"You two are jerks," Renie said to them as her mother led her into the other room.

"Renie, sit down."

"Okay, but maybe you should sit down. You're the one who's sick."

"I'm not sick Renie. I'm having a baby."

Now, Renie was sick. She turned and ran to the bathroom her mother came out of.

"That didn't go as I expected," said Liv as she walked back into the kitchen. "I'm pregnant Billy, in case you hadn't put two and two together."

"Sorry I swung you around."

"It's okay. First trimester, I would've gotten sick whether you swung me around or not."

Ben was grinning from ear to ear and couldn't help circling Liv's waist with his big arm. He whispered something in her ear that Billy was glad he couldn't hear.

Renie came around the corner and looked as green as Liv had a few minutes before.

Billy followed Ben's lead and put his arm around her waist. "You okay?" he whispered in her ear.

"No."

Billy laughed. Renie would be learning a great deal about sharing in the next few months.

"So since you're not riding, can I take Micah out after breakfast?"

Liv started to say something, but caught Billy's smirk. "Hell no, you're not riding my horse Billy Patterson."

"I have a soft spot in my heart for him."

After her accident, it was Billy who waited by Liv's side until the ambulance came. Then, it was Billy who took care of Micah, made sure he didn't have any injuries, and trailered him home. He worked with him every day while Liv was in the hospital making sure he stayed in shape.

"I'm sorry Billy. Of course you can ride Micah."

"Thanks Livvie. I kinda miss ridin' him."

Billy held Renie's hand on their way out to the barn. "You doin' okay?"

"It's all a little too much. I should've gone to Spain."

"Huh? To Spain? What're you talkin' about?"

"Nothing. It's not important."

Before she could scoot away from him, Billy stopped her. "What's in Spain Renie?"

"Nobody."

"Nobody? Renie, what the hell? Nobody? Who's in Spain? Answer the question."

"It's nothing Billy."

"This the same nobody you learned more about yourself from?"

She jerked her arm away from him. "Yes Billy. It is. You had Willow, I needed somebody too."

"Willow's my daughter Renie. That's a little different."

"Yes it's different, she requires your undivided attention for the rest of her life. While Jace only needed my attention a few hours a day."

"Jace? Is that a name?" He smiled. "Is he an actor or somethin'?"

"Shut up." She couldn't help but smile herself, because now Billy was laughing, doubled over laughing. "It isn't that funny."

"Yes it is. For Christ's sake Renie, you couldn't have found a regular ol' cowboy? Somebody named Stetson? Or *Maverick*?"

She and Billy had good times making fun of the young bull riders who came out the chutes with names like Tuf or Stran or Cody. Jace was just as bad, she had to admit it.

"Tell me about him."

"No. It's none of your business."

"Everything about you is my business."

"I don't want to talk about him Billy."

"He know about me?"

"Yep. Well, sort of."

"What's that mean?"

"You said it yourself Billy, I talk in my sleep."

Billy leaned over and put his hand on his knees, as nauseous as he suspected Liv and Renie felt earlier.

Chapter Fifteen

"You are such a hypocrite."

"What? How am I a hypocrite?"

"You had a baby with somebody. And then, you lied to me about it."

"What...in...the...hell...are you talking about?" Billy took deep breaths between his words and stood; so mad he was afraid he would hit something.

"You told me you'd never been in a relationship. Was that so you could get in my panties Billy? Is that what you tell all the girls, so they think they're *special*?"

"Is that what you think? Is that why you left?" The anger flowed out of his body as he began to realize that was what she thought.

"There wasn't anybody who mattered Renie. Not ever."

"You expect me to believe Roxanne didn't matter?"

"No, she didn't matter. If Mr. Johnson hadn't sought me out at the rodeo in South Dakota, I would have forgotten she existed."

"I don't believe that for a minute."

"Renie," he rubbed his eyes and then ran his hand through his hair. "I'm not sure how to say this without making everything worse."

"Say it Patterson. Tell the truth. It'll be good for your soul."

"I had sex with a lot of women. A lot. I don't remember most of them. Hell Renie, I'm not sure I remember any of them."

"Thanks Billy."

"I don't mean you."

Renie had saddled up Pooh and was headed out to ride.

"Will you at least wait for me?"

"Can't say I still want to ride with you Billy."

"Stop it dammit."

Renie stopped and glared at him.

"Just stop it. This is hard enough without you adding to it." He had Micah ready to go, and motioned for her to follow him.

"I slept with a hell of a lot of women Renie. None of them meant a damn thing to me. And maybe that makes me a horrible person, but there isn't anything I can do to go back and change it. So that isn't something we're gonna talk about."

She continued to glare at him.

"What we do need to talk about is you, and me, and my daughter. That's what we need to be talking about, not all this other shit."

"The other shit matters to me Billy."

"Okay, what part of it? Let's do this. What else do you want to ask Renie?"

"How many times?"

"How many times *what*?"

"How many times did you have sex with Roxanne?"

"A couple times maybe."

"How long were you seeing her?"

"Are you not hearing anything I'm saying? I wasn't seeing her. I *fucked* her. Maybe twice, but I don't remember. I'm running out of patience with this conversation."

"Tough shit. You want me to meet your daughter, there are questions I want answers to first."

His head felt as though it was splitting in two. All her life Renie had been the most exasperating woman he'd ever known. Even as a little girl she was like this. Half of him wanted to wring her neck; the other half loved her more than life itself. It had always been this way, even before he realized what he felt for her was love, the all-encompassing forever kind of love.

He sighed. "What else do you want to know?"

"It doesn't matter."

"Wait a minute. You said there were questions you wanted me to answer before you meet Willow. What are they? Let's do this Renie. I'm not goin' home without you."

"*What?*"

That wasn't what he meant to say. He didn't know where it came from, but now that he'd said it, he couldn't take it back. He could tell her the truth though.

"I didn't mean it that way. I meant I'm not goin' home until you and I have come to an understanding. I'm not goin' home without knowing you're a part of my life again. Is that better?"

"I'm not going home with you Billy. You better get that through your head right now. That isn't happening."

"Okay, I got it. Now back to what we were talking about. What are the other questions?"

"I don't remember. Drop it Billy."

"This is it girl. I'll do this once. You want answers, get 'em now."

A few minutes went by before she said anything, but Billy could tell there was something she was stewing about. It was a matter of time before she'd spit it out.

"How could you not know Billy?"

He'd wondered that himself more times than he could count. He shook his head. "I wish I had an answer. I don't. I don't know how I didn't."

She watched him. She knew him. He was telling her the truth. And not having the answer bothered him. He was torn up about it.

They came to a gate that was closed. Renie jumped down to open it, but Billy beat her to it. When she put her hand on the latch, he put his on top of it.

"Look at me," he whispered. "You know me. Better than anyone. No way in hell I would've knowingly gotten somebody pregnant and walked away. No way I'd do that."

He wouldn't have. And if he had known, she would've lost him forever, because he would've done whatever he thought was right for Willow, and Roxanne. Billy Patterson was a good man deep down. No one knew him as well as she did, and he was right, it would've been different if he'd known Roxanne was pregnant.

"Don't kick me out of your life over this. Please don't. Try to get to know her. She's a baby Renie."

"I'm not sure."

"Please. I'll beg you if that's what it takes."

"I need time…"

"Time? It's been eight months. How much more time do you need?"

She got back on her horse, pushed Pooh into a gallop and rode back to the barn.

She didn't know how much more time she needed, and him yelling at her about it wouldn't help her figure it out. Her biggest problem was that she didn't understand her attitude any better than he did. What was she afraid of?

He was right, Willow was just a baby. What was it that she expected to happen that made her unable to face meeting a baby?

It didn't take long for Billy to catch up to her on Micah. Her mother's horse was much younger than Pooh, and Billy knew how to push him.

"I'm sorry."

"Don't be. I don't know what's wrong with me. I'm the one who's sorry."

"Does this mean you'll meet her?"

"I didn't say that."

"I know you didn't. But does it?"

"Bring her here. I'll meet her if you bring her here." That way if it were too much, at least Renie would have her own mother's support to make it easier. She wouldn't be alone with Billy and his baby; Billy and the life he had without her.

He hadn't said anything, so she turned and looked at him.

"If you're waiting for me to say no, you'll be waiting a long time. I'll do whatever it takes. You want Willow and me to come visit you here, no problem. Tell me when."

"Thanksgiving."

Thanksgiving? He didn't think his parents would mind much. It wasn't as though she was asking him to come for Christmas. That might have been a problem, taking Willow away from Grandma and Grandpa for her first Christmas with them. Thanksgiving was different.

"Okay. Thanksgiving." He hated that he'd have to wait that long to see Renie again, but he'd waited eight months; he could wait a little longer if that's what she needed.

"You'll come here."

"We'll come here."

"Where will you stay?"

"Where do you want us to stay?"

She was chewing the inside of her lip. He wished he could understand why this caused her so much anxiety. He tried hard to put himself in her position, but he couldn't. Maybe if he could get her to talk about how she was feeling, he could understand, and help her figure out a way to make it easier.

As hard as it was to be away from Willow, something told him that Renie was the one who needed him more right now. Willow was in good hands with his mom and dad. Renie needed to be in his hands. She needed to know that he loved her, as much as ever. And just because Willow was in the picture, it wouldn't ever change how he felt about her.

"So are you going home now?" she asked, as though she was reading his mind.

"Nope."

"When are you going home?"

"I haven't decided yet. But isn't gonna be today, or tomorrow. It might not even be the day after that."

"Why?"

"Why what?"

"Why aren't you going home?"

"Because you need me to stay."

It was all she could do not to cry. The tears she fought were of relief. He was right; she did need him to stay. She needed to know she mattered.

When they got back to the barn and were walking the horses inside, Renie reached out and took his hand in hers.

"Thank you for staying."

"I love you Irene Fairchild. I'm stayin' until I'm sure you believe it."

Once the horses were settled, Billy pulled her closer and lifted her, so her legs wrapped around his waist. One hand held her bottom while the other circled behind her neck, pulling her in, so he could get his lips on hers.

"How soon do you think we can be alone?"

"Soon, I think." She unwrapped herself from him and planted her feet back on the ground. "My mom is pregnant."

"Yes, I know. How are you feeling about it?"

"Weird."

He laughed. Poor Renie. There was a lot she'd be getting used to. And all of it had to do with babies.

* * *

Jace could not get Irene Fairchild out of his head. He and Tucker had been traveling all over Spain, eating, drinking, and having fun. He loved hanging with Tucker, and under normal circumstances, he loved the female attention he and his twin seemed to get wherever they went. But this time, Tucker was enjoying the attention all on his own. The girl he spent the summer with at the dude ranch was under his skin.

He'd told her he'd be back in Colorado for Thanksgiving, but they hadn't made any plans beyond that. He thought about calling her, but talked himself out of it. A couple days ago, he broke down and sent a postcard to her. Ben Rice was his cousin, his mother had his address, and so he went ahead and did it. Now he questioned whether he should have. It wasn't so much sending the postcard that he questioned, it was what he wrote.

> *Don't think I've ever been as thankful as I will be this Thanksgiving. Counting the days until I see you again. Love, Jace.*

He might have gone too far, but they'd spent the entire summer sharing sheets, and then instead of going straight home, she came to Aspen and stayed with him a couple extra days. She had to be feeling the same things he was. Had to be.

He talked to Tucker about it before he sent it. His advice was to say what he felt. If it bothered her, then she'd say so. That was typically Tucker's advice. Say what you feel. Do what you want. Jace believed he shared the same philosophy. Until he met Irene Fairchild. There was something about her that made him rethink his approach. He cared more about what she thought than any other woman he'd ever known.

He hoped he didn't scare her off by so boldly telling her what was in his heart. Even when she left that day in Aspen, he hadn't used the word love, as much as he'd been tempted to, as much as he'd been feeling it for her. When Jace told Tucker he was in love with her, Tucker said he knew.

"You'd know too, if it were me."

Jace supposed he would.

"I miss her man."

"Yeah, I feel that too."

It was the twin thing. Not something they hadn't felt before, or heard before. That's how twins were, people said. Jace couldn't say it was true with other twins, but it was true for Tucker and him. Even when he was still in the States and Tucker was in Spain, he felt what his twin was feeling. It was the reason he still came, even though he'd wanted to stay in Colorado, and spend more time with Irene. He knew his twin needed him, so he came.

* * *

Billy was sitting at the counter in the kitchen, talking to Ben while Renie went to check on Liv. He pulled a magazine out of the pile to read it, and the postcard fell out of it. He wouldn't have paid any attention to it, except he saw it was from Spain. He flipped it over and read it.

There it was again, the knife in his heart. It was the way the guy signed it, "Love, Jace," that bothered him the most. He wondered if Renie knew he planned on seeing her at Thanksgiving. She couldn't have, or she wouldn't have asked him to come with Willow. Right?

He set the postcard back down on the counter. When he saw her coming, he tucked it under one of the other magazines. He didn't want to bring it up, and ruin their time together. He'd gone eight months without having her in his arms, in his bed. They had a lot of time to make up for.

"How's she doin'?" Billy asked.

"She's good. Tired, but good. And happy." Renie smiled at Ben who smiled back at her.

"You gettin' used to the idea of bein' a big sister yet?

"I'm already a big sister Ben."

That made Ben smile all the more, that Renie considered his boys her "brothers."

"I hope they're as okay with it as you are."

Renie figured Jake and Luke would be more okay with than she was. They were still little boys, or at least Luke was. Luke would be thrilled about not being the baby of the family anymore. And Jake would be happy about it. He seemed happier when he believed everyone around him was happy. When they weren't, Jake worried. Renie put him through hell the last eight months. She'd known it, but she hadn't known how to change it.

"When will the boys be back?" she asked.

"Tonight. I miss 'em so much."

Ben was close to his boys. He hated to be away from them when his band was on tour, and he hated to be away from them when they were with their mom. Like Jake, Ben liked everyone close, and everyone happy.

"When will you tell them?"

"Soon. Maybe tonight. You two gonna be around? It might be nice to tell them with the whole family here."

"The whole family? Your mom, dad, and everybody?"

"No, I was thinking *our* whole family," Ben winked at her.

She looked at Billy.

"Okay by me. What time's dinner? There are a couple things I wanted to do before then, if we have time."

Renie blushed, and Ben started to laugh.

"Go do what you gotta do, and be back here by seven," Ben said, still laughing and heading out of the kitchen.

"Nice Billy," Renie said once Ben had left the room. "Tell my stepfather we're gonna go have sex, why don't you?"

Billy shrugged his shoulders and smiled. Yep, he could get away with most anything with his blue eyes, that smile, and those dimples.

"Do you need to call home?" she asked him.

"Nah, we did a little Facetime while you were talkin' to your mom."

"What? You did what?"

"Facetime," he said, showing her his phone. "You know what that is right?"

"Yes I do Billy, but it isn't something I would expect you to know about."

"I'm more techno than you. It's one of those things you don't want to admit about me. It's okay, if you think the whole cowboy thing is sexier, we'll stick with that."

They were back at the house Billy was staying in.

"Why didn't you get a hotel room? There are plenty of them around here, and the rooms are cheap since the season hasn't started yet."

Why hadn't he? Because he wanted to have crazy, loud, anywhere-he-wanted-to-have-it sex with her. That's why. He didn't want to be confined to a hotel room, where she didn't feel comfortable, or they had to worry about someone hearing them.

"I don't like hotel rooms. I spent too much time in them when I was on the circuit." That was another thing, he didn't have sex with Renie, they made love, and it wasn't something he wanted to do in a hotel room. He'd had too much sex in hotel rooms.

"Are you officially retired Billy? I haven't paid much attention to circuit news."

Billy hadn't announced it yet, but word was out that Billy was raising his kid, whose mother had died. As much as he didn't want to ride saddle broncs anymore, he didn't want to face the gossip and small-mindedness there would be out on the circuit. It was time he made the official announcement.

There was a Bose dock for an iPod in the family room. Billy set his phone in it, scrolled through his music and hit play.

"Dance me to your beauty with a burning violin," played through the speaker and Billy put his arms around Renie. "Dance with me darlin."

Renie melted into him and let him dance her around the room.

"I love havin' you in my arms, feelin' your body up against mine." His lips trailed down the side of her face, down to her neck. She arched back and Billy continued his way down to her shoulder. He reached down and unbuttoned her shirt, then pushed it off one shoulder so his lips could touch more of her skin.

He moved her across the floor, to the bedroom, moving her shirt off her other shoulder as they went. Instead of dancing her to the bed, he backed her into the wall, pushing her up against it, while his hands found the zipper on her jeans, unfastened them, and pushed them over her hips and to the floor.

He wanted her there, where she was, up against the wall. He wanted to feel her legs wrapped around him, clinging to him. He wanted her to need him, to hold her, to love her, to remind her that he was the man for her. The only man for her. The only man who knew every inch of her, and how to make her feel better than she ever had before.

"Billy," she whimpered.

He grasped her thighs, and she put them around his waist. He slid inside her, and she gasped.

"Tell me Renie, tell me how much you want me."

"You know I do Billy. I want you so much."

"Only me Renie. Tell me I'm the one you want."

"Only you."

"Say my name."

"Billy…"

"Who do you love?"

"I love you Billy," she cried out.

"I love you Renie," he answered.

He laid her on the bed, and she watched as he took off his clothes, in too much of a hurry before. He stretched out next to her and turned her face toward him, looking her in the eye.

"Renie?" he said softly, gently.

"Yeah Billy?"

"I didn't use a condom."

"It's okay. We're okay."

"How are we okay?"

"I'm on the pill Billy. I have been for a while."

Chapter Sixteen

They made love again, and again. Billy was frantic in his need for her. She put her hand on his chest, over his heart, and he moved over her again, pushing her legs apart with his.

"Billy, stop. We have to get back to the house."

"Don't wanna. I need you, just you, just us."

She pushed against his chest with both his hands. "Billy, stop."

He did, and looked into her eyes. "I can't lose you," he said.

She moved her hands to his face. "You won't."

"Do you swear that to me? That there's no one else. Is that something you can swear to Renie?"

She sat up and moved so she was next to him, instead of under him.

"Did you hear me? Did you hear what I asked you?"

"I'm here with you Billy. I wouldn't be if there were someone else."

The look on her face made his heart stop. He'd gotten carried away in his need for her, his need for her reassurance. He'd never felt this way before. He'd never cared about anyone enough to need reassurance from them. *He hated this feeling.*

"Come on," she said. "Let's take a quick shower before we have to leave." She smiled at him and pulled him to the bathroom with her.

"Yeah? You gonna let me get you clean Renie?"

"Yes I am, right after you get me dirty again," she smiled.

They were a little late to dinner, but Ben and Liv didn't seem to notice. Luke greeted them at the front door and threw his arms around Renie's waist.

"What's going on Luke? It's hasn't been that long since you've seen me."

"I know, but I missed you," he answered, glaring at Billy when he did.

"You remember Billy don't you Luke?"

"Yeah, hi," he said, not making eye contact with Billy.

Billy reached out his hand to shake Luke's hand, and Luke turned his back on him. Renie grabbed his shoulder. "Luke, that wasn't very polite."

Luke turned back around and shook Billy's hand. "Hi," he said again, but still no eye contact.

Jake stood off to the side, but approached Billy when he heard Renie admonish Luke.

"Hi Billy," he said, and made the first move to shake his hand.

"Hey Jake—wow, that's quite a grip you've got there buddy." Billy pulled his hand out of Jake's grasp.

"Dinner's ready," Liv shouted from the kitchen. "Boys go wash your hands." She looked at Renie and Billy. "You two can sit down, almost everything is on the table. Ben will bring in the rest."

"I take it I'm on the Rice boys' shit list," Billy whispered to Renie.

It took Renie a minute to realize he was talking about Jake and Luke.

"What was that puzzled look on your face all about? Who'd you think I was talking about?"

She had no intention of talking about Jace Rice. But at first, that was whom she thought he meant.

Renie's prediction had been correct about how Ben's two sons would react to news that soon they would have a little brother or sister. Both of them were overjoyed, and Luke had a million questions. He told them he thought Liv was too old to have more babies, just as his own mother told him she was.

"Never at a loss for inappropriate commentary, are ya pard'ner?" Ben said.

Liv laughed and kissed the top of Luke's head. He was being honest; there wasn't anything wrong with that, she commented.

Billy was distracted throughout dinner, and nobody missed it.

"What's going on with you two?" her mother asked when she and Renie were cleaning up the kitchen.

"He's bringing Willow here, for Thanksgiving."

"He is?"

"I'm sorry Mom. I should have asked first."

"Don't be silly, you don't need to ask. In fact, Ginny and I were talking about Thanksgiving a few days ago. Ben and I will be happy to host it here. I'll invite Dottie and Bill. They usually host a big dinner for the ranch hands, so I'm not sure they'll be able to make it, but it surely would be wonderful if they could."

Liv said she planned to invite Paige and Mark too, and asked Renie how she felt about inviting Blythe.

"Are the two of you speaking yet?"

"Why wouldn't we be?"

Renie hadn't thought about Blythe at all. Which made her a terrible friend, but they'd gone weeks without talking before, how was this different?

"She's hurt and confused that you never told her you were interested in Billy. She feels bad about asking you to fix her up with him."

"Oh," Renie answered. "I hadn't thought about that."

There was so much she hadn't thought about in the last eight months, much of which involved other people's feelings. How many other people had she inadvertently hurt?

"I'll call her tomorrow. I feel awful about it. It hadn't occurred to me that Blythe would be upset."

"You've been living in your own little world the past few months, and I suppose you've been entitled to it." Liv sighed. "We're used to you being the strong one in our little patchwork family. It's been difficult for us to get used to how different you've been."

"I'm sorry Mom."

"Don't be. What I'm saying is that we need to cut you some slack and let you show your emotions, in the same way the rest of us do.

"Speaking of Thanksgiving, did you see the postcard that came from Jace?" her mother whispered.

"No, I didn't. Where is it?"

Liv pointed at the stack of mail on the kitchen counter. "You might want to look at it later, when Billy isn't around."

"By the way, he's not going back right away."

"He's not?"

And Then You Dance

Billy joined them in the kitchen. "What are you two talking about in here?"

"Thanksgiving. My mom is asking your mom and dad to join us. Paige and Mark too."

He wrapped his arm around Renie's waist and rested his chin on her shoulder. "We'll all be back together again."

"We'll do it here. Maybe your folks can get someone else to host Thanksgiving back at your place this year. They've been doing it every year for as long as I can remember."

"They'll figure it out. They'll want to be here."

Liv picked up the landline to call Dottie. She was anxious to get the plans in the works since Thanksgiving wasn't that far off.

"You ready to leave?" Renie asked him.

"Whenever you are. No rush."

"Why don't we challenge the boys to a game of foosball, and let them win. Maybe they won't be…"

"As mad at me?"

Renie laughed. "Yeah, that's what I was thinking."

"It's sweet how they are so protective of you."

"I've been wretched to be around these last eight months Billy. They haven't shy about telling me so."

She'd been wretched? Hearing so made him happy. If she was miserable, it had to have been because she missed him as much as he missed her. If it hadn't been for Willow keeping him distracted, he would've been wretched too. In fact, he had been. He hadn't seen many people while they were apart, so there wasn't anybody to call him out on it.

"Not sure how I'll be able to stand being away from you again."

"I can't come to Monument Billy. I've committed to working at the Goat for the season, and we're getting busy already." It was an excuse, she could take time off if she needed to, but it would cause a hardship for the rest of the staff, so she wasn't being completely dishonest about it.

Billy knew it too. But, he didn't say anything and Renie was glad he didn't.

"What should we do tomorrow?" he asked her.

"I have to work tomorrow night, but during the day we can do whatever you'd like to do."

"Hmm," he said, pulling her closer. "I can come up with a couple ideas to keep us busy."

"I'd like to ride Pooh again. I missed her so much."

"How come you didn't—"

"I couldn't."

"What?"

"As long as she was with you I knew I'd have to talk to you again someday."

"I felt the same way."

"Why did you bring her here?"

It had been a really hard decision, he told her. He had hoped things would work out as they had, although he never dreamed they would work out this well.

"If you refused to talk to me, maybe I would've trailered her back to Monument."

***

Two days later Billy started thinking about going home. They agreed to talk to each other on Facetime, and Billy showed her how to use it on her phone.

"As long as we both have a cell signal, we can see each other whenever we want to," he told her. "Maybe you could talk to Willow on it too."

"We'll see."

Renie was shutting down again, he could sense it. The last few days had been heavenly. They'd spent every moment together. He'd even gone and hung out at the Goat while she worked. Until the last couple of minutes, it seemed like old times.

"Not today," he said.

"What?"

"I'm not going back today."

"Wait. Why not?"

"Because you still need me here."

"You can't stay here forever Billy."

"Willow is in good hands, happy as can be, and you're not. So I'm not leaving yet."

"It's okay—"

"No, it isn't okay. I'm not leaving until I *know*, in my heart, you won't shut me out of your life again."

She wanted to tell him he was wrong, that she'd be fine if he went home. But he was right. As soon as he said he was thinking about leaving, she started to freak out about how hard it would be for them to be apart again. She did need him with her, and although she knew he had to get back to Monument, back to Willow, she was thankful she'd have another day or two with him.

"What about after Thanksgiving?"

"After? You mean Christmas?"

"No, in general."

"I don't know Renie. We have to wait and see how things go. We'll keep talking, that's the important thing. Keep talking, keep communicating, and keep making sure we're on the same page."

He sounded so…adult. He had changed in the last few months, more than she had. He'd grown up. But, he hadn't left her behind. Maybe that was one of the things she'd been worried about. Billy was so much older than she was. What if he woke up one day and realized she was still a kid? She felt like one, whether he saw her that way or not.

She quit college, gave up her dream of being a vet. She worked as a wrangler at a dude ranch for the summer, and now she was waitressing in a bar. Even to herself she sounded like a kid who didn't know what she would do with the rest of her life. How could she expect anyone else to view her differently?

***

Dottie arranged for a local catering company to provide Thanksgiving dinner for the hands at Patterson Ranch. This was the first time since she married Bill that they wouldn't be home for Thanksgiving. She didn't mind though. It was getting to be a lot of work, and this was their first Thanksgiving with Willow. The baby girl wouldn't know the difference, but for Billy, and for Renie, and their two families, this was a step in the right direction.

"How do they seem?"

"Since we rarely see them, I'd say they seem to be doing well," Liv laughed. "It's taken me a little while to get used to it, but I have. When they're here, they seem happy."

"It's when Billy comes home that it gets tricky."

"You are dead-on right about that. I'm surprised he's still here to be honest with you. I didn't expect him to stay this long."

"He didn't expect to either, but when he called this morning he said Renie wasn't ready for him to leave yet, so he had to stay."

"That doesn't sound like Renie."

"It isn't her. It's him. He knows her well enough to be able to gauge what she needs better than she can herself."

Dottie encouraged Billy to trust his instincts. Willow was fine; in fact, she and Bill were enjoying every minute with their granddaughter. They were in no hurry for Billy to get back. And Willow didn't know the difference. She'd be happy to see her daddy, but she'd settled in at their house without a hiccup.

"I'm sure he misses Willow though."

"He does, but he went a long time missin' Renie too."

"I'm so happy you'll be here for Thanksgiving. I've invited Paige and Mark too, and Blythe is coming with them."

"You're gonna have a crowd sugar. How early do you want me to get there to help you?"

"Would tomorrow be too soon?" Liv was joking, but she missed Dottie and Bill so much. She couldn't wait to have them here.

"You're sure you have room for us at the house? We can get a hotel room."

"Heavens no! I'm so excited to have you stay here. This is a big house, bigger than mine, and we've never had it full."

The Pattersons and Cochrans were coming for Thanksgiving, along with Ben's parents, his brothers, their wives, and a few of the guys in CB Rice. Liv had never cooked

Thanksgiving dinner herself. She and Renie spent the holiday at Patterson Ranch for as long as she could remember. She was as nervous about it as she was excited.

"We'll make plans to drive over on Monday. That will give us plenty of time to catch up and do what we need to do for dinner. Order the turkeys now though."

"I don't even know how to do that Dottie."

"No problem sugar. I'll order them from here and have them delivered to you. Give me the final count of how many you're expecting, and I'll take care of it."

"Thanks Dottie. You're a lifesaver, as usual."

"You're like my own Livvie, you know that's how Bill and I feel about you. It's as though I'm spending my first Thanksgiving at my daughter's house."

That made Liv teary-eyed. She still hadn't told Dottie she was pregnant, and she'd asked Billy not to either. Since she'd be here in less than a month, Liv wanted to wait and tell her in person.

Getting through the month would be as hard for her as she knew it would be for Renie and Billy. Maybe not quite as hard, but she would be on pins and needles the entire time, both in excitement, and in worry.

***

"This is one of the hardest things I've ever had to do," Billy said. "I wish I didn't have to go home."

"It's okay. I'm happy you stayed as long as you did."

Billy was feeling better about the two of them, so when he hit the seven-day mark, he decided to go home. He'd be back, with Willow, in less than three weeks.

His parents were coming to Crested Butte on Monday, but he wanted to come the Friday before, so he and Renie had time alone with his daughter. He made arrangements to rent the same place he was staying in this week, that way if Renie was feeling too uncomfortable, or overwhelmed, he and Willow wouldn't be staying in Ben's house. She could escape if she felt the need to.

"You're being so great about this Billy. I don't think I could be as great about it as you are."

"What do you mean?"

"You're being so patient with me. If I were in your shoes, I'm not sure I would be."

He put his hands on each side of her face and looked into her eyes. "You are one of the two most important people on the face of the earth to me. I'll do anything, *anything*, to make this work. I can be patient. But, I can't be away from you for very long."

Renie watched Billy drive away from the ranch house. She stood outside long after she couldn't see his truck. A feeling of loss hit her almost instantaneously, along with a feeling of dread. The next time she saw him, Willow would be with him. She prayed she didn't react to the baby the same way she had the first time she saw her.

***

"You should call her instead of showing up unexpected," Tucker said to Jace while he was packing his bag. "Give her some notice."

"Why?"

"Well mister cock-sure-of-himself, maybe she's moved on. Got another guy."

"Okay, I'll call her. After I get home."

Tucker and their parents were staying on two more weeks, but they'd be back in Aspen in time for Thanksgiving. Jace was hoping he could talk Irene into coming to his parents' house for the holiday. And if she wouldn't, he planned to finagle an invite to Ben's instead.

***

Renie pulled her cell phone out of her pocket, knowing it was Billy calling. As she hit the answer button, she glanced at the screen. It wasn't Billy, it was Jace.

Chapter Seventeen

"Hello?"

"Irene! Hi, it's Jace. How are you?"

"I'm good. How are you?"

"Happy to be back in the States." *Closer to you.*

"I…um…wow. I didn't expect to hear from you."

"At all? Or this soon? Did you get my postcard?"

His postcard. She'd forgotten all about it. Her mother had mentioned it to her, but then she never thought about it again.

"I, uh, didn't get it."

"Oh, damn. Well anyway, it said that I was looking forward to seeing you. When can I?"

She didn't know when he could see her, and she didn't know how to tell him.

"How about later this week? What are you doing with yourself anyway?"

Let's see. She'd reconnected with the love of her life, they were trying to figure out how to spend their lives together, she was about to meet his one-year-old daughter, and she was even considering going back to school. It was a lot of information to tell someone she hadn't been sure she'd ever talk to again.

"Are you there?"

"Yeah. Sorry. I'm not sure Jace."

"About what? What you're doing with yourself?"

"About later this week. There's a lot going on."

"How about this, let's meet for a drink, or coffee. The pass is still open, it won't take me that long to get there."

"Well..."

"It's just coffee Irene. Then you can tell me whatever it is you don't want to tell me on the phone."

She forgot. He knew her too. Maybe not as well as Billy did, but he knew her.

"Okay. When?"

"Tomorrow."

"That works, let's meet at..."

"I'll pick you up at the ranch, that way I can see Ben and Uncle Bud and Aunt Ginny too. It'll be great to see them again."

Oh. This was turning into more than coffee. He wanted to stage a mini-family reunion.

"I'll leave early and text you when I do."

"That sounds..."

"I can't wait to see you Irene. I missed you."

"Me too." Wait, what was she saying? Why was she telling him she'd missed him?

"Great. Tomorrow it is then. I'll get there around nine. But as I said, I'll text you when I leave Aspen."

He sounded so excited. Too excited. She should tell him not to come. But he was right, she had a lot to tell him, and it would be easier to do in person.

***

"Good morning."

"Hi Mom."

"That's not a very enthusiastic greeting. What's up? Missin' Billy?"

"Yeah, I miss him." He'd been gone less than two days. They were back to texting and talking several times a day, but it didn't make it any easier. They talked via Facetime too, but he hadn't asked her to talk to Willow yet. Maybe he was waiting for her to ask.

"There's more."

"There is? What's up sweet girl?"

"Jace is back in town. He wants to come to Crested Butte and have coffee with me."

"Oh. You haven't talked much about him. Are you…you know, going to?"

"Yeah, I am. I figured it would be easier to see him face-to-face. Oh, by the way, do you know where that postcard went? He asked about it, and I told him I hadn't seen it. I'd hate for it to be in plain sight when he gets here tomorrow."

"It's right here," Liv said, pulling it out from under a stack of other mail. "I need to sort through this today. Wait, did you say when he gets here *tomorrow*?"

"I know. He wants to see Ben. Bud and Ginny too."

"That sounds like more than coffee."

"That's what I thought."

***

Jace texted as promised, at seven. Renie had two hours before he'd be there. She'd forgotten to tell Ben he was coming, so she hoped her mother had. She didn't want Jace to have any reason to come to the ranch after they had coffee, so she wanted to be sure he saw everyone on the front end of his visit.

"You want coffee, or are you waiting for your date to have some?" Ben said when she came upstairs.

"Oh good, Mom told you."

"I can't wait to see him myself. How 'bout you?" he smirked at her.

"Stop it."

"What?"

"You know what."

"Aw come on, have fun with it. You have two cowboys chasin' your skirt. This is how life is supposed to be at your age."

"They're not chasing my skirt, and I have to tell Jace about Billy today. I don't plan on seeing him again."

"Okay," Ben said, with a lilt of reservation.

Renie went downstairs to take a shower and get ready. Jace would be here too soon as it was.

She heard a truck drive up, and she looked out the window of the family room. It was Bud and Ginny, not Jace. The closer it got to the time he'd be there, the more nervous she got. When her cell phone rang it made her jump.

"Hey Billy."

"Hey sweet girl, how are you this morning?"

"I'm good. How're you?"

"I'm not good. I miss the hell out of you."

"I miss you too."

"Ten more days, if I can wait that long. I may pack little miss Willow in the truck and head over later today."

"What? No, you can't do that!"

"Huh? I was joking. What's going on with you?"

"Nothing. I'm not…"

"What? Ready yet? I know. That's why it was a joke Renie."

She didn't answer him.

"What else is goin' on? There's somethin' you don't want to say."

"Jace is coming over from Aspen to see Ben and his parents. He'll be here in a little while," she blurted out.

"Jace? The guy from the ranch? Why is he coming to see Ben and his parents?"

"He's Ben's cousin. Their grandfathers were brothers."

"How long have you known this?"

"That they were cousins?"

"No Renie, that he was coming for a visit."

Renie didn't like the tone of Billy's voice. "Since yesterday afternoon. I didn't even know he was back from Spain."

"When were you going to tell me?"

"Stop it. He's a friend, and he's Ben's cousin. You're starting to sound a little…I don't know…angry."

He was angry. Ben's cousin signed a postcard to her with the word *love*. She hadn't mentioned that he was related to Ben. What else had she left out?

"How long's he stayin'?"

"For a couple of hours. I mean, I don't know. For coffee."

"He's driving from Aspen for coffee?"

"Billy, stop it. You're making too much of nothing."

He wished he could put Willow in the truck and drive straight there. Or ask Ben to fly over and get him so he could meet this Jace character for himself.

"Okay, but I want you to call me after he's gone. I want to see your pretty face. I miss you so much."

"I miss you too."

She saw Jace drive up to the house an hour later. He looked good. Really good. And she was surprised she noticed. She was even more surprised at the surge of excitement she felt when she saw him smile. Jace was such a good man, a nice man, and one whose company she enjoyed very much. She hoped he wouldn't mind if they were just friends from here on out.

She went out the front door and waited for him on the porch.

"Well there she is," he said, walking up the steps. He pulled her into his arms and drew her into a kiss before she could protest. More surprising than the surge of excitement she felt when she saw him, was how unwilling she was to pull away from his kiss. It felt good to be in his arms, better to have him kissing her.

"Wow," he said. "I missed you more than I thought."

Renie stepped back, out of arms' reach. "Good to see you Jace. How was Spain?"

He laughed. "It was fun. Tucker is…well, he's a lot of fun to be around."

"Oh yeah? And what kind of trouble did you two get yourselves into?"

"Oh girl, you know me too well." He threw his arm over her shoulder and they walked into the house.

Jake and Luke were standing in the family room. It was obvious that they had been looking out the window.

"Close your mouths," she said. "You'll catch flies leaving them open that way."

Luke stepped forward to say something and Ben put his hand over his son's mouth. He leaned down and whispered, "Not a word out of you."

"But—"

"Not. A. Word."

"Not even hello?"

"That's it, nothing else. No questions. Got it Luke?"
"Got it Dad."

"Well hey there Jace. I bet you weren't as old as Jake here the last time I saw you."

"I don't think so. Hey Uncle Bud, Aunt Ginny." He hugged them both.

"My goodness," said Ginny. "You have grown into a *fine* looking young man." She looked at Renie and wiggled her eyebrows.

"How are your mom and dad?"

Renie walked over to her mom while Jace caught up with Ben and his parents.

"She's right. He is a *fine* looking young man."

"Stop it, Mom. You're not helping."

"What? I'm stating fact." She tapped Renie's arm. "Where are your manners young lady? Introduce me to him."

"Jace, this is my mom, Liv."

"Liv," he answered, "I've heard so much about you. It's a pleasure to meet you."

"I cannot say that I've heard as much about you," she winked. "But it is a pleasure to meet you too."

Renie blushed and swore she'd wring her mother's neck later, when they were alone.

"How was Spain?" Ben asked.

"Good. My parents and Tucker are still there. They'll be home next week, in time for Thanksgiving." He looked at Renie. "Which I wanted to talk to you about, by the way. I'm hoping you don't have any plans."

"Oh we have big plans, her—"

Ben clamped his hand over Luke's mouth.

Jace looked at Renie.

"We'll talk about it later," she said softly.

"Are you hungry? Can we get you some breakfast?" Ben asked.

"Uh, no thanks. Irene and I are heading out for coffee."

"Irene—" Ben clamped his hand over Luke's mouth again.

He bent down and whispered, "What part of not another word didn't you understand? Now not another word."

"Okay, sorry." Luke pouted.

"Am I missing something?" asked Jace.

"No one calls her Irene, that's all," answered Jake, who had remained removed up to that point, other than introducing himself.

"They don't? What do they call her?" he smiled at Renie.

"Renie!" answered Luke, moving far enough away that Ben couldn't stop him.

"Renie huh? That's interesting." He was smiling at her still, and reaching for her hand. "Ready to go?"

"Sure, if you are. You didn't get to spend much time with your family though," she said quietly enough that she hoped he heard her.

"I'll catch up with them later. I can't wait to hear what you've been up to."

"Jace can you stick around and have dinner with us?" Ginny asked.

Oh great. This was what she hadn't wanted to happen.

"I'd love to," he answered Ginny, but was still looking at Renie.

And Then You Dance

"Where to?" he asked when they were in the truck.

"There's a place on Elk Avenue called Rumors. We could go there."

"Sounds good." He took her hand. "Speaking of rumors, I heard one about you having a nickname. Renie huh?"

"It's what my mom calls me. Other people too."

"So you don't like it?"

"No, I didn't say that. My name is Irene. There are some people who call me Renie, that's all."

"So what do you want me to call you?"

"Irene. As you always have." In fact, she liked that he called her Irene. And that no one else did.

"I like to be different, especially when it comes to you, so if everyone else calls you Renie, I'll stick with Irene."

"Thanks." She looked out the window.

"What's up sourface?"

"I thought you were going to call me Irene."

"When you don't have the sourface on. What're you thinking about?"

"Nothing. Do you know your way to Elk Avenue?"

"Sure do. And I guess you'll tell me whatever it is that you've got to tell me once we're there."

She barely nodded her head, but she knew he caught it. He squeezed her hand, hard, and didn't let it go.

"I like this place," Jace said, after they'd ordered and found a place to sit. "I especially like the little bookstore next door. I'd love to wander through it later."

"Sure, we can do that. It's such a beautiful fall day, I thought we could walk through town." Elk Avenue had wonderful little shops and restaurants scattered over the course of several blocks. The side streets had them too. It was easy to spend several hours walking around downtown.

"I'd love that." His elbow rested on the table and he put his chin on his fist, moving closer and looking into her eyes. "Tell me how you've been?"

"I've been fine. How have you been?"

He raised his head from his chin, reached over and touched her cheek. "Come on, talk to me. What's been going on with you?"

"My mom and Ben are having a baby," she blurted out, not meaning to.

"Wow! That's great! Good for them." He must've realized she wasn't smiling. "Or…it's not good for them?"

"No, it is good for them. I'm happy…for them."

"But not happy for yourself?"

"It isn't that, but, how would you feel if your mom and dad told you they were having another baby? Wouldn't it be a little weird?"

"It would be very weird, but I don't know, my mom and dad are so much older than your mom and Ben. Don't get me wrong though, I hear what you're saying. I get that it's weird for you." He smiled and kissed across her knuckles.

She saw what he was doing. She was watching him. Yet she had no desire to pull her hand away. She'd forgotten how easy he was to be with—and how much she liked him.

The rhythm they fell back into was an easy one. It was mid-afternoon before she knew it.

"Are you hungry?" Jace asked her.

"Starving. I didn't realize how late it had gotten." She looked at her phone and cringed. There were four texts from Billy and an equal number of voicemail messages.

"Did you forget about something?"

"What? No. It's just later than I thought."

"Somewhere you need to be?"

"No, not really." She excused herself and went to the ladies room. She couldn't very well call Billy, and if she texted him, what would she say? He was probably already furious with her; she might as well wait until later and deal with it all at once.

"You sure everything's okay?" he asked when she came back to the table.

"Yes. There's something we need to talk about though."

"I figured there was." He was frowning.

"It's about Billy."

"Figured that too." He leaned back in his chair, further away from her.

"I've known Billy almost all my life…" she began the story.

"He's coming for Thanksgiving." It wasn't a question. It was a statement.

"He is," she answered.

Jace rubbed his hand over his face. "I'm not sure what to say. I guess I'm relieved you weren't 'with him' during the summer. I'm not sure how I would've felt about that."

"I wouldn't have done that Jace."

"I know you wouldn't. But…"

"But what?"

"What about today?" He looked at his phone. "I've been here several hours now. And I haven't been shy with my, uh, affection."

She knew he was right, and she didn't know how to answer him.

"I didn't feel the way I thought I would when you got here," she said.

"No? How did you feel? Or how didn't you feel?"

"I'm happy you're here."

"Ouch woman! I guess you mean that in a good way, but wow, you didn't expect to be happy to see me?"

"Honestly?"

"Please."

"No. I didn't. I didn't expect to feel the way I'm feeling at all."

He leaned forward and ran his finger down the side of her face. "How are you feeling Irene?"

"I want you to kiss me."

"Not a problem." He leaned closer and rubbed his lips over hers. "It's my pleasure," he added.

He kissed her thoroughly. Any ideas she'd had about the two of them having an innocent, friendly visit were long gone. And she had no desire to stop what they were doing.

It was a warm and sunny day, so they were sitting outside on the patio at the Brick Oven Pub. It shouldn't have surprised her when someone stopped at the table to say hello.

"Hey Renie, how are you?"

"Good Will. How are you?"

"Will?" Jace asked. "Will Rice?"

"Yep, that's me."

"I'm Jace. Jace Rice."

"Jace? No kidding, how the hell are you?"

Will pulled up a chair and sat down at the table with them. They spent a few minutes catching up before Will settled his gaze on Renie.

"How did you and Jace meet?"

Jace answered before she could. "We both worked at Black Mountain Ranch this summer." He went on to tell Ben's brother how he'd recently returned from Spain.

"How long will you be on this side of the hill?"

"I'd planned to stay a few hours, but then Aunt Ginny invited me for dinner."

"That's right, she called to tell me there was a family dinner, mentioned somebody was in town, but I didn't quite catch what she was talking about. Great, then. Maeve, that's my wife, and I will catch up with you later."

Will was eyeing Renie and she knew what he was thinking. She hoped he didn't want to talk about it. He got up from the table instead, but rested his hand on her shoulder.

"And you? I'll see you later too, won't I?"

"He know about Billy?"

"Yep."

"Then you're in for an awkward conversation. He couldn't have missed the lip-lock we were in when he approached the table."

It was Renie's turn to put her hands in her face. More than Will, she was worried about Billy. She had to call him, but she had no idea what she would say.

"What's happening with him?"

"I'm sure he's furious."

"Let's go back to the house. You can call him from there. I'll make myself scarce. Maybe I'll visit Uncle Bud and Aunt Ginny for a while."

"Why are you being so nice about this?"

"Oh, I'm not. Not at all. I fully expect you to be honest with him Irene. And I'm not leaving. I'm staying for dinner, and I plan to be sitting next to you when I do."

Jace dropped her off at Ben's, but didn't come in. He drove away before she'd gotten inside.

"Oh dear, what's happened?" her mother asked.

"He's going to Bud and Ginny's. I need to call Billy."

Renie was downstairs with her door shut before Liv could ask her another question.

Chapter Eighteen

Billy was nearly frantic. It was all he could do not to call Liv, but Renie was an adult and calling her mother because he was worried about her was not an appropriate thing to do. In fact, if anything had happened to Renie, he knew Liv would contact him.

No, Renie was out with this Jace guy, the one she'd spent the summer with. Who taught her more about herself.

Willow started to cry, and he realized he hadn't been paying attention to her. This wasn't good. He was so upset about Renie, he'd forgotten his baby girl. *Shit*. What kind of dad was he?

He picked her up, and snuggled her against him. Once she had his undivided attention, she calmed down. More warning flags shot up around him. Maybe Renie's instincts were dead on, and it would be harder to juggle the two of them than he thought. It broke his heart to think she might be.

His cell vibrated in his pocket and he set Willow down on the floor to answer it. As soon as he did, she started to wail again.

"Hey," he answered. "Can you hang on a minute?"

He didn't wait for Renie's answer; he set the phone down so he could pick Willow up again.

"Hi," he said once he had his baby girl settled. "Where are you?"

"I'm home."

"Yeah?"

He was pissed, and he didn't care if she knew it. She would've been pissed to if the situations were in reverse.

"Billy, I—"

Willow started to cry again.

"Hey Renie. Willow's fussy. I need to take care of her. I'll call you later."

He hung up. *He hung up on her.* Because Willow was fussy. She knew that wasn't the only reason he had. But still. Wasn't that the very thing she was most worried about? That Willow would always come first? Their entire lives would revolve around Willow, whether Renie was ready for that kind of life or not.

She wasn't even twenty-four. Was that the life she wanted? She wasn't sure it was.

She came back upstairs, boots on, ready to go for a ride. Boy was she glad Pooh was out in the barn and no longer at Billy's.

"Where are you off to?" Liv asked.

"Riding over to Bud and Ginny's."

"Did you talk to Billy?"

"Yep, for about three seconds. He hung up on me because Willow was fussy."

"Oh dear."

"You got that right. Ya know, I don't need this shit from him. He wants it all, and he doesn't care how much he tramples on everyone around him to get it."

Liv knew now wasn't the time to say it, but at that moment, Renie could've been talking about herself as much as she was talking about Billy.

And Then You Dance

She vowed to stay out of it. Right after she called Dottie.

***

"Wow, that was quick," Jace said when Renie walked into Bud and Ginny's house.

"Yep."

"Did you make your phone call?"

"Yep."

"Okay, I guess you don't want to talk about it."

"Not now I don't."

Ginny walked into the kitchen. "Oh! Hi Renie. I didn't know you were in here."

"I just got here. Bud's putting Pooh in the barn. I'm not intruding am I?"

"No, not at all. I was about to start dinner. We've got a crowd coming tonight to see Jace."

Renie rolled up her sleeves. "Put me to work then."

Jace watched her maneuver her way around the kitchen. It was clear she was pissed. He wanted to ask her about her conversation, but didn't want to do it in front of Aunt Ginny.

She was here though, and that had to mean something. He walked over to where she was and kissed her cheek. She turned, smiled at him, and kissed him on the lips. Yeah, he didn't care about how her conversation with Billy went. If she was kissing him, she was his, at least for the next few hours.

***

Billy knew he'd handled that the worst way possible with Renie. Everything she was worried about, that Willow would be his first priority, he'd thrown into her face. And he hung up on her. Way to drive her straight into someone else's arms.

He heard the back door open and turned to see his mother standing in his kitchen.

"Should we change our plans for Thanksgiving?"

Shit. What had she heard and how had she heard it already?

"Billy, I love ya," she said after listening to his side of the story. "No mama could love her son more, but I have to be honest with you. You are an idiot."

"I'm an idiot? You're siding with her? She's been off doing who knows what with another man and you're siding with her?"

"No, I'm not. I'm not siding with either one of you. I'm just saying that you're an idiot. Don't you think you should have at least let her talk? Tell you what's going on?"

"Why? So she could tell me that she'd spent the day with another man? No, thank you."

"How do you know that? What if you had spent the day with Liv?"

"That's different. She's Renie's mom."

"Yes, but she's another woman. That would've been completely innocent on both your parts. Maybe this was innocent too."

"Nope, not the same thing at all. I never had sex with Liv. Sorry to be blunt Mama, but that's the difference."

"Okay, well here's a question for you then. Are you going to act like such a jackass that she has no choice but to pick the other man instead of you? 'Cause that's the road you're on Billy. You're gonna drive her right into his arms instead of yours. Is that what you want?"

"No. It isn't."

"So what are you gonna do about it."
"I don't know."

* * *

The place was a madhouse; there was no other word for it. Between Ben and his brothers, their wives, Jace, Ben's two boys, Bud and Ginny, and her and her mother, Renie was completely overwhelmed. The only other time in her life that she was around this many people having dinner was Thanksgiving, at Patterson Ranch in their dining hall, when all the cowboys and families came together to celebrate.

What would she do about Thanksgiving? Billy was bringing Willow, and Dottie and Bill were coming too. She and Billy needed to talk about today, and resolve things before the two of them ruined the holiday for everyone else.

Blythe was coming with her parents too, and she had a lot of making up to do with her friend. In fact, she wouldn't be all that surprised if Blythe decided not to come.

She couldn't blame her; she knew she'd been a lousy friend to her for the last year. If you counted how long she had been dishonest with Blythe about how she felt about Billy, she'd been a lousy friend for years.

Renie needed some fresh air. She went out and stood on the porch. A few minutes later, Jace joined her.

"What's going on in that pretty head of yours?"
"I messed things up today."
"With Billy?"
"Yeah, with Billy."

He put his arm around her, and she rested her head against his shoulder.

"I'm sorry Jace, but Billy has been…a significant part of my world for most of my life."

"You love him."

"More than anything."

"This thing with us, what do you think that's all about?"

"I like you Jace, very much. I love Billy, but I like you, and I'm attracted to you. I'm not sure what that says about me."

He turned her in his arms, so he was facing her.

"You can't ignore it. At the very least, you need to figure out why."

"Why what?"

"There must be something that's missing with Billy that you find with me. I'm not saying this because I'm crazy about you. Even if I walk away from you right now and never look back, you'll still need to figure out this thing with Patterson."

"You're being awfully nice about this."

"Yeah, I care about you…there, I admitted it," he teased.

"It's that thing, you know, the nothing ever bothers you thing."

"As I've told you before, this bothers me, a lot. But, there isn't much I can do about it. If he didn't mean something to you, you wouldn't be out here fretting about it."

She turned so her back was to him, but he kept his arms around her waist.

She saw a truck coming down one of the ranch roads, but didn't pay much attention to it. The Rice family employed a lot of ranch hands; it wasn't unusual to see a truck or two out on the back roads.

As it got closer, she realized it was on the main road, and it was heading toward Ben's place. Something about it didn't seem right to her, and she stiffened.

And Then You Dance

"What's up?"

"I don't know. Something about that truck…"

"Maybe you should say something to Ben."

"Yeah, maybe."

She turned away from Jace and dug out her cell phone.

We need to talk, she texted Billy.

I know we do, he answered.

Where are you?

Here.

Here? As in Crested Butte? Had she just seen his truck?

"Jace, would you mind telling Ben I took his truck? I'm heading up to the house." On the ranch, most everyone left their keys in the ignition, it was a habit.

"Wait, do you think you should go alone? I can go with you. Or maybe let Ben go if you're worried about it."

"It's okay, I know who it is." She was walking to Ben's truck as she said it. She pulled away, and caught sight of Jace, still standing on the front porch. She hated to do this to him, but what she'd done today to Billy was worse.

It didn't look as though anybody was home when he pulled up, but Renie texted him saying they needed to talk a minute ago. Maybe she was home alone. He knocked on the front door, but there was no answer. He turned around and saw the headlights of another truck coming toward the house. He leaned against the porch railing and waited.

"Hi," she said as she jumped out of the truck and walked toward him.

"Hi."

"You drove all the way here."

"Yep."

"How come?"

"'Cause my mama told me I was being a jackass."

She stood in front of him now. She reached out and put her fingers through his belt loops, pulling herself closer to him.

"About what?"

"What you spent your day doin'."

She let go of his belt loops, put her arms around his waist and her head against his chest.

"I'm sorry."

"About what?"

"About today."

"Do I even wanna know?"

"No. You don't. But you need to."

"Shit," he said. "I was afraid of this."

"Let's go inside."

Renie pulled her vibrating cell out of her pocket as she walked in the front door. "Hey Mom."

"Renie, is everything okay?"

"Yeah. Billy's here."

"Oh."

"Jace knows, or at least he knows I left."

"He came in and told Ben."

"I gotta go Mom, but everything's okay."

Billy was waiting for her on the sofa in the family room when she came in. Somehow he'd managed to light the fireplace during her brief conversation. She sat next to him, tucking her feet under her as she did.

"You hung up on me."

"You spent the day with another man." He ran his hand through his hair. "I don't wanna do this. I don't wanna go back and forth with you about who did what. Just tell me what the fuck is goin' on."

"I don't know how to explain it." Renie got up and started pacing in front of the fireplace. She stopped and held her hands out, as if to warm them, but then kept her back to Billy when she started to speak.

"I was happier to see him than I expected to be. I expected to have a quick cup of coffee and tell him goodbye."

"But that didn't happen."

"He says there's something I'm missing with you, that I find with him."

Billy didn't say anything. She turned around to look at him, and his eyes were closed.

"It isn't just Willow. There are other things I'm worried about Billy."

"What other things?"

"I wish I could explain how I'm feeling. But, I can't. All I know is that I love you. Anything beyond that…"

"What are you afraid of? That's what it comes down to. There's something you're afraid of."

She shrugged her shoulders.

"You're right, ya know. You were feeling this way before I found out about Willow. That night in your apartment, you were afraid of me. It near broke my heart Renie, to think you could ever be afraid of me."

He stood in front of her, but didn't touch her. "We should have talked about it then. I should have talked about it, asked you about it. Before we made love. I think about that moment all the time, seeing that look in your eyes. *That fear.* It almost brings me to tears."

She looked up at him. There were tears in his eyes. She reached up and touched his face.

"Billy—"

"I love you Renie. Do you know how much? Can you feel it comin' off me? Too much to be able to handle thinking that you could ever be afraid of me."

"I'm not afraid of you."

"You are. You can't deny it. You have to face it. You have to face whatever it is you're afraid of."

"Not you. Us maybe, but not you. I love you Billy, I have my whole life. I know you'd never hurt me…"

"No, you don't. And that's what you're afraid of. I'm a risk. A huge risk. Because your heart is in it. This other guy? He's not a risk. He hasn't climbed into your heart yet. And I pray he never does."

Billy turned and looked at the fire. "That's why I'm here ya know. Not because I'm some jealous asshole. I'm here because I don't want him to have the chance to mean something to you."

Renie went back to the couch, but Billy stayed where he was.

"If things were different, if I didn't have Willow, I could stay and fight for you. But I can't. I feel as though I'm being pulled between the two most important people in my life. I can't take care of you or her the way I want to. If I take care of you, I'm not there for her. If I'm there for her, I risk losing you."

She could see the pain on his face. It ran through his body as he said the words. How could she be the cause of such pain? What was wrong with her? How could she do this to him?

"I don't know what the answer is, but I do know this. If you're thinking that leaving me is the answer, *I'm here to tell you that isn't it.*"

"Are you sure Billy? I feel as though I'm asking you to choose. And I know you can't. I mean you can. You have to choose your daughter."

"Does it really come down to that? I can't believe it does. I won't. You haven't even met her Renie. You haven't even tried. You have to try. Isn't it worth it to try?" He sat down next to her and gripped her shoulders.

"Isn't it?" he demanded.

She started to cry, tears pouring down her cheeks.

"What are you so afraid of?"

"I...don't...know," she said between sobs.

"She's just a baby. I wish I could understand it. If I could, I'd be able to help you. Is there anything you can say that will help me understand?"

"I don't understand it myself Billy. If I don't understand the way I feel, how I can explain it to you?"

He let go of her shoulders and sat down next to her on the couch. When she leaned into him, he put his arm around her. She rested her head on his shoulder and took a deep breath.

"What about Thanksgiving?"

"You tell me. My whole family is comin' to Crested Butte. And they're doin' it for us. If you don't want it to happen, you better say so right now."

"No, I want it. But, I mean, do you?"

"*Of course I do.* Jesus Renie, it's the thing I'm waiting for to start the rest of my life."

"You think everything will fall into place? That easily."

"I don't think it. I hope for it. I pray for it. I want to believe it more than anything."

"And what if it doesn't?"

"We deal with it then. I wish now we hadn't waited. The longer we wait, the more anxious you get. I'm right about that, aren't I?"

"I don't think it's her. I think it's you."

"Yeah?"

"I don't know if I can share you," she whispered.

"I know," he whispered back.

Billy spent the night, in Renie's room, but left at sunrise. Jace spent the night too, at Bud and Ginny's.

He wanted to know what happened last night, but wasn't sure how to go about doing it. He called Ben.

"Yep, his truck was here last night, but when I got up this morning it was gone. I know Renie's out ridin' Pooh. Dad said she came down to the house a little while ago to ride her home."

Damn. She'd been here, right outside, and he missed her.

"Mind if I come up to the house? I want to say goodbye, at least."

"Come on up," Ben laughed.

"What's so funny?"

"If Liv and I have a girl, I don't think I'll live through her courting years. When I met Renie she was already grown up, and I gotta tell you, I'm about ready to sit both you and Cowboy Patterson down and threaten you within an inch of your lives."

"I hear ya," he laughed. "I want what's best for her," he said more seriously. "I care about Irene. I'd like to be the man that puts a smile on her face, for the rest of her life. Although I'm beginning to think I don't have a prayer in hell up against…what did you call him? Cowboy Patterson."

"See ya in a bit Jace. And good luck. Never liked Patterson all that much myself, but can't say I disagree with your assessment."

Jace was waiting near the barn when Renie rode up on Pooh.

"Good morning," he said.

"Hey."

"Wanted to say goodbye."

"Heading back?" She looked in the direction of the pass. "It's a beautiful day for a drive home."

"Yep, it is." He took off his cowboy hat and walked toward her. "I hoped we could talk before I go."

She climbed down and took Pooh's reins. "Sure. Of course. I owe you an apology."

"Nah, you don't. I figure things are hard enough for you right now without me complicating them."

"True. They are," she laughed.

He was close enough to touch her face, so he did. And when she leaned in closer to him, he lost what little resolve he thought he had. His palm held her cheek as he leaned in to kiss her. When she kissed him back, he grabbed her around the waist and pulled her into him.

Chapter Nineteen

Her arms came up and circled around his neck, keeping him close to her. She pulled away from his kiss and rested her forehead against his chin.

"I was supposed to be apologizing to you, not making it worse."

"Uh, I'll take worse, along with that kind of apology anytime you want to give it to me," he answered.

She let go and walked Pooh into the barn.

"I'm serious Jace. I can't do this. I mean…"

"You're in love with him."

"I am, but I heard what you said yesterday. Something between us doesn't work. Even before he became a dad, he saw it."

She looked away from him, shook her head, and laughed. Then looked back at him. "You're so much alike."

"Oh man, I wish you wouldn't say that. Jeez Irene, no man wants to be told he's so much like the guy he's trying to steal you away from."

She laughed again, but she was frowning.

"Billy and his family are coming for Thanksgiving. I need to figure things out by then. You know…what I want, how I feel, who I am." She took a deep breath. "And what the hell is wrong with me."

"I'd like to help."

"You just confuse me more. You *don't* help."

"No, I'm serious." He held both his hands up. "Hands off, I promise. Talking only."

She raised her eyebrows at him as if to say she doubted him.

"How was your ride?"

"Too short."

"Wanna go back out? If we did, we could talk, and you'd know for sure I wouldn't be trying to kiss you."

"Okay. That sounds nice. I miss riding with you."

"I miss riding with you too."

"Ben won't care which horse you ride."

"What about that one?" he said, pointing to Micah.

"Uh, no. That's my mom's horse and nobody rides him but her and…"

"And? Who?"

"She lets Billy ride him."

"Why him? Not you?"

"I'm sure she'd let me if I wanted to, but I don't. And the reason Billy gets to ride him is because he took care of him after my mom's accident."

"Your lives are entwined."

"You have no idea."

They rode out over the hills of the Rice Ranch, quiet at first.

"Why don't you tell me about him? Forget who I am, just talk about him."

"Jace, really? I can't do that."

"I'm serious. Tell me what you feel. I won't lie and tell you hearing about him won't hurt, because I know you love him. But, on the other hand, you need somebody to talk to. I'm here, and I'm offering."

"We already did this."

"No, we didn't. You told me about *him*, not about you and him. Tell me what's got you so tied up in knots."

"If it was that easy," she laughed.

"It is. Start talking. Try a pros and cons list. Here's the good stuff, and here's the bad stuff."

"I can probably handle that."

Once she started it was easy to talk about the good things about Billy. There were so many things she loved about him. She talked about the Billy she knew when she was a little girl, and how kind he was to her. Sometimes she felt as though Billy was the only person who really saw her. When she thought no one was paying attention, she'd look at him, and he'd be watching her. Studying her.

She told Jace about the day she rode Pooh out into the meadow the first time, and how Billy didn't tease her about giving a girl horse a boy's name. He told her that day to listen to her horse as much as she talked to him, and now she realized that was what Billy did with everybody. He listened more than he talked. He paid attention.

"Confidence," she said. "That's another thing. Until I met you, I'd never met anybody as confident as Billy Patterson." That had been a deal-breaker, she told him.

"And when my mom got hurt, I don't know what I would've done without Billy. My mom was impossible to deal with," she laughed. "Between trying to hide her condition from Ben, to being the biggest pain in the ass in the world, she was also very depressed. I'd never seen my mom that way. Billy helped so much. He was there every step of the way. No one else thought about me, everyone was worried about my mom. And rightly so. But not Billy. He worried about me."

"What else?" Jace asked.

Renie talked about how much fun Billy was. He made her smile, he made her laugh. He was the first person she felt like a woman with, instead of a kid.

If Renie ever needed anything, she knew Billy would do everything in his power to make sure she got it. Everyone else had given in to her about school. When she said she wasn't going back, no one argued with her. Not Ben, not her mom, but Billy had. He pushed and pushed her, to at least consider going back.

"Is there more to this superhero, or is that it?"

"There's more, but I don't think I feel comfortable talking about it."

"Door's open, pretend I'm a priest or something."

"Jace—"

"I'm serious Irene. You have this one opportunity to talk about whatever you want. It may not come again. And I'm not watching a clock trying to hurry you along."

"Okay, but remember, you asked."

"I'm ready, give me your worst."

"He was my first...you know."

"Yeah?"

"Yeah. I wanted him to be. But, I didn't think he saw me that way, as a woman, rather than a little girl. I was the sidekick, and I assumed one day he'd find someone who was *more*...and I'd get left behind."

Jace stopped his horse, and she pulled Pooh in as soon as she realized it.

"What?"

"I'm not here to comment. I'm here to listen."

"If you have something to say, say it."

"Think about what you just said. Figure it out for yourself."

"Which part?"

"You heard me, figure it out for yourself."

"I was afraid he'd find someone else?"

He shrugged his shoulders.

"It's the reason I told my mom to sell him her ranch."

"Why?"

"Because I knew that I wouldn't be able to stand watching him from afar. The Pattersons would never give up their ranch to another family. I knew one day it would be where Billy lived, with his wife, and their children. I knew it would rip me to pieces to see him with someone else. I've loved him for so long."

"Keep going."

"About this, or pros and cons?"

"So far I haven't heard any cons, and I'd sure like to. But if you have more pros, keep goin'."

She could talk for hours about the virtues of Billy Patterson. He was, after all, her favorite person on the planet. But what about the not so wonderful stuff? That was harder.

"He slept around a lot. Before me. I guess that isn't much of a surprise." She looked at Jace and raised an eyebrow.

"What? We're talkin' about Billy, remember?"

She thought back to the first time she met Jace, and how she wondered if he greeted all the new girls who came to the ranch personally.

"He's stubborn."

"Keep goin'. I like this part."

"He's selfish."

And Then You Dance

"Care to elaborate on any of these condemnations? I'm enjoying this."

"Before we became...romantic...Billy took me for granted. He expected me to be around when he wanted me to be." She laughed. "He'd call me and ask me to dinner, and then expect me to cook it for him.

"He relied on me to be there for him. He never asked, he expected. And, of course, I was. I wanted to be around him whenever I could be."

She looked at Jace, who nodded his head. "Go on."

"He was the saddle bronc champ year before last."

"That's a con?"

"It's not a pro or a con. It's just something about him. Part of what makes him who he is. Cowboys like him, the good ones, are some of the best men on the planet. They're honorable, and gracious. They know their lives ebb and flow by the luck of the draw of the horse, or the bull. Don't get me wrong, there's a lot of skill necessary to get to their level. And with it, there's an expectation, a code among them, that they'll have humility. You know, 'work hard, stay humble.'"

He nodded again.

"You're one of them too. I don't know why I'm even telling you this."

"First, thank you. Second—keep talking about Billy."

"Doesn't stop any of you from being cocky, Billy included. I doubt he gave much thought about any of the women he had sex with."

She rode for a while without saying anything.

"I didn't believe him at first, about Roxanne. He told me he'd never had a relationship, or a girlfriend, and I didn't believe him. When we went to Texas, when he found out Willow was his baby, I thought he lied to me."

"What changed your mind?"

"He did. We argued about it, and I realized he was telling me the truth. I should have known he wouldn't lie to me about something like that."

"So we're back to pros."

"He's a good man. I know it in my heart."

"So where's your damage comin' from?"

"What do you mean?"

"There's something that's holding you back. Keeping you from taking the next step with Billy. Is it the baby, or is there more to it?"

"That's what he asks me. I don't have an answer for you anymore than I do for him. Or myself."

"Without the baby, would you be with him?"

"I don't know."

"So…"

"So? What? You're obviously trying to get me to come to an epiphany, and I'm not seeing it."

"There is something that's holding you back from giving in…trusting him."

They rode another few minutes in silence. Irene was thinking hard on what he said. It was so obvious to him, but he wasn't a shrink. And what if he was wrong? He wanted to help her, but there wasn't a lot he could do or say if she couldn't see what was so obvious to him. He could lead her to water, he couldn't make her drink it.

"What about this? Worst-case scenario…you and Billy. What would that look like?"

He hit on something with that question, because now she was crying.

"I can't."

"Sure you can. You've gone this far. What is it? What's the worst thing you can imagine happening between you and Billy?"

She still didn't answer him, but she knew what her answer was. The tears streamed down her cheeks.

"Say it out loud."

"No."

***

"I don't think this is a good idea," Dottie said to her son.

"I'm not askin' you Mama."

"Billy!"

"I'm sorry, I don't mean to be disrespectful to you, but there's gotta come a day I figure out what I'm gonna do in my life without asking my mama's opinion."

He had a point. She doubted many men his age talked to their mama very often, let alone consult her on most of their life decisions.

"I'm just sayin'—"

"Don't just say anything. I gotta do this. And if it blows up in my face, then I'll know who to blame."

Dottie picked up Willow from where she sat, happily playing while they talked. "Grandma's gonna miss you baby girl."

"It won't be for that long."

"I know, but I miss her when I'm away from her for an hour, so I'm gonna miss her more now."

"I know what you mean. I miss her when she goes to sleep."

He took Willow from his mother and hugged her. "I love you so much." He nuzzled her neck, and she giggled.

"Dadadada," she said, and opened her mouth to give his cheek one of her special kisses.

"Do you have everything packed?"

"Nah, I haven't even started packin' Willow's stuff yet."

"Give her to me. I'll pack her stuff, and you can start loading the truck."

He kissed Dottie's cheek. "Thanks Mama."

"Gives me a few more minutes with my little angel."

***

"Thank you," Renie said to Jace when they got back to the barn.

"You're welcome. I hope it helped."

"It did."

"I think you figured it out."

"I guess I did, but I need time to sort through it all."

"I'm a phone call away if you want to talk more."

"Thanks Jace."

He ran his finger down her cheek. "We both know this is the end of the road for us, other than as friends."

She took a deep breath and let it out slowly. "I'm so glad you feel that way."

He didn't. Or he didn't want to. But listening to her talk about Billy all afternoon convinced him that even if she decided she wanted to be with him, it would be temporary. Irene loved Billy. All she needed to do was conquer her fears, which may not happen quickly enough for Billy, but it would happen eventually.

***

"This is gonna be our home for a while baby girl," Billy said the next morning as they drove into town. He stopped by the realtor's office, signed the final paperwork and picked up the keys.

"Everything will be finalized tomorrow morning," she said. It didn't matter, he had the keys, and he was ready to get his baby girl settled in. There was a lot more happening tomorrow, important things, which he needed to focus on.

He patted his pocket, as he had every three or four minutes in the last couple of hours. Yep, it was still there.

He hoped he could get Willow to take a nap so he could unpack the truck. This was one of those times he could use his mama's help, or anyone's help. Then it occurred to him. There was someone he knew who understood the position he was in better than anyone else. He couldn't believe it had taken him this long to realize it.

***

"Hey-o Billy. What's up?"
"Hey Livvie. I called to ask your help with somethin'."
"Yeah, what's that? What can I do for you?"
"Could you come into town?"
"Which town?"
"Crested Butte."
"You're here?"
"Yep."
"Sure. Where are you exactly?"

He gave her the address, and filled her in on some of his plans. She told him she'd be there inside of a half an hour. "Let me find Ben and tell him where I'm going."

"Sure. Just don't mention it to Renie."
"Not a word, I promise."

"Bold move," she said when he answered the front door. "Not unlike you though." She reached out for Willow, who held tighter to her daddy.

"Oh no, you've forgotten me. I haven't been around enough." Liv started to tickle Willow who got over her shyness quickly once she heard Liv's voice.

"They say they remember voices more than faces." Willow reached out for Liv who took her from Billy. "Let's go find something to play with, shall we? Where did your daddy put that bag full of toys I know he brought with him?"

Willow pointed to a canvas bag sitting in the middle of the living room floor.

"When does the furniture arrive?" Liv asked.

"I haven't gotten that far."

"Where are you planning to sleep?"

"I brought Willow's travel crib, the one she uses when she's with my parents, and an air mattress for me."

"You go unload the truck, we'll play, and then your daddy and I will talk. Sound good?"

Willow started babbling a mile a minute and Billy escaped to unpack the truck.

"Do you want me to order in food?" Liv asked as he made one of his trips inside with stuff.

"Sure. That Stash place was good."

"Perfect. I know their number by heart."

Billy had most of the truck unpacked by the time the food arrived. Luckily the house had a built-in microwave so he could heat up Willow's baby food, which she had little interest in once she saw what her dad and Liv were eating.

"I don't want pizza to become her favorite food," Billy said, watching her dive into a piece.

"If it does, she'll live. Kids crave what they need. Tomorrow she may try to swipe your banana, or dig her fingers into a salad."

"Sounds as though you remember a lot about raising a baby."

"I do, but I've also been reading baby books," Liv laughed and rubbed her tummy. "It's been a long, long time since I had a little girl around." She kissed the top of Willow's head when she said it.

"Hoping for another one?"

"Oh, it doesn't matter. Ben would say differently. He's terrified of being a little girl's daddy. Says he doesn't know how to do girls. He'll figure it out if that's what we have."

"Do you want to know ahead of time?"

"I do, he doesn't. He says that if it is a girl, he'll have that much more time to worry."

It took another hour before Willow settled down enough to go to sleep. Billy closed the door softly behind him, turned the baby monitor on, and set in on the floor near where Liv was sitting cross-legged.

"You said you had a lot you wanted to talk to me about."

"I do. And it starts with a phone call I got yesterday afternoon."

Chapter Twenty

"Yeah," he said when the call came in from a number he didn't recognize.

"Patterson? Uh, this is Jace Rice calling."

"Jace Rice. Unexpected."

"Yeah, I know. But hear me out for a minute before you decide you don't want to talk to me."

"I'm all ears."

"Wow," Liv said when he finished the story.

"I know, right? Gotta give the guy credit. He cares about Renie."

"Obviously," she shook her head and laughed.

"What?"

"I hope I'm having a girl."

"Why's that?" Billy laughed too.

"Those Rice men have some mighty big *huevos,* don't they?"

"Ha! That's great Livvie. And yeah, they must."

"Seriously though, he made a valid point."

"What was it like, raising Renie on your own?"

"You know, I never thought of it that way. My mom and dad were hugely supportive, and then when they passed away, your parents took us in, so to speak.

"She made it easy though. She was a good baby, a good little girl, even as a teenager, she never got in any trouble."

"Renie's always been a rock…on the surface."

"Until recently anyway. She's been a bit of a mess lately. Thanks to you." Liv teased.

"Thanks a lot. But seriously, I appreciate this."

"I know you do. And I'm happy to help. I hope you can get through to her."

"Have to. Can't live without her."

Liv's cell phone rang. "It's Ben." She got up to take the call.

***

Billy meant it. He had to get through to Renie because there was no way he could consider a life without her in it. He wanted Willow to grow up in a house full of love, the way he had. And without Renie, it would be half what it should be.

"I'm heading back to the house now, but I'll see you tomorrow."

"You're sure she's not working?"

"Ben called and confirmed it. He also made sure that Will knew not to let her switch shifts with anyone."

"Okay, I'll see you around three tomorrow then. Thanks again Liv."

"Make her believe Billy, and then make her happy."

"I'll do my best, you know I will."

She kissed his cheek on the way out the back door.

Billy filled the air mattress and carried it into the room Willow slept in. He kissed her cheek.

"Big day tomorrow baby girl. Big day. Most important day of your daddy's life."

He spent most of the night staring at the ceiling, planning the next afternoon over and over in his head.

***

It was almost eleven by the time Renie came upstairs. Liv was a nervous wreck by the time she did.

"Hey there."

"Morning Mom."

"How did you sleep?" Liv kissed her daughter's forehead.

"Okay."

"What's wrong honey?"

"The same thing that's usually wrong. I'll give you three guesses."

"Are they all Billy?"

"First he drives all the way from Monument to Crested Butte, in what started off as a jealous rage over Jace. Now that he's back home, he's uncommunicative. He frustrates the hell out of me."

"When's the last time you talked to him?"

"I talked to him for a few minutes yesterday. We sent texts back and forth a few minutes ago."

"And what's he saying?"

"Nothing. He's busy."

"How did you leave things with Jace the other day?"

"We agreed to be friends. You know, he's such a good man. I wish things were different."

"You do?"

"No, not different that way. I love Billy, but I don't know whether it will *ever* work out between us. I'll love him forever anyway. It's not something another man will want to live with."

"No, probably not." Liv sat down at the kitchen table next to where Renie nursed a cup of coffee.

"Sometimes I feel as though I wasn't the best mother I could be to you."

"Huh? Where is this coming from?"

"You are so independent. It seemed as though nothing ever bothered you. At least on the surface. I wish I would've paid better attention honey."

Renie started to laugh.

"How is that funny?"

"It's something I've said to Jace. That nothing ever bothers him. He set me straight on that mighty fast. I feel the same way he does."

"And how is that?"

"A lot bothers me."

"You're good at hiding it."

"Yep."

"Tell me how you're feeling about Billy and Willow."

It took Renie a few minutes to start talking, but when she did, she told her mother about her ride with Jace, and what they talked about. Listening to her daughter, Liv's respect for Jace Rice increased more by the minute. There was part of her that agreed with Renie, it was too bad things couldn't be different. Jace was a good man. He'd make someone a great husband someday.

"That's why I want to talk to Billy. I want him to know how I feel. Telling Jace about him I realized that I've never told Billy those things. And now he's so…distant. I feel as though we're never on the same page."

Liv hoped the look on her face didn't give anything away. They were definitely on the same page this time.

"What are your plans for the rest of the day?"

"I don't know." Renie walked to the window. "Maybe I should drive to Monument and have this out with him once and for all."

Oh God, what was Liv supposed to say now? "Uh...I heard there was a storm coming over the pass, I don't think you should risk it." Liv hadn't heard that, but doubted Renie ever listened to weather reports.

"Seriously Mom, I talk big. Can you imagine me confronting Billy that way? I don't think so. I do want to talk to him though."

Thank goodness, thought Liv. Billy better put his plan into action soon. "Why don't you go for a ride honey? The fresh air will do you good, and the weather won't stay this nice much longer."

"I think I will, especially if there's a storm coming in. Thanks Mom."

That would buy her time to call Billy and find out what his plan was. She wished they'd talked more about it yesterday.

"Will you calm down?" Billy said when she called him.

"I know, I'm a nervous wreck."

"She isn't going anywhere. She'll take a ride, talk it out with Pooh for a while, then...knowing her, she'll come in, eat, and then crawl in bed with a book."

Liv laughed at how well Billy knew her daughter. That was exactly what she'd do. And then when she least expected it, he'd show up and whisk her away. By then, Liv would be at his new house with Willow. She wished she could send Ben in her place so she could be home when Billy got here.

***

"Your daddy looks so handsome, doesn't he baby girl?"

Liv's level of nervousness earlier was nothing compared to how nervous Billy was now. She didn't think she'd ever seen him nervous, about anything.

"Are you gonna be okay?" he asked her.

"Me? What about you?"

"It's the rest of my life Livvie. And your life too, right Willow?" Billy kissed Willow for the hundredth time since Liv had gotten there.

"She calms you down."

"Yep. She's the only one who does, other than Renie."

"It'll be fine."

"I'm hoping for a hell of a lot better than fine Liv."

"Yeah, that's what I meant." She reached up and kissed his cheek. *"Bonne chance!"*

"Thanks, I think. Oh, keep your eye on this one, she took a few steps today."

"Billy! Are you kidding? Willow took her first steps today? That's a huge milestone."

"I know it is Liv. Jeez. I got it recorded for Grandma and Grandpa. And you can see it tomorrow if you want to. In fact, I'm sure you'll see it with your own eyes in a few minutes. If you put her down that is. You can't be holdin' her all the time, you'll spoil her."

Liv grinned. She loved seeing Billy as a father. If anyone had asked her years ago what kind of daddy he'd be, she wouldn't have known what to say. Now, she couldn't imagine a better dad in the world, except for Ben, of course. He was great with his boys, and would be with their baby too. She rubbed her belly and smiled.

"Ben's gone, right?"

"Yep, he and the boys are at a movie, and they're going to eat afterwards. Then they're coming here."

"Okay, I gotta get this show on the road. Bye-bye Willow. Daddy loves you so much. Bye Livvie, thanks again for this." He was out the door before Liv could answer him.

He pulled the truck over twice on his way to the Rice Ranch. He wished he'd had a drink, but he didn't want Renie to smell alcohol on his breath. It wouldn't have helped his nervousness anyway.

***

Renie was getting irritated with Billy. She texted him an hour ago, and he still hadn't answered her. What the hell was he doing anyway? Maybe he was busy with Willow, and surprisingly, that part of it didn't irritate her. It made her smile. In fact, she planned to ask him to text her pictures. Maybe they'd even try Facetime tonight. That was if he ever answered her.

A knock on the door startled her. As much as she didn't want to crawl out of bed, she had to. Ben and her mom were out with the boys for the afternoon, and she was home alone. She looked in the mirror as she walked past it. It wasn't a pretty sight; she should take a shower soon.

She opened the door without looking, and took a step backwards. It was Billy, and she wasn't sure she'd ever seen him look as good as he did at that moment. She looked him up and down, leaning against the door jam.

"Hi."

"Hi yourself," he smiled at her.

God she loved his smile.

"You gonna invite me in or feast me with your eyes out here on the porch sugar?"

She remembered another night he said almost those same words to her. She stepped aside and waved him in.

"I've been texting you."

"I know."

"You couldn't have told me you were in town? It would've been nice if I had at least taken a shower today," she laughed. "And look at you cowboy...so handsome."

"Why thank you ma'am." He handed her the daisies he held behind his back. "For you."

"Wow. Flowers. Thank you, they're beautiful. My favorite."

"I know they are."

"What's going on Billy? When did you get into town?"

"We'll talk about that later. Why don't you go take a shower and get ready?"

"Ready for what?"

"Just get ready. Like you're goin' out."

"Goin' out where?"

"Jesus girl, look at how I'm dressed and figure it out."

There he was, the Billy she loved so much. She missed him, his self-assuredness, his cockiness. It was one of her favorite things about him.

"Don't want to help me get ready?"

"Yes I do. But I'm not gonna. We'll never leave this house if I do and I've got plans. So stop temptin' me and *go get ready.*"

"Okay, okay. I'm going," she walked toward the stairs, but turned around and smiled at him. "I'm so glad you're here Billy."

"Whoo-wee Renie. I told you to quit temptin' me. You keep smilin' at me that way…"

She ran down the stairs before he finished his sentence.

Billy took a deep breath in when she came upstairs. She had on a dark gray cashmere sweater. She knew he loved it. It was so soft, he loved holding her and sliding his hands up under that sweater. Oh God, he needed to stop thinking about sliding his hands anywhere on her body, or his plans would be shot to shit.

"You look beautiful," he said as she stood in front of him. He looked her up and down. She had a tight black skirt on that came just above her knees, black tights and little black ankle boots. She left her hair loose, the way he loved it, down over her shoulders. He could eat her up, she looked so good.

"Let's go," he said, pulling her toward the door. "Do you have a jacket?"

"Will I need one?"

"We'll be out late, so yeah."

She grabbed a black leather jacket off the coat rack near the front door.

"Where are we going?"

"You'll see."

Billy drove toward town, but kept going, in the direction of the ski area. When they passed it, she had no idea where he was taking her.

"Billy?"

"We are going to see the most beautiful view of the sunset in all of the valley."

And Then You Dance

"Okay." At least that explained why he was in such a hurry, the sun would be going down soon. She wondered how he knew about the view though.

They stopped at a curve on the side of the road. Billy backed the truck in and turned it off. He was right, the view was spectacular—in the other direction.

He got out, walked around to her side, and opened the door. "Come with me," he said.

He'd lowered the tailgate of the truck when he came around, and Renie saw he had blankets and pillows in the back, along with two glasses and a bottle of wine.

"Ooh, romantic."

"That was the plan." He lifted her up so she could easily scoot back on the blankets. He opened the wine and poured her a glass first, then one for himself.

"Are you hungry?" He hadn't thought to bring anything to eat for this part of their evening.

"No, I'm fine," she snuggled into him and watched as the sky turned different colors.

"Good." He turned his head toward hers and kissed her. It was heaven, being here with her, kissing her. *Heaven*. He took her wine glass and set it down along with his, so he could kiss her harder, and hold her, feel her against him.

"We're missing the sunset," she whispered.

He tucked her back against him and turned to watch it.

"Billy, I was kidding."

"I know you were. But we're here for a reason. So you're right, let's watch it."

He brought her in closer, and she tucked one of her legs in between his. "Are you cold?" He grabbed another blanket and threw it over them.

"No, I'm fine," she said again.

"Renie?"

"Yeah?"

"I think I figured out what you're afraid of." He heard the catch in her breath, and felt her body tense up. "And there are some promises I want to make you. Important promises."

She didn't say anything, but he hadn't expected her to.

"The first thing I want to promise you is that I'll never, ever stop paying attention to you. I mean it. Forever Renie—for the rest of our lives."

He handed her glass of wine back to her, and touched it with his.

"That's the first promise."

"Okay."

He didn't say anything else for a few minutes. He wanted each promise he made her to sink in. He wanted her to have plenty of time to think it over and say anything she wanted to say.

"It's beautiful here, isn't it?" he said as the sun sank further behind the mountain.

"It is. I never knew about this place. I've never driven farther down this road than the ski area."

"Most people don't. That's part of what makes it special. If you keep going, you eventually come to Gothic Valley. We'll come out here and hike sometime."

"I'd like that."

He waited a few more minutes.

"There's another promise I want to make you Renie."

"Okay."

"I promise that we will always have special moments, just like these. Time that we set aside for us. Just the two of us. Forever Renie—for the rest of our lives."

She looked into his eyes, but again, didn't say anything.

They sat in silence until the sun tucked all the way behind the mountain. He moved the blankets off of them.

"Come on, time to move on to our next stop." He took her by the hand and pulled her toward the tailgate. He lifted her off and carried her back to the passenger door.

"Billy, what are you doing?"

"This way I get to hold you a little bit longer."

"You can hold me as long as you want to Billy. We could—"

"Nope. I've got a plan and I'm stickin' with it. I don't care how hard you try to tempt me into doin' somethin' else."

The way she smiled at him though, he wanted to drive back to Ben's house, and take her straight to bed. But that wasn't what tonight was all about.

Instead, he drove into town, and parked in front of a little cabin on a side street. Renie immediately recognized where they were. Soupcon was one of the most romantic restaurants in Crested Butte. They served French food, in two *prix fixe* seatings. It didn't look as though they were open, however.

Once again Billy came around and opened her door for her. He took her hand and led her to the front door of the cabin. When he opened it, she gasped.

The entire dining area was awash in candlelight. One table was set, in the center of the room. The rest of the tables were bare, except for their tablecloths.

"Wow," she murmured. "It looks so beautiful."

"Welcome Mr. Patterson," a gentleman Renie didn't recognize greeted them. "Thank you for joining us this evening. Mademoiselle?"

He led them to the table, and before he could pull out Renie's chair for her, Billy stepped in front of him, and did it himself. The man stepped back and smiled.

When Billy sat down, the man disappeared into the back.

"Who is that?" she asked him.

"That's Tal. You've never met him?"

"I know Jason, but I've never seen Tal before."

The sous chef rarely came out of the kitchen, but Renie was happy to be able to put a face with the name. Jason, the head chef, was more often the face of the team renowned in the valley for their superb cuisine.

Renie realized the wine glasses on the table had already been poured. She took a sip. It was the same wine they'd been drinking before.

She looked around. "Are we here alone tonight?" You couldn't get into the restaurant without a reservation, and they were usually booked weeks in advance.

"Tonight? Yes, we are."

"Why?"

"Because I requested it."

He took her hand in his and brought it to his lips. "Look at me," he said. "There's another promise I want to make to you."

He waited until he was sure he had her attention, that she was looking in his eyes, listening.

"I promise that I will always listen to you, even when you aren't talking."

"Billy—"

He picked up her wine glass and handed it to her, before picking his up and touching it to hers. "Forever Renie—for the rest of our lives."

Jason came out from the back with their first course.

"Foie gras with brioche toast points on a bed of truffled apple and chive greens with raspberry coulis, sauternes gelee and demi glace," he said before disappearing back into the kitchen.

"Billy this is so…romantic." She kissed him, hard, on the lips.

He reached around and grasped the back of her neck with his hand, holding her there, kissing her more deeply. "I love you so much," he murmured before moving away from her.

Chapter Twenty-One

Music played softly in the background. The voice was so familiar. It dawned on Renie who was singing. It was Ben, but in a way she'd never heard him perform before, just his voice, accompanied by a piano.

"What is this?" she asked.

"Hmm?"

"The music. What is it?"

"A gift, from Ben."

"Why?"

"Because I requested it."

"I've never heard him this way," Renie murmured.

"Beautiful, isn't it? Like you."

He brought her hand to his lips again, and kissed across the back of it. "Dance with me," he said.

He stood and held his hand out to her. Someone turned the music up slightly, and he moved her across the open floor.

"I love having you in my arms."

She leaned further into him.

"I remember the first time I held you this way. Close to me. Your body touching mine, this way." He kissed her neck, below her ear, softly. "I wanted you then Renie. I wanted to make love to you that night. Did you know? Did you feel it?"

She knew exactly when he meant. And yes, she'd felt it. "I wanted it too Billy."

He led her back to the table when the song ended, and pulled her chair out for her. When she was seated, he moved her hair over her shoulder, leaned down and kissed the back of her neck. She shivered as the current from his lips ran throughout her body.

He sat, and this time Tal came out from the kitchen.

"How is everything?" he asked.

"Wonderful," Renie answered.

Jason joined him with their next course.

"Spiced carrot soup," he said. "With paprika-roasted crab, and pistachio dust. *Bon appetit.*"

The two men disappeared again.

Billy raised his glass. "Another promise Renie."

She raised hers too, and waited.

"I promise to dance with you, hold you close, touch your body with mine. I never want us to lose that connection."

This time Renie touched her glass to his first. She closed her eyes, took a deep breath, and opened them. The smile she gave him, he could conquer the world in the name of that smile. "Forever Renie—for the rest of our lives."

They were both quiet, looking into each other's eyes.

"What *is* this?" she murmured.

"He calls it *Patience.*"

Oh, love, it's a difficult thing for me
I always want too much
And end up lonely
Over my head
Awkwardly
Hands in my pockets
Laugh in the wrong place and want to leave

Cause I'm not patient and I should be
Because I know I have it in me

"I love it. Is he recording it?"
"He said he might be."

Tal came out and cleared their plates. He refilled their wine glasses and once again, disappeared.
"Another dance?" Billy asked.
"I'd love it," she answered.
This time Billy moved slower, and kissed her. Their bodies stopped moving as their lips sought each other's. Billy ran his hands down the sleeves of her sweater.
"So soft," he said. "My favorite."
"Why I wore it."
"When you came upstairs and I saw you in it, all I could think about was running my hands under it, feeling your skin, caressing you with my hands." He slipped his hands under her sweater and circled her waist, slowly inching up.

The song ended, but he continued to hold her close to him, his hands touching her, moving slowly up and down her back.

"I promise to show you with my eyes, my hands, my lips, and every other part of my body, how much I love you, how much I desire you."

He began to sway again, to the music, dancing her back closer to the table. "Forever Renie—for the rest of our lives."

"I love you Billy." She held him tighter and lay her head against his chest.

"Our next course should be coming at any moment, although right now, the only appetite I seem to have is for you."

He pulled her chair out again, and as before, he moved her hair to the side, to kiss the back of her neck.

"I love it when you let your hair down Renie, when you let it fall over your shoulders. You wore it this way for me tonight, didn't you?"

"Mmm hmm," she murmured, falling back against him.

When Jason came out from the back, Billy sat back down.

"Elk tenderloin with truffle-whipped potatoes, baby carrots, and roasted baby beets," he said, setting a plate in front of each of them.

They sat quietly after they finished their entrée. More of Ben's music serenading them.

That's when I met your mother,
The girl of my dreams,
The most beautiful woman I'd ever seen.
She said boy can I tell you a wonderful thing
I can't help but notice you staring at me
I know I shouldn't say this
But I really believe
I can tell by your eyes
That you're in love with me.

"This is such a different style for him."
"He said he's never written this way before."

"He loves her so much, doesn't he?" she asked.
"He does."

Billy stroked her face. He looked into her eyes and she could see it, feel it—how much he loved her.

"I promise to love you, with everything I am and everything I'll ever be, to give you my heart, to hold in your hand, forever Renie—for the rest of our lives," he said.

She closed her eyes, and smiled.

"You are so beautiful," he said.

"So are you," she answered.

Jason joined them once again. "Your final course this evening," he said, setting one large wine glass between the two of them. "Strawberries, raspberries, and blackberries, with Grand Marnier and Crème Anglaise." He winked at Renie before he left them alone.

"Billy, this has been a magnificently romantic evening. I love it so much, and you so much, for doing this. I want you to know what it means to me."

"I would do anything for you." He gripped the back of her neck and brought her head to his, until her forehead touched his. "*Anything.* I love you so much. I cannot live without you. Do you understand me?"

There was a cry in his voice that she understood all too well. She felt it in her soul, whenever she thought about losing him. What if she lost him? How could she go on if she lost him?

And then, as if he could read her thoughts, he said, "I promise to do everything in my power to never, ever leave you—forever Renie, for the rest of our lives."

She cried then. Because that was her fear. What if she had to go through life as her mother had, without him, the love of her life?

What if she fell in love with Willow too, and Billy left them both? How could she go on…without him? She wasn't as strong as her mother was. She wouldn't be able to do it. She couldn't raise Willow on her own, without him.

His eyes bored into hers. Even through her tears she could feel the heat of them. He understood. That was what he was trying to tell her. What he'd been trying to tell her all night.

"Oh God, Billy," she cried. "I'm so scared."

"I know," he whispered.

He took her hand. He slipped something on her finger. She could barely see it through her tears. It didn't matter what it looked like. What it meant mattered.

"Marry me Irene Louise Fairchild. Love me and let me love you, forever, for the rest of our lives."

"Yes Billy, I'll marry you," she answered. "And I'll love you, and let you love me. Forever—for the rest of our lives,"

The drive back to the ranch was serene. That's what he was feeling. Serenity.

"Where is everybody?" she asked when they drove up to the house.

"Camp-out."

"Camp-out? It's freezing. Where did they go?"

"My house."

"Your house? All of them? Don't the boys have school tomorrow?"

"I'll take you there tomorrow. It's in town."

"Billy what are you talking about?"

"We have a house in Crested Butte now. You and me. And Willow."

She gasped. "*What did you do?* You didn't sell the ranch did you?"

He looked at her and smiled. "No, of course I didn't sell the ranch. Silly girl."

"But, you bought a house here?"

"Yep."

"Why?"

"Because I wanted to. Are you ready to go inside?"

"I guess so. Are we staying here tonight? Alone?"

"Yep, we are."

"Then, yes. I'm definitely ready to go inside."

They were just inside the front door when Billy spun her around, and ran his hands under her sweater.

"Everything else off, except this," he murmured.

She led him into the great room and motioned for him to light the fireplace while she started to undress. "Light the fire," she grinned.

"Oh baby, you have no idea how hot my fire already is."

Renie spread a blanket out in front of the fireplace, and tossed a couple of pillows on top of it.

"C'mere, so I can hug you," Billy said. "God, you're so sexy."

He sat down with his back up against the coffee table. Renie sat in front of him. She leaned back and closed her eyes.

"I want to remember every moment of this night." He moved his hands up from her waist to her breasts. "I love this sweater," he said, nuzzling his cheek against her shoulder. "But not as much as I love what's under it."

Renie turned around to face him. "Kiss me."

"God, I can feel your heart pounding under my hand," Billy said. His kiss was hard and raw. "Tonight is the night we started our forever Renie."

His body was tight with everything he'd been holding in for so long. All of the emotion he'd felt for the last eight months, the uncertainty of what would happen between them, came flowing out of him.

He wasn't gentle, he plundered. He didn't give, he took. And she was as eager as he was, her passion for him was that of desperate need. She was no longer afraid, there was no fear. When she trembled, it was with longing.

Renie wanted to remember every moment as much as he did. She wanted to wrap it up and keep it in her heart, so when she felt doubt, she could pull it out and blanket herself in it.

She wrapped her body around his, taking what she wanted—tasting, savoring, lingering.

And then suddenly, everything changed. What was once frantic between them became a slow dance of hands and lips and murmurs. Billy started to stroke his hands, slowly, over her body. "I want to own every inch of this body." He kissed down the side of her arm, then her waist, and down her hip. Her lips began taking their ownership of his body too.

"I've got to be inside you Renie. I need to be. I want to fill you, join with you, never be separated from you."

"Hurry," she answered, and again their pace changed. They were lost in each other, delirious as they quivered together.

Billy reached up and held her face in his hands. "You and me, forever—for the rest of our lives."

"Billy," she whispered, half hoping she wouldn't wake him. She wanted a few minutes to look at him. They hadn't talked about when yet, but soon Billy would be her husband. They would spend the rest of their lives together, as friends, as lovers, as soul mates. They would be partners, companions on life's journey.

Tomorrow their journey would begin. And the first step would be meeting his daughter. The little girl Renie had been so afraid to share him with. She prayed she'd have the strength to let those fears go, and learn to love her without hesitation.

He told her, in all his promises tonight, that he understood. He promised to pay attention to her, to listen, to plan special moments for the two of them. And most importantly, he promised not to leave her.

Her brain told her it was a promise he didn't have power over, but her heart knew that Billy understood how great that fear was for her. The more they talked about it, gave it words, the more that fear would distillate.

Her love for him was something pure, the essence of who she was. Acknowledging, rather than burying, her feelings would bring them closer together, instead of driving them apart. She should have trusted Billy would know that. He knew how she felt, he knew what to say, he knew how to comfort her. All those months she'd gone without his comfort, when it was the thing she needed more than air, or sustenance.

Billy was awake and studying her. "You are so lost in thought. Every memory I have of you there is a component of it that involves me wonderin' what you were thinkin'. There is always somethin' goin' through this beautiful head of yours," he stroked her hair and moved it away from her face. "I want to be the man who gets the rare and special privilege of being the recipient of your thoughts. The one you trust enough to share them with. To get the gift of you. Will you let me be that man?"

"You are that man Billy. Every thought has been yours, because they are all of you. All my life you have been the voice, the face, the smile in my head. Even when I couldn't talk to you, I heard you. And I felt you. I never doubted that you loved me. Not ever."

"We talked about us tonight Renie. We need to talk about Willow. I need to know how you're feeling, what you're thinking."

"I don't feel as afraid. I'm not as worried about how I'll share you with her, because I know there will be a part of you that you keep just for me."

"Always. There will always be a part of me that is for you alone. And if we give Willow brothers and sisters, there will still be a part of me that belongs to you. In the same way that no matter how many people I have to share you with, I know there is a part of your heart you'll keep separate for me."

"You know me so well. You know the perfect thing to say. Don't you?"

"It isn't so much that I know what to say, it's more that I know what to feel. I can feel you. When you're scared, I feel it. When you're worried, I feel it."

She smiled and started to speak. He put his fingers on her lips to silence her.

"That's how it's always been for you, hasn't it? Even when you were a little girl, you knew how I was feeling."

"Yes," she answered simply.

"That's why I'm grounded when I'm with you, because you do that for me."

"I do."

"I want to be the person who grounds you."

"You do Billy. You're the only one who ever has."

"We need to talk about Jace too."

"Oh Billy, it isn't necessary, we're—"

"Friends. I know. You're good friends. Jace is a good guy. And you know, he's also family, in a weird and convoluted third-cousin-in-law way."

"Why are you talking about him as though you know him?"

"Because he called me."

That made her pay attention. "He did?"

"Yep. He did. That's how good of a friend he is to you."

"Oh." Her brow furrowed, and she started to tuck her hands under her legs. Billy took her arm and pulled one back out.

"Listen to me." He put his hand on her chin and turned her head, so she was looking into his eyes. "There wasn't anything Jace said to me that I didn't already know. He cares enough about you to want to make sure of it."

He winked then. "Before he gave me his permission to ask you to marry me."

"You're kidding."

"I am…a little," he laughed. "I talked to your mom too."

"That explains the conversation she and I had this morning. She was apologizing for not being a better mother to me."

"Oh no," he shook his head. "I gotta tell you, she was a nervous wreck. I thought sure she would blow the whole surprise because she was."

"And that explains even more."

"Hey, can we go get into a real bed?" he said, changing the subject. "If we sleep on the floor all night, no matter how romantic it is, I won't be able to move tomorrow. You gotta remember, I'm *a lot* older than you are. And you're the one who's gonna have to take care of me."

"I've had fantasies about you sneaking into my bedroom Billy…let's see if we can play out some of those tonight."

Billy was up in a flash. "You wanna play out fantasies sugar, I'm your man." He kissed the side of your face. "I'm your man no matter what," he said more seriously.

"Before we go to sleep, I promised I'd text your mom. And if I don't, she'll make Ben crazy 'cause I'm sure she's pacin' the floor wondering what's happening with us. This next part is important. Are you paying attention?"

"Yes Billy," she rolled her eyes at him.

"How do you want to handle things with Willow tomorrow? Do you want them to come back here, and bring Willow with them? Or would you rather you and I go to the house."

"I don't know. What do you want to do?"

"I don't think it matters."

"There."

"You're sure."

"Yep. Positive."

"How did you go from not knowing to being so positive?"

"'Cause you bought a house. And even though I'm not sure why you did, I'm guessing it'll be our home at least part of the year."

"Yeah, still not following what this has to do with Willow."

"Let's christen our new home together, the three of us. As a family."

"I like it." He leaned over and kissed her. "I also bought it so we could have a place near your mom."

"I know."

"I want our family to grow Renie. There isn't anything I want more than for us to have another baby. I want to start working on that right away."

"Maybe we should stop talking and start working on those fantasies I mentioned then."

* * *

Renie woke up to the sounds of Jake and Luke clomping down the stairs to throw their stuff from their "camp-out," in their bedrooms, they were arguing about something on top of it.

"Jeez, have they ever heard of inside voices?" said Billy.

"You better get used to a lot of noise if you're serious about us adding to our family."

"You know what I realized?"

"What's that?"

"We're both only children."

"You *just* realized it?"

"No, that's not what I mean. I mean I don't have any experience with sibling rivalry, and that kind of shit. Do you?"

"We'll buy books."

"Yeah, I bet my mama's already thought of that. You should see all the books she bought me after I brought Willow home. And she was on my case every minute to make sure I read 'em too."

"Billy?"

"Yeah baby?"

"Let's go. I don't want to wait anymore."

He got up and hugged her. "Sure, of course, we can go as soon as you want."

She got up and pulled a duffel bag out of her closet. She started pulling stuff out of drawers and throwing them in the bag. "We can come back and get more later, but for now I want to have enough clothes with me, so we don't have to worry about it for a few days. Oh. Wait."

Wait? What was wrong? Shit. He'd just started to get comfortable. He pulled her into a hug, and rested his chin on the top of her head. "Tell me."

"It isn't Thanksgiving yet. Maybe you need to get back to the ranch. I didn't think…I'm sorry."

"Everything you assumed was right. *We* aren't goin' to the ranch, until *we* decide we want to. I'm not on a timetable. Okay? Willow's here, you're here, that's all I need in life. Doesn't matter where we are as long as we're all together."

Ben was in the kitchen making breakfast when they came upstairs. "Well good morning," he said.

"Good morning," they both answered.

"I hear congratulations in order."

Renie held her hand out for Ben to see her ring. The smile she had on her face melted Billy's heart. That was happiness right there. If happiness had a look, it was on Renie's face.

The ring had belonged to Dottie's mother. The art deco designed featured a single, round, two-carat diamond in the center, ringed with eight small sapphires. Between each of the sapphires were small round diamonds. On the outside were diamond-filled leaf patterns.

"Wow. Gorgeous. And you picked that out all on your own Patterson? Didn't think the cowboy had it in him."

"You throw that word around an awful lot for bein' pretty close to one yourself Rice."

"Oh stop. Are you two going to spend the rest of your lives calling each other by your last names? That'll be as annoying as it is confusing." Renie put one hand on each of their shoulders. "And Ben, the ring belonged to Billy's grandmother. I've never seen anything this beautiful. I'm so honored to have it."

"Yeah, okay, it's nice. I'll give you that," answered Ben. "But, I'm not very happy with him right at the moment," he said with a growl.

"Why the hell not?" Billy answered with an equal amount of indignation.

"I heard all about your proposal last night. Put me and the little song I wrote for Liv when I proposed to shame."

Renie hugged Ben. "Your proposal to my mom couldn't have been more perfect, and you know it."

Ben smiled at her. He said a lot with his smile. When you were given the gift of one, you knew he really liked you.

"Ready?" Billy asked.

"Yep, let's go. Bye Ben. Say goodbye to the boys for me too. They're downstairs fighting, and I don't want to get in the middle of it this morning."

"Wait, what? You're leaving? I made breakfast." He waved his hands over the huge breakfast he had just finished preparing.

"Sorry Ben," said Renie. "We're having breakfast at home this morning."

"Good luck with that," he mumbled. "You don't have a refrigerator let alone anything to eat breakfast on."

"Oh...yeah...I guess I left that out Renie. We don't exactly have anything *in* the house yet. We just have the house."

"Then we'll have to stop and get coffee and some of your favorite pastries on our way home."

"See?" Billy said to Ben. "See how she is? And she's mine. All mine. She's perfect, and she's all mine."

Ben rolled his eyes but smiled as he waved them off.

Chapter Twenty-Two

"Well, hi there," Liv said softly when Billy and Renie walked in the back door.

"Is she asleep?" he asked.

"Just dozed off," she whispered.

Billy took Willow out of Liv's arms. When he did, she rubbed her face against his chest. "Dadada," she murmured and smiled. Her voice sounded so sleepy, but she picked up her head and looked straight at Renie.

"Bah," she said and then continued on with an unintelligible string of babble.

Renie got closer to Willow and her daddy. "Hi," she said softly.

Willow tucked her face into Billy's chest again, then turned and gave Renie a shy smile.

Not knowing what her reaction might be, Renie took a deep breath, and held her hands out to see if Willow would come to her. She didn't even hesitate.

Billy thought he might pass out, he'd been holding his breath so long. He watched as Renie walked over to the blanket Liv had spread out on the floor that was covered with Willow's toys and books. She sat down, still holding Willow in her arms, and picked up a stuffed monkey with one hand.

"Who's this?" she asked.

"Mun," Willow answered taking the monkey from Renie's hand. She held it up to Renie's lips. Renie gave the monkey a kiss. Then Willow brought the monkey to her lips and kissed it too.

Billy turned to look at Liv, who was trying to wipe the tears away before anyone noticed. They were falling from her eyes too quickly for her to catch them all.

He put his arm around her. "Thanks," he said.

She rested her head on his shoulder. "They're beautiful," she answered.

Willow put her head down on the pillow and stretched her little body out. She patted the pillow. "Seep," she said pointing at the blanket.

Renie stretched out right beside her. She tucked her arm under Willow's head; the baby snuggled up against her.

"You okay?" Billy whispered.

Renie nodded her head.

He put a blanket over the two of them, and then kissed each of their foreheads. He went back to where Liv was standing, near the back door.

"That was a little slice of heaven, watching that," he said while Liv gathered her things.

"It'll take time, but if you let them get to know each other on their own terms, it'll seem like no time at all."

"Okay, Grandma," he winked at her.

"And no interfering. As soon as you start telling Renie how to act around Willow, it'll blow up in your face."

Billy laughed out loud. "Because I've always had luck telling Irene Fairchild how to act. Give me a break Livvie."

"I'm just saying, let her learn the way you did. You had time alone with Willow to figure it out. I'm not saying you should leave them alone, just be sure to give them enough space."

"You done?" he smirked.

"No. I'm not. You screw this up Billy Patterson, and I'll tell *your* mother."

He kissed Liv goodbye and came back to where his girls were stretched out on the blanket. He snuggled up on the other side of Willow, who had drifted off to sleep. "Can I join you?" he whispered.

Renie nodded again, and then closed her eyes. Billy closed his too, dozing, but shaking himself awake every so often; to make sure he wasn't dreaming. Willow had her head on Renie's chest, her little arm tucked into Renie's side. He could tell by their breathing that they were both sound asleep.

When he woke up, the two of them were in the kitchen. He wasn't sure how long he slept, but he was starving.

"Find anything good to eat in there?" he said to them.

Willow came running at him and jumped on top of him, smiling and covering him with kisses. She stopped, turned toward Renie and held out her hand. "Bah," she said.

"I'm dying to know what Bah means," she laughed. "I think it's her name for me."

Billy looked at Willow, and then pointed to Renie, smiling at her. "Mama," he said. He pointed back at his baby girl, "Willow." Then back at Renie, "Mama."

"Bah-ma," Willow answered.

"Okay," he said. "Bah-ma. We'll start with that."

He looked back at Renie who appeared unfazed.

"You okay?"

"Yes Billy," she rolled her eyes at him. "I've grown accustomed to your no-holds-barred approach to things. Willow and I met an hour ago, and you're introducing me as 'mama,' why wouldn't I be okay?"

The look on her face told him she was kidding, or at least not mad at him.

"I'm starving. Are you as hungry as I am?" he asked.

"More."

"Wanna have dinner with me?"

"Who's cooking?"

"You are."

Renie laughed. "Then we better go shopping. I'll need a stove, a refrigerator, pots and pans…"

"Maybe we better eat out for the next couple of days." He picked up Willow. "Or go to Grandma's house. Wanna go to Grandma's house Willow?"

"If you're referring to my mother, I can't wait to see the look on her face the first time you refer to her as 'Grandma.'"

"Too late."

"Huh?"

"While you and Willow were sleeping, we had a conversation. I snuck it in to see how she'd react."

"And?"

"I don't think she even noticed. She continued right along with the lecture she was in the middle of givin' me."

Renie held out her hands and Willow maneuvered over to her. "Let's go see Grandma then. And Grandpa too."

"Oh I'm gonna love this," said Billy. "*Grandpa Ben.* This is gonna be *good*."

"She likes you," Billy said on the ride to Ben and Liv's.

"I like her too." Renie turned around to look at Willow who had dozed off in her car seat. "She's easy to like."

"So are you."

She was very easy to like. Easy to love too. But the likability part, Billy believed that was what Willow was responding to.

Even when she was a little girl, Renie had a sense of calm about her that soothed everyone around her. He hadn't been worried as much about how Willow would respond to Renie. He had been more worried about how Renie would respond to Willow. So far, it was good.

He wondered how long it would take before he'd let himself breathe easy, how long it would be before he felt they were really going to be okay.

When they got to the house, Luke was on the front porch waiting for them.

"Did you bring Willow?" he asked.

"Nope, we left her back at the house."

"What?!"

"Luke," Renie said, messing up his hair. "He's kidding. She's in her car seat."

"Are you gonna get her out?"

Billy started to say something, but Renie interrupted him. "Yes, Billy will get her out. What's up Luke?"

"Nuthin'," he said, looking down at his feet. "She's kinda fun to play with I guess."

Ben came out on the porch. "Willow follows Luke around wherever he goes. And she laughs at everything he says. Little bit of hero worship."

Billy lifted Willow out of the car, who squealed with delight when she saw Luke. "Down," she said, clear as could be.

"Hey *Grandpa,* got any cold beer."

Ben smiled at Billy and raised his hand. Renie closed hers around his before he could make a gesture that either of the kids might mimic.

"I'll get even with him," he whispered to Renie. "Thinks he's so damn funny. I'll get him when he least expects it."

"Hey there. Didn't want to order take-out tonight? Can't say as I blame you," said Liv.

"Hey Mom." Renie hugged her hard. "Thank you so much."

"Oh sweet girl, I'm not exactly sure what you're thanking me for, but you're welcome anyway."

"For everything, basically."

They heard a loud crash, followed by a wail out of Willow. Billy went running toward the porch, Renie and Liv followed. Ben was out in front of them.

"I'm sorry Dad, I don't know what happened," Luke was standing near Willow, and he was starting to cry himself.

"What did she hit?" Billy shouted as he tried to find something to stop the blood that was flowing from the gash in her head.

"Here," said Ben, handing Billy his shirt. "Head wounds bleed like crazy. It looks worse than it is." He turned to Liv, "Go get the keys to the truck baby."

Renie walked over to Luke, who buried his head up against her. "She'll be okay, it'll be okay," she said to him over and over again.

Billy caught her eye while he was waiting for Liv to bring the truck around. "You can stay here—"

"No, I'll go with you." Renie leaned closer to Luke. "You stay here with your dad okay? We're taking Willow to see a doctor, but I meant what I said. She'll be okay."

"Okay," he said, still sniffling.

"Renie, can you drive?" Billy asked her. Willow was still screaming and trying to wiggle out of Billy's arms.

"Of course." She took the keys from her mom and started to get into the truck.

"Bah-ma," Willow started screaming between her wails, still trying to wiggle away from Billy.

Renie looked at him; he was as white as a sheet.

"Mom, can you come with us?" Renie said. "Can you drive? Billy, get into the back seat with Willow."

Liv took the keys from her, and Renie climbed into the back seat. Since there wasn't a car seat in Ben's truck, she could scoot to the middle, and sit right next to them.

"Are you okay?" Billy asked her.

"I'm fine, and you are too aren't you precious? You're gonna be fine, aren't you?" Renie kept repeating soothing words to Willow who continued to do her best to escape her father's grasp.

"How's the bleeding?" she asked.

Billy lifted Ben's blood-soaked shirt up, afraid of what he'd find. "Looks as though it stopped."

"Let's keep the shirt where it was, but why don't you try to move her over to me."

"Are you sure?" Billy looked down at his daughter who he was holding around the waist with one arm while he kept the shirt pressed against the gash with the other. It dawned on him that he was holding her so tightly he might be hurting her.

"You want to come sit on Bah-ma's lap Willow? You can if you want to."

Willow reached out to her, and Renie lifted her to her lap.

"You're gonna get blood all over you."

Renie glared at him.

"Sorry, here," he handed her the shirt to put up against Willow's head.

"You doin' okay back there?" Liv asked from the driver's seat.

"We're okay Mom. Thanks for driving."

"I'm a better driver than a nurse," Liv answered. "The time I had to take you to the emergency room, Bill had to go with me. Do you remember that Billy? You were a teenager."

"I remember every second of it," Billy answered looking out the window.

"You do?" Renie whispered.

"We thought you broke your arm. I've never been so scared in my life. Until maybe now."

"Why?"

"Why what?"

"Why were you scared?"

"Because you were." He rubbed his hand over his face. "And I had no idea how to make you feel better." He rubbed Willow's back. "She's calming down now that she's with you."

Renie kissed Willow's forehead. "Feeling better little one?" she whispered. Willow was still crying, but the wailing had subsided.

"You're so good with her," he said and looked back toward the window.

Liv looked in the rear view mirror, she could see Billy's reflection in it. He looked like a man in pain, and it wasn't just worry. He looked as though he was about to cry.

"The town clinic is open. They should be able to take care of her here," she said pulling into the parking lot.

"Billy get out here and help Renie, then I'll go park."

Billy was already halfway around the truck before she finished her sentence. Willow let him take her, but looked back to make sure Renie was following them.

They were in the back by the time Liv came inside.

"Hey Liv, how are you?" said Linda who manned the front desk.

"I'm doing okay, better than they are," she laughed a little. "I was the driver." She shuddered, "I'm way better with car keys than I am with blood."

"Skittish are you?"

"Yes, I could never have been a nurse."

Linda laughed. "Who was that with Renie? I told them to go back and we'd catch up on the paperwork after they saw the doctor."

"That's Billy Patterson and his daughter, Willow. Soon to be my son-in-law and grandchild."

"Oh." Linda raised her eyebrows.

"What?"

"Renie know what she's taking on?"

Linda had known Ben all his life, and consequently knew a lot about his family, and Liv, and now Renie. She made it her business to know as much as possible about the town's residents.

"She's known Billy a long time," Liv said before she stopped herself. She didn't owe Linda any explanations and neither did Renie.

Willow needed six staples to close up the gash in her head. When the doctor asked them what happened neither Billy nor Renie could answer him. They hadn't pressed Luke to tell them, they were more worried about getting Willow into town.

Billy didn't look as though he was getting any more color in his face. "Are you okay?" Renie asked him softly. The doctor had given Willow a shot to numb her before he put the staples in. That had been rough, but Willow was calmed down and playing with the buttons on Renie's shirt.

"I don't know," he answered. He got up and paced in the small space of the room they were in.

"She's doing better Billy. And she'll be fine."

"I know she is."

"Then what is it?"

He turned and stared at her for what seemed too long. "Can we talk about it later?" He averted his eyes from hers.

They both sat in the back seat with Willow again on the way home while Liv drove. By the time they got to the house, Willow was sound asleep.

"Do you want to stay here tonight?" Liv asked them. "Ben can run to town to get her porta-crib. That way you can sleep in a bed tonight instead of on an air mattress. And if you need anything we'll be here to help."

Renie looked at Billy, who didn't appear to be listening. "Billy, would that be okay?"

"What? Yeah, sure. Whatever you want to do is fine."

"Billy—"

"It's fine. Okay?" He got out of the truck and carried Willow inside.

"What's going on?" Liv whispered.

"I have no idea," answered Renie. "He's been acting this way since we saw the doctor."

"Post adrenalin-rush maybe."

"I get the impression he's angry with me about something."

"Why would he be angry with you?"

"Again, no idea."

"Where are they?" Renie asked Ben when she got inside.

"Downstairs. He wanted to make sure she stayed asleep."

Liv asked Ben to go into town to get the crib, and he told her his parents had one at their place. He'd run and get it.

"I better go check on them," Renie said once he'd left.

"Okay sweet girl. Let me know if you need anything."

Liv couldn't read the look on Billy's face on their way to the clinic, or his behavior on the way back. He was troubled by something, more than Willow's accident.

She went in search of Luke to see how he was feeling. He was playing a video game with Jake. Both of them were unusually quiet. She sat down with them, but let them keep playing. From where she was she could see the door to the bedroom where Renie was with Billy and Willow, and wondered about the conversation taking place in that room.

"Billy?" Renie said softly when she walked into the room.

"Shh," he answered. She turned on the small lamp on the dresser on the other side of the room so she could see where she was going.

She sat down on the bed. Willow was asleep between them. They stayed quiet for a few minutes. Renie lay down and let her eyes close.

"I don't understand it."

"Hmm? What did you say?" She must've dozed off.

"I don't understand why you did it."

"Did what Billy? What are you talking about?"

"Come on, let's not talk in here. I don't want her to wake up." His voice was a cross between a snap and a whisper.

They went out of the door and saw Liv and the boys in the family room.

Liv looked at them and then asked the boys to come upstairs with her. She thanked them for being so quiet, but suggested they give Billy and Renie privacy.

"Thanks," Renie murmured as they walked by.

Renie slid down the wall outside the bedroom door, and Billy sat down across from her with his back against the opposite wall.

"Tell me what's going on Billy."

"It hurts. It hurts that it took you so God damned long. And for no reason."

"*What* are you talking about?"

"*You*. You're so good with her. As though there's never been a problem. So why? Why did you take so *fucking* long Renie?"

She raised her knees up in front of her, crossed her arms over them and put her head down.

"Don't you dare hide from me. Answer me dammit. *Why?* You put me through hell, and now you act as if…"

"As if what Billy?"

He started to speak, and shook his head.

"You act as if you…care about her." His knees came up and he put his head down on his arms as she had. "It's makin' me fucking crazy."

Renie moved across the hall and sat up against him. "It wasn't her Billy. It was never Willow."

"Well what was it then? Huh? What? I'm trying to understand how you could go from not wanting to know her to being so good with her."

"I thought yesterday…I thought you understood."

"I did, part of it. But now…it seems as though it was all for nothing. All the hurt, all the time we were apart. There was no reason for it."

She didn't answer him. She got up, walked into her room, grabbed her shoes and jacket, and went upstairs. "Stay with her," she snapped at him.

She didn't see her mother when she got upstairs, but Ben was sitting at the table with the boys. They were eating ice cream.

"Where ya off to?" he asked her.

"Going for a walk," she said and slammed the front door closed behind her.

"What was that all about?" Liv asked, walking back into the kitchen.

All three of them shrugged their shoulders.

Liv found Billy sitting on the floor outside of the bedroom when she went downstairs.

"What's going on with you Patterson?"

"I'm pissed."

"I never would've guessed." She paused. "What are you pissed about?"

"That it's fine. It's all fine. Why the hell did it take us eight months to get here if there's no fucking problem?" he took a deep breath.

"Shit Liv, Willow loves Renie. Here I thought I was gonna have to run interference between them, ya know? But no, she's fine. And I'm not talkin' about Willow, I'm talkin' about Renie. Did you see her? *She was fine.* She was better than fine. She's great with Willow."

Liv took a deep breath herself, and waited for a couple of minutes before she answered him, trying to figure out how best to do it.

He didn't give her a chance. "I missed her so much. And there wasn't anything I could do about it. I couldn't leave Willow to come chasin' after Renie. Not when she was so little." He put his head back down on his arms.

"It's got to be one way or the other Billy. You have to decide which it will be and stick with it."

"What the hell are you talkin' about now Livvie?"

"You can't tell her you understood how she felt one minute, and then turn around and tell her you don't understand her actions the next. Her feelings drove her actions."

"But *she's fine.*"

"Billy, you know her. When has Renie *not* been fine?"

He didn't answer her.

"If you stopped for a minute and paid attention, you might find she's not fine. You might find she's scared to death by all of this. It's what she does. She keeps her feelings to herself when she thinks it might upset someone else. She pretends as though everything is fine until she gets to the point where she implodes. That's what these last eight months have been about. They haven't been about you, or about your daughter. They've been about *my* daughter."

Billy still didn't speak, but he was looking at her.

"Instead of being mad at her, maybe you should talk to her and see how she is. You won't find out by looking at her Billy. Jesus, haven't you learned anything?" Now Liv was mad, at Billy.

"Okay, okay, settle down now," he said. Jeez, he didn't need Liv mad at him now too.

"Don't you tell me to settle down Billy Patterson. Do you realize your mother was the only person who realized what was going on with Renie? I didn't know how she felt about you. I never saw it, and I'm her mother. How do you think that makes me feel?"

She stood. "So pull your head out of your ass Billy, go find her and tell her you're sorry."

"But—"

"Go!" She stomped her foot and pointed at the stairs.

"Willow."

"Oh for Christ's sake, I'll stay with Willow. Go find her."

Billy figured he didn't have much choice.

"Where is she?"

"I don't know!" Liv was yelling at him now. He'd better get going or she would wake Willow up, or maybe hit him or something.

When he went out the front door, Renie was sitting on the porch steps. He sat down next to her.

"Hey," he said.

"Hey," she answered.

"I'm sorry."

"I don't know what to tell you Billy, just because things seem—"

"Stop." He put his hand on her arm. "I'm sorry. I shouldn't have said any of that."

She looked away from him.

"This won't be easy, I know that. And I'm sorry I got mad at you."

"But?"

"Nope. No buts. I'm sorry, and I'm not gonna make any excuses."

"But you're still mad at me."

"Yeah, I am. And I might be mad at you for a while, but that's my problem. And it isn't so much that I'm mad at you, I'm hurt. You hurt me."

She started to say something.

"But," he said before she could. "That's how I feel if I'm thinkin' about *me*. If I start thinkin' about *you*, I'm not mad. I have to keep workin' on it Renie."

"I thought you understood."

"I did. I do. I get confused sometimes. Your mom told me that I can't tell you that I understand how you felt, but then turn around and say that I don't understand what you did. That made a lot of sense to me. I'm hurt by your actions, but I understand how you felt. It's gotta be one or the other."

"And?"

"I'm here and I'm not goin' anywhere. Unless you come with me, that is."

He took her hand in his. "You didn't throw your ring out in the pasture. That's a good sign."

She laughed. "I wouldn't do that Billy."

"Nah, you wouldn't. Sounds more like somethin' I'd do."

Chapter Twenty-Three

"Hey Mom," Renie said when she walked in the front door.

"Hey honey, or should I say honeys."

Renie set Willow down. She ran over and wrapped her arms around Liv's legs. "Gah-ma."

"Oh you are melting my heart little girl. Did you hear that? She called me Gah-ma."

"Better than Bah-ma," Renie answered.

"What brings you two here this morning? Not that you ever need a reason."

"Billy is painting Willow's bedroom and the house smells. I thought I should get Willow out of there."

"Are you getting settled in okay?"

"Yeah, almost everything is finished, except her room."

Billy and Renie had been busy furnishing the house. She felt as though all she did lately was wait for furniture or appliances to be delivered. They'd gone to Denver the week before and stocked up on kitchen stuff, bedding, towels—all the essential little stuff they could fit in the back of Billy's truck.

"Have you talked to Paige lately?"

"Yep, I talked to her this morning?"

"Did she say anything about Blythe?"

"Yes."

"She's not coming, is she?"

"No honey, she's not."

"I've been trying to get in touch with her, but she's not responding."

"She's upset Renie. Part of her feels stupid about how she pestered you about Billy. The other part of her is mad that you never told her how you felt. And then, you disappeared on her. She's not just mad, she's hurt."

"Sounds familiar."

Liv set the dish down she had in her hand, and motioned to Renie to come sit next to her.

"There's something I've been wanting to talk to you about, and now is as good a time as any."

"Oh no. Mom, if you're about to tell me you're mad at me too, I'm not up for it."

"No, that isn't it at all. Do you want to hear what I have to say?"

"As long as you don't yell at me."

"Oh honey, I never yell at you."

"But you scold me."

"I won't do that either. Well, maybe a little, but in a good way."

"Great."

Willow toddled over and climbed up on Renie's lap. "You love me don't you Willow? You'll protect me from Gah-ma."

"Gah-ma," she said, looking at Liv, who pulled her phone out of her pocket and handed it to Willow to play with.

"Don't do that, she'll want to play with everyone's phone now."

Liv pointed to herself. "Gah-mas get to do whatever they want. That's the beauty of it. No rules for gah-mas."

"Okay, let's get this over with. Scold away."

"Honey, you need to learn to stand up for yourself."

"Huh?"

"I mean it. How much of Blythe's crap have you put up with over the years? My guess is that it's been a lot. She doesn't want to talk to you? Send her an email. Say you're sorry you didn't tell her how you felt about Billy. You don't have to say anything more than you're sorry.

"We all need to accept that you need time and space too, in the same way everyone else does."

"Mom, I can't."

"You can. And you have to sweet girl. I don't want to hurt your feelings, but the days of Renie the doormat are over. I won't stand for it any longer."

"I am a bit of a doormat sometimes."

"Sometimes?"

"Back off Mom, I'm agreeing with you."

"Good. So apologize and tell her to get over it. Tell her she owes you some slack. Demand it."

Renie looked at Willow. "Gah-ma's feisty today. My goodness!"

Liv kept Willow entertained while Renie used her laptop to send Blythe an email.

"Okay, done," she said a few minutes later.

"Good. Do you feel better?"

"I do, but at the end I begged a little. I want her to come for Thanksgiving. I couldn't help myself."

"Speaking of Thanksgiving…has Billy talked to you about it?"

"No. About what?"

"He asked Ben to invite Jace and his family."

"He did *what*?"

"I was afraid this would be your reaction."

Liv was back to keeping Willow occupied while Renie called Billy. She went out to the front porch to do it, but Liv could still hear part of the conversation, and her daughter was not happy.

"Billy, why would you do this? And more importantly, why didn't you discuss it with me first?"

"I know, I shoulda talked to you about it. But Renie, it felt like the right thing to do."

"*Why?*"

"Now wait a minute girl. Aren't you the one who told me you and Jace were friends? Doesn't make sense that you're gettin' this upset about me invitin' one of your *friends* to join us for Thanksgiving."

"Just because I said we were friends doesn't mean we should start spending holidays with him."

"Listen, he's Ben's cousin—"

"Who up until last month he hadn't seen for *years*."

"And, as I was saying before you interrupted me, which was rude by the way, he helped me Renie. He didn't have to do that."

She still didn't know what that meant. Billy told her Jace called him, but not much more than that. What, were they friends now too? That might be a little awkward.

"Doesn't matter anyway sugar. The deed's done."

"Ben didn't think it might be a good idea to ask me about it before he did it?"

"Nah, I told him you were fine with it."

"Billy!"

"Come on now. We gotta do it sometime. We're gonna be runnin' into him at family gatherings, might as well start now."

"Fine. But next time, at least talk to me about it."

"You're not mad at me are ya? 'Cause if you are, why don't you see if your mama can babysit Willow while we, ya know, have make-up sex."

That put a smile on her face, as he knew it would. "No, I'm not mad at you Billy."

"Damn. Wanna see if your mama will babysit Willow anyway? I'm craving a little alone time with you darlin'."

"How'd it go?"

"Not much I can do about it now. It isn't as if I'd ask Ben to un-invite him. It will be awkward though."

"We'll have a full house honey, you can avoid him at least part of the day."

"Thanks. That helps not at all. By the way, Billy wanted me to ask you if you could babysit Willow."

"Of course I can. When?"

"Tonight. Too short notice?"

"No, it's fine," she chuckled. "We don't have any plans. Better get your babysitting in now," she rubbed her belly. "Soon I'll have my hands full, won't I Willow?"

Willow rubbed her belly too.

"We've been talking about the new baby, haven't we?"

"How are you feeling anyway?"

"Great. Much better now that the morning sickness has subsided."

We're on tonight, she texted Billy.

Why we gotta wait til tonight? he answered. Which made her laugh, then blush.

"Go ahead," Liv said.

"What?"

"Go. We're good here. We'll see you tomorrow."

"You're sure?"

"Leave Renie, before I change my mind."

"Thanks Mom," she said, leaning down to kiss her cheek. "Bye-bye baby girl."

"Bye Bah-ma," Willow answered.

"Call us if she gets too fussy."

Renie left Willow's diaper bag, and they hadn't taken the porta-crib back to Ben's parent's house, so Willow had everything she needed for the night.

"Okay, we'll call you." Liv smirked. "We won't call them will we baby? We'll have a great night, just you, me and Grandpa Ben."

"How's he taking to being called Grandpa?"

"He grumbles, but he loves it," she winked. "Now, go!"

Renie stopped and picked up a bottle of wine, cheese and crackers, and strawberries on her way back to the house. It would be their first night alone since the night Billy proposed. It hadn't stopped them from making love every night, but there was something different about knowing Willow wasn't in the next room, and they wouldn't have to worry about her waking up at an inopportune moment.

"Come here girl," Billy greeted her at the back door. "What's this? Wine? You must not be too mad at me."

"I can't stay mad at you Billy. You know that. Especially once I see those damn dimples."

He wrapped his arms around her waist and nuzzled up against her hair. "I love you Renie."

"I love you too Billy."

"Come show me then."

***

Blythe gave in and agreed to come to Thanksgiving with the warning that Renie owed her, and she expected her to fix her up with a hot skier. Great, thought Renie. Maybe she'd placate her by taking her out to the Goat one night while she was there. There'd be a couple contenders for hot skier at the Rice family's bar. Maybe CB Rice, or at least Ben would consider playing over the weekend. It had been a long time since she'd seen them play, and she didn't think that Billy or Blythe ever had.

***

By Monday, Ben and Liv's house was full. Dottie and Bill were staying in Renie's room, Paige and Mark were in Luke's room, and Luke was bunking with Jake in his room.

Jace and his family would be staying in the main house with Bud and Ginny.

"I'm proud of my mama," said Ben. "She didn't try once to talk us into having dinner at the main house instead of here."

"Oh no, do you think she wanted to? I don't want to offend her. Ben why didn't you say something sooner?"

He wrapped his arms around her. "I think she's more than happy to pass the gauntlet to you Liv. Maybe next year one of the other daughters-in-law will host."

Liv raised her eyebrows. She couldn't imagine either one of her sisters-in-law hosting a crowd of people.

"No?" Ben laughed, picking up on her thought process. "Well maybe you and my mama can switch off every other year."

"Let's see how I do this year before we etch a schedule in stone. I've never done this before."

"It'll be great, and I'm helping. So's Dottie. You think you'll get to do much yourself?"

"You're right, not much. Dottie is used to cooking for a group much bigger than ours."

They'd had good times over the years spending the holidays with the Patterson family. It was hard to believe that soon they'd be family in earnest.

"Did I tell you Renie asked if I'd consider getting the band to play at the Goat Thursday night?" Ben told Liv.

"On Thanksgiving?"

"Yeah, most of them will be here with us for dinner anyway. Will and Maeve said they wouldn't mind manning the bar. Renie said she'd work too. No one ever has anything to do Thanksgiving night, that's why movie theaters are so crowded."

"You don't mind?"

"Nah, I'm looking forward to it. We don't have to serve food, just drinks. Maybe it'll become a tradition. Thanksgiving night at the Goat."

Liv had to admit it sounded like fun. Even if it was just family and friends, the place would be packed.

It felt like old times, having the Cochrans and Pattersons with them for Thanksgiving, even if they were in Crested Butte instead of Monument.

They were headed to the ranch; Renie to see Blythe and spend the day with her. Billy was tasked with bringing Willow to the house. He figured no one cared about seeing him; it was his daughter they were dying to get their hands on.

"Billy?"

"Yeah darlin'?"

"I'm worried about you and Jace."

"Why? You think he's gonna challenge me to a dual over you or somethin'?" He picked up her left hand and brought it his lips. "You're wearin' my ring, your fate is sealed. I'm not givin' you up for anyone."

"It's just that the two of you are a lot alike."

"Handsome, charming, lady-killers, that sort of thing?"

"Yeah that. Stubborn and maybe a little over-confident too."

"We'll be fine. You gotta remember, we're guys. We handle things differently. We'll give each other a ton of shit, jabs mired in humor…don't worry, we got this."

***

Renie took Blythe downtown. They would have breakfast, shop, spend too much money, and things would be fine between them. She hoped.

They hugged when Renie came in the house, but Blythe was unusually quiet. And sullen, which wasn't as unusual.

"We're going to Izzys, sometimes it gets crowded and there's a long wait, but it's worth it."

"That's fine." She was sulking.

"Come on Blythe, are you going to act this way all day? I told you I was sorry."

"I thought I was your best friend."

"You are my best friend."

"Then how come you never told me how you felt about Billy? I feel like such an idiot. All the times I asked you to fix me up with him, and you didn't say a word. You lied to me Renie."

"I didn't lie to you Blythe."

"Yes, you did."

"I just didn't tell you. I didn't tell anyone."

"That's bullshit. I distinctly remember you telling me that you thought Billy was serious about someone. Remember that? Was it you?"

That had been before she and Billy went from being friends to being more. And Blythe was right, she had lied to her.

"No, it wasn't me."

"See?"

"I didn't tell anyone. It wasn't just you. I couldn't admit how I felt to anyone."

"That's the part I don't understand. Why not?"

"It was too personal."

"Too personal? I'm your *best friend*."

"I'm sorry Blythe. I don't know what more I can say."

"Maybe we're not as good of friends as I thought we were."

"Don't go there. It isn't that way."

"It isn't? Will you tell me the truth from now on? Will you talk to me about how you're feeling? Because I'm not sure I'll feel comfortable talking to you when I know how much you hold back. Do you ever give me your honest opinion, about anything?"

No, not always. And there was a reason she didn't. She never wanted to hurt Blythe's feelings. It was easier to tell her what she thought Blythe wanted to hear, than tell her what she really thought. That included when Blythe hurt her feelings. It was all part of her life as a doormat. She took on the annoyance, sometimes even the hurt, to spare her friends' feelings.

"I'm working on it."

"What does that mean?"

"My mom gave me a lecture about being a doormat the other day. So I'm working on not being one. It isn't easy. I've had twenty-three years practice hiding my feelings."

"She's right. It's time to stop doing that."

Renie wondered how Blythe would react if she got what she wanted, and she told her how she felt. She doubted their friendship could withstand it. Blythe was used to doing things her own way, and getting whatever she wanted. Especially when it came to Renie. How would Blythe react when she told her to find her own hot skier, and leave her out of it?

When they got back to the house, Liv was sitting at the table and had her feet up on a chair, with a pillow under them.

"Mom, is everything okay?"

Liv started to laugh. "They're babying me. Because they've forgotten I've already had one," she shouted in the direction of the kitchen.

That's right, her mom hadn't told Dottie or Paige she was pregnant before today. She'd wanted to wait until she could do it in person.

"What?" asked Blythe. "What is she talking about?"

"My mom is having a baby."

By the look on Blythe's face, you would have thought Renie said Liv was giving birth to alien triplets. "Blythe, be nice."

"But—"

Renie put her hand over Blythe's mouth. "I'll work on telling you how I'm feeling. You need to work on the opposite. We don't always want to hear what you're thinking Blythe."

"Bravo!" There were claps and cheers from her mother and Paige.

"'Bout time you stood up for something Renie," said Paige. "I'll enjoy finding out how you feel about things."

Renie rolled her eyes. "It hasn't been that bad."

"She never hesitates to tell me when she doesn't like something," Billy shouted from the family room. "Never has, never will."

"Oh hush up you," she answered.

"See? That's how she talks to me. Tells me to shut up, tells me she doesn't like what I'm wearin', hates my cooking."

"As if you ever cook."

"I made breakfast once."

"What time is dinner? I'm thinking about going for a ride. Blythe are you up for a ride?"

"I will be if you let me ride Pooh." Blythe was skittish around horses. Whenever the two of them rode together, Renie let her ride Pooh, knowing her horse would be gentle.

"Of course. I'll ride one of Ben's. He won't mind."

"Hey can I get a kiss before you leave again?" Billy shouted.

"Somethin' wrong with your legs cowboy?" she answered.

She went into the family room and saw that Willow was passed out on his lap.

"The boys wore her out. I know I should put her in bed, but I miss her sleepin' on me."

"I love seeing the two of you this way."

"She's usually hangin' on you lately, not me so much anymore. Thought I'd take what I could get."

Renie bent down and kissed Willow's forehead, and then turned to kiss Billy. He put his hand on the back of her neck and held her there. "Give me a real kiss darlin'. And later, you and me are gonna do some dancin'. Got it?"

"Got it." She loved to dance with Billy. She had all her life, from the time she was a little girl to the first time Billy realized she wasn't a little girl anymore, to now. Soon they'd be dancing as husband and wife. She couldn't wait for that day to come.

"It's so weird." Blythe said on their way to the barn. "It's almost as though I'm watching a brother and sister kiss. Ew."

As they were walking in the barn door, a truck pulled up and honked the horn. Renie turned and saw Jace climbing out. The other man looked so much like him, it had to be Tucker.

"Hey there," he shouted to Renie and ran over to her.

"Who. Is. That?" Blythe asked.

"Jace. I'll introduce you."

"There are two of them? Oh my God, I've died and gone to heaven."

Here she was, faced with her first test, and she couldn't do it. She wanted more than anything to tell Blythe to stay away from Jace, but she couldn't bring herself to. Plus, whoever Jace chose to spend time with was no longer any of her business. Maybe Blythe would end up liking Tucker better anyway.

Jace picked up Renie and swung her around in a circle. "I hear congratulations are in order," he said when he set her down.

"Yep. I'm uh, you know, engaged."

"I'm happy for you," he answered softly. "Sad for me, but happy for you."

"Who's this?" Tucker asked.

"This is Irene," Jace introduced her. "Irene, meet Tucker. And this is…I don't know who this is."

"This is Blythe Cochran," answered Renie. "Her mom and my mom are best friends. We are too. Have been since we were five years old."

Blythe blushed as she shook each man's hand.

"Nice to meet you," she said to both.

"You too," said Jace, with a look on his face Renie had seen before. But just once, the first day she met him at Black Mountain Ranch.

About the Author

My books are filled with things that bring me joy: music, wine, skiing, families, artists and cowboys. Not always in that order.

I'm an author, speaker, editor, teacher, blogger, and in my spare time—became certified as an executive sommelier.

I bring years of experience in the publishing world to all I do. I've edited and designed more than two hundred books, including fiction, non-fiction, children's books, coffee table, and cookbooks. And then one day, I decided to write my own.

I'm an east coast girl, who spent half her life on the west coast. But now my husband, our two boys, and I happily call Colorado home.

Also available in the Crested Butte Cowboy Series: book one, *And Then You Fall*, book three, *And Then You Kiss*, and book four, *And Then You Fly*. Coming soon, book five, *And Then You Dare*.

You can find me here:
Website: http://www.heatherabuchman.com
Twitter: http://twitter.com/heatherabuchman
Facebook:http://www.facebook.com/Heather-A-Buchman

More from author Heather A. Buchman

CRESTED BUTTE COWBOY SERIES
And Then You Fall
And Then You Kiss
And Then You Fly

COMING SOON
And Then You Dare

EAST AURORA LINGER SERIES
Linger - Book One
Linger - Book Two: Leave

Made in the USA
San Bernardino, CA
05 March 2015